SOMEWHERE
ALONG
THE
WAY

SOMEWHERE ALONG THE WAY

ANNA GOMEZ

OPEN ROAD

INTEGRATED MEDIA
NEW YORK

ISBN: 979-8-3372-0085-9

This edition published in 2025 by Open Road Integrated Media, Inc.
180 Maiden Lane
New York, NY 10038
www.openroadmedia.com

To my parents,
because I miss them very much.

SOMEWHERE
ALONG
THE
WAY

PROLOGUE

"Hi," he whispered, quietly tiptoeing through a children's waiting room doorway. She'd been sitting by herself, surrounded by torn-up books and tiny cups and saucers laid out in front of broken dolls. "What are you doing?"

"I'm having a tea party," she replied. "You were gone a long time, Papa."

Her father sighed and took his place next to her, crossing his legs on the floor and motioning for her to come closer. The little girl scooted toward him and settled on his lap. With practiced expertise, he spread out the frills of her yellow dress over her knees and tightened the braids on her hair.

"Why can't I come out, Papa?" she asked, her big brown eyes looking up at him. He thought of her mother and how he saw her in this little girl every single day. "Why can't I see my grandma and grandpa?"

The father bristled at her question but tried to remain composed. How could he tell her she'd never see them again? "Well, the doctors and nurses are trying to make sure they're taken care of."

"And then I can see them?"

"Hija," he said, pulling her close.

She tucked her head under his chin and waited for him to continue.

"Granny and Grampy . . . they fell asleep and went to heaven."

"You mean they had a heart attack or a stroke? Like Ellie in *Up*?"

If this moment weren't so profound, he would have laughed. How could he forget how smart this six-year-old was? Her keen intuition? How old was her soul?

"Why, Papa? Why would that happen? Grampy walked to church every day. Granny vacuumed all the time."

"Their hearts got tired, I suppose," he answered.

"Did they get tired because they were helping to take care of me?"

"Oh no!" the father exclaimed. "Don't ever think that. They'd get mad at me whenever I'd take you to Auntie Elma's instead."

"But . . . we had so many plans. I wrote them all on the calendar. Our trip to Atlantic City to go on the rides this summer."

"We can still do all that," he said, releasing his hold on her so she could lean forward to reorder the cups and saucers and change places between the yellow and blue doll.

He watched as she focused on the tea kettle and poured imaginary tea into the cups. It wasn't unusual for her. She didn't dwell on sad things. She kept moving.

"So, I don't have a mom, and now I don't have a granny or a grampy anymore," she said, matter of fact like she was reciting a poem or spewing words from memory.

Her simple words crushed him, and when she looked up at him, his heart began to break. He took a deep breath and held it, afraid to release all the pain he had inside.

What she did next would define their relationship as father and daughter. It would empower him and fill him with conviction.

She grabbed his hands in hers and held them tight before leaning forward and kissing him on the cheek. "Don't worry, Papa. I'll be okay. The only one I need is you."

PART 1

CHARLOTTE

CHAPTER 1

These weren't snacks. They were meals. Large aluminum trays brimming with meat, chicken, lasagna, noodles, and rice. It was ten o'clock in the morning, for heaven's sake.

Next to the long plastic table stood two oversized orange coolers. She lifted the lid off one of them to find soft drinks, water bottles, and beer. *Beer?* Out of the corner of her eye, she saw a small tray of cheese and crackers, store-bought spinach dip, and a bag of Doritos.

He would have laughed and pointed that out to me, she thought, allowing herself the tiniest of smiles. *"A mix of cultures. Aren't we so lucky to be living here?"*

"We know who brought that, Charlie." She could hear him saying, too.

There it was again. That searing pain in her chest. It caused her to clutch her heart. This physical pain was so consuming that it debilitated her, numbed her, and kept her from crying. The pain trapped her tears. Charlie had to choose: tears or pain.

Why not both?

"Charlie?" A tall, skinny man in a gray suit placed a hand on her shoulder. "Are you okay?"

"Sorry, Kent," she answered with a murmur, pushing her shoulders back and walking toward the table. She ran her finger along one of its edges before pulling back the foil that covered a stew, releasing a whiff of soy sauce and vinegar. Kent wiggled his nose and sniffed. Charlie turned her face away from him, afraid he would sneeze. "What are we going to do with all this food?"

"We can announce that there will be refreshments after the service," he replied.

"Okay. Who brought all the rice and adobo?"

"Your Auntie Elma's cousin," Kent confirmed.

"And I suppose Dad's side brought the crackers?"

"Your Uncle Pete. And the beer. He said your dad would approve."

Still distracted, Charlie glanced through the doorway and across the hall. Chunks of snow formed a trail from the lobby to the gathering place, and a maintenance man showed up every few minutes to mop the wet footprints left by the visitors' heavy boots. The constant influx of people through the revolving doors brought in a taste of the damp, bone-cold Brooklyn air in February.

A few hours ago, Punxsutawney Phil saw his shadow. Charlie had never understood it but had always been intrigued by how people allowed their life to be defined by . . . well, in this case, a groundhog. But then again, she found herself listening to the radio every year, just like she read her horoscope or followed astrologists on Instagram. She was waiting for something, always counting on something better coming her way.

Six more weeks of winter was right, anyway. At least in her case. *At least this year.*

From where she was, Charlie could see two people kneeling at her father's casket, the rest seated on banquet chairs. There were over forty of them, and their actions were repetitive and familiar. Signs of the cross, hands on the casket, rosary clutching, shoulders shaking, whispers and prayers, and words of condolence. They were the hankie generation, from a time when blowing your nose into a disposable piece of something was such a waste of money. They'd lived in the era of cloth diapers and clothespins. The women held those hankies, dabbing their eyes, while the men had them tucked into their pockets. Charlie's father was like a son to them. Abandoned by his wife, raising a daughter on his own. The Sunset Park community had adopted and parented him from the time he was a young man.

Directly facing the other doorway, she spotted the three Missys—Missy Smith, Missy Donahue, and Missy Malone— with some others she knew from high school. Dressed in all black, their necklines and wrists dangling with gold, their hair coiffed, and their nails impeccably done, they whispered quietly, shielding their mouths with their hands. She could name the designer purses they flaunted on their arms. She'd only started buying them last year. These women had them all their lives—first from their daddy's money and now from their husband's. Auntie Elma convinced her father that attending a prep school in King's County and paying thirty thousand a year in tuition was the only way Charlie could gain future entry to an Ivy League school. Seeing the three Missys brought back the teenage trauma of going to a school where every parent owned a business, an estate, or an entire football team while she was known as the daughter of a limo driver.

Papa, Missy's dad, bought her a Range Rover for her sixteenth birthday.

Your car is so much cooler, hija! I bet you don't know anyone else who owns a stretch. You can sleep in it, eat in it, and party in it.

In the years to come, he would call it her party bus. It became a running joke between them.

Charlie was supposed to be out in this crowd of people who loved her father, allowing them to comfort her. But what placated her was this place, being in the break room, surrounded by the food her father loved and the beer he consumed too much of.

"You sure you're okay?" Kent asked again. How he'd changed over the years. He was Party Boy Kent in high school, and look at him now, the owner of a funeral home.

"Sure I am," she lied. "How much do I owe you for this? You know, he didn't have any insurance, but I can write a check—"

"Don't worry about that now," Kent assured her. "It won't be much."

Charlie nodded, her chest still numb and heavy. "Thank you."

"We should probably start with the service. Did you want to say a few words?"

"Uh." Charlie avoided his eyes, her gaze fixed on his lapel's round, shiny button. It was some sort of holy medal that she knew, but even after all those years in Catholic school, she couldn't remember the saint's name. "I don't think I can. But I know my Auntie Elma would be happy to do so."

Auntie Elma looked eerily composed when she walked up to the podium. That was such a far cry from the way she'd thrown herself onto his hospital bed as the machines stopped beeping. Charlie always thought Auntie Elma was in love with her father. After all, what woman would devote all this time to help raise a daughter that wasn't even hers? But there sat Joe, her husband of twenty years, and then their only son, Justin, who was as smart as he was good-looking.

Auntie Elma swayed sideways, pausing briefly in front of the coffin to pay her respects. Charlie was ready to spring into action, certain she was going to faint. But on she went, tapping the microphone to get everyone's attention. For a few seconds, Charlie couldn't help but look lovingly at her father's image. He was only fifty-five, his hair just starting to gray, but his spirit was strong and youthful. He drove a limousine during the day and spoke of the famous New Yorkers who were his regulars: Al, Tony, Ryan, Anne, Sarah J. He called them by their first names and asked them to autograph their ride tickets for her.

They'll be collectors' items someday, hija.

Anne and Ryan sent flowers, which stood out, especially these massive white wreaths with specially imprinted wide ribbons.

Until Auntie Elma's voice broke through her thoughts.

"Thank you all for coming today. For those who don't know me, my name is Elma. Edgar and I have been friends for over thirty-five years. I was his best friend—" She stopped and looked at Charlie. That pain, again. Sharp and stabbing. "I am a close family friend," she corrected herself. "Right now, I am doing the unimaginable. I never thought I'd be here standing in front of you under such traumatic circumstances. Edgar was beating prostate cancer. He was in the process of recovering. So this is a shock to all of us. Never in a million years did we ever think we would be where we are today. He . . ." she choked before swallowing loudly, ". . . was taken away from us too soon. But before he succumbed, he wanted to make sure we knew that he had a great life and how thankful he was to all of you for being a part of it. And that he leaves to us his whole heart, his daughter, Charlie, to cherish, to nurture, and to love with all our hearts, just like he did all these years."

Auntie Elma beckoned her to come forward.

No. Charlie shook her head. It was too much. This pain. Going up there and vocalizing the fact that he was gone? She wasn't ready. This couldn't be real. Just two days ago, he'd gone off oxygen and told her he was feeling better. She'd sworn he'd recovered from the virus, the pallor in his cheeks banished, the weakness and coughing subsiding. The last time she'd called him, he'd said he could walk once around the ninth floor of the hospital. All good signs. She'd known he'd have to build his strength back up, but he'd assured her they'd be discharging him soon.

Shortly after, he'd felt a tightness in his chest. Then, the high fever returned.

The chemo had made him thin and weak. Maybe Charlie had always known he'd never be the same, terrified that any type of infection would shred his insides. And that's exactly what it did.

"Charlie, we are here for you. We will always be here for you. We have lost the kindest, most genuine man we have ever known."

Charlie glanced at Auntie Elma's husband, who shifted uncomfortably in his seat.

"But most especially, Charlie has lost her father, her best friend. Our deepest condolences and prayers go to you. At least now we know he rests with your grandparents, Wilma and Bert."

A woman from the audience ran up to give Auntie Elma her hankie.

Don't do it, Auntie Elma. I saw her using it a few minutes ago.

She blew into it loudly, pausing with her mouth agape when she saw the line of people starting to form. About thirty of them were leaning against the wall and squeezing themselves along the narrow aisle between the rows of chairs. Aunt Elma broke into a wide smile. "Well, I didn't even have to ask. It looks like we're going to be here for a while. Everyone is limited to a minute each, and Tia Malou, do not, I repeat, do not start wailing into the microphone!"

The tributes lasted over an hour, and there was a mixture of tears and laughter delivered by the people whose lives her father touched.

He could fix anything.

He recycled my speaker wires and used them to fix my clothes dryer.

He sang like Frank Sinatra.

Did you know that he was Muhammad Ali's driver?

He was like a son to us. To all of us.

He never asked us for any help but would give anyone the shirt off his back.

We single women always wondered why he never dated. It was our loss.

He was so well-read. He loved history. But he also loved Hallmark movies.

He was a diehard 49ers fan. That traitor.

And although no one could see her as she stood covered to the side by her father's giant portrait, Charlie held her head high.

Screw the Missys of the world. She'd been the daughter of the King of Sunset Park.

CHAPTER 2

"Charlie. Wake up."

The light of dawn streamed through the dust-laden blinds, illuminating the powdery remnants floating through the air. Little streaks of orange seeped through every opening, trying to invade the darkness Charlie had grown accustomed to in the month following his death. She slept through everything. Every sound, every noise. The crackle of potato chip packets and wrappers lodged between the creases of her comforter, the shrill of ambulances and police sirens, people yelling and screaming on her street, car alarms, laughter . . . nothing fazed her or aroused her from her self-induced stupor. Not even the empty juice boxes and the chewed-out chocolate bars strewn atop the piles of dirty laundry covering her bedroom floor.

Charlie squeezed her eyes shut for a few seconds, determined to go back to sleep. It had been her only respite for weeks, and it pissed her off that the pills were losing their effectiveness. She'd taken a double dose the night before. They should have been working well into the late morning.

"*Charlie.*"

Charlie's body shuddered from head to toe. A gust of frigid

air caused her to pull the ends of her comforter over her head. *Was it. . . ? Could it be? Let me dream some more.*

She stayed still, afraid to make a move. But when she realized what was happening and the possibility of it, she shot straight up, eyes wide open, eager to confirm that the voice she heard was his.

"Papa? Is that you?"

He sat on the side of her bed, just like he used to when she was a little girl. Charlie would talk his ear off and tell him about her day from when she woke up until she went to bed. As the years went by, those moments grew less and less, her teenage memories overshadowed by her determination to move away. She'd worked hard to get into Harvard and planned her grades and achievements since she was a high school freshman. She opted for business because of its stability. That was her goal: stability. Predictability. Safety. She breezed through school, excelling with a photographic memory and hating every minute of the path she had chosen to take, so far from who she thought she was, who she longed to be. She wanted a life where she could create colorful stories, travel the world, and live in the moment.

Of course, none of that was practical. So Charlie graduated summa cum laude with a degree in business and now works at a global consumer goods company as their youngest-ever chief revenue officer. Stable. Predictable. Colorless.

Her father smiled at her now and nodded. "Yes, Charlie. It's me."

"Am I dreaming?"

"Probably," he said, his blue eyes looking so young and alive. Charlie noticed a full head of hair on him and his favorite gray suit. It was way too big for him, a hand-me-down from Auntie Elma's husband, but he carried it off with ease. Her father was a beautiful man, and he knew it. Always the schmoozer with the ladies, he could talk anyone into a business proposition, and he'd done it for as long as she could remember. Always working on a new idea, none of them ever taking off. But then he got sick, and the chemo zapped all his dreams away.

"Listen, Charlie. Do you remember when you turned eighteen and decided you wanted to find your mom? You asked Auntie Elma to help you, but then you went to college and never brought it up again. Why was that?"

She thought back to that time. "I realized I didn't need to find her. I had you. And Auntie Elma and Auntie Elma's million relatives. I was grateful."

He turned to look around the room. "You haven't left this apartment in five weeks."

"What do you mean? I've gone to the grocery store a couple of times."

"Going to the little store across the street doesn't count." He held both arms up and turned from side to side. "And what is with this wreckage?"

"I . . . I just—"

"This is not you," he interrupted. "You hate mess. And I've never seen you eat so much chocolate."

"You're dead! Give me a break, Papa. You were the only one I had. And now you've left me. I'm still trying to figure out how to live my life without you."

"By what? Killing time?"

"Why not? You always told me that time heals all wounds."

"Oh, my darling daughter. Wounds can also fester and grow if left uncared for. Healing only begins when you try to move forward. I've had my time. I'm happy now, free from pain, and watching you from where I am. Life is so beautiful, Charlie, and you have so much more to live. You can't waste another moment by living in the past. I hope that, in my own way, I've been able to show you how happy you made me and how joyful my life was because I had you. And how proud I've always been to be your father."

"How, Papa? How am I supposed to keep going?" Charlie was a blubbering mess, swiping the tears from her eyes so she wouldn't lose sight of him. There he was, speaking to her like it was a normal day, and they were sitting at the table for dinner. He was her source of support and cheerleader, helping Charlie with her thesis and rehearsing her presentations with her whenever she needed an audience.

"By focusing on yourself and doing the things that make you happy. Promise me, Charlie. Promise me you'll take your life back. Promise me that today will be the last day you will live a life of regret."

"I would give everything to have you back. I feel bad I never got to spend more time with you after I got promoted. I was traveling so much, working so many hours, I—"

"We texted each other every day. While you were on the train, every day."

"That wasn't enough. I realize that now."

"Hija," he said, reaching out to touch her.

Charlie yanked his hand forcefully and brought it to her face. He smelled like Dior's Eau Sauvage, his favorite cologne. She could feel him. He was real. The familiarity of his skin, mottled and dry, calloused from all the manual labor he'd done through the years, his right thumb deformed by arthritis.

"I love you with all my heart. I will always love you. You have given me all the happiness a father could ever ask for. And now, I want to give you one last gift. Speak to your Auntie Elma. She has your mother's letters."

"My mother? Letters?"

"Your mother wrote to me regularly from the time you were born. I kept all her letters. Saved them until you were old enough to get to know her. I thought that maybe I could give them to you once you had your own daughter. She was the love of my life. And you were her gift to me."

"But . . ." Charlie stammered. She couldn't find the words. "You said she left."

Truth be told, at that moment, she couldn't care less about who left who or even about those letters. She cared about her dad being there. She squeezed her eyes shut and prayed so hard for him to stay. Maybe he was still alive, and the past four weeks had been nothing but a bad dream.

"I have to go, Charlie. I'm so sorry I didn't give them to you. I thought we had more time. I kept hoping things would change," he reasoned. "Read those letters. Get to know your mother. And find the joy and resilience in them. And please," he said, smiling as he gently brushed his thumb across her cheek, "stop sleeping your life away. From this day on, live your life in the sunshine. You brought so much light into my life. Share that light with others."

"Don't go, Papa. Don't leave me," Charlie wailed. "Tell me how I can get past this. How do I survive when my home is in you?" The more she reached for him, the more he backed away, stepping away, moving back, further and further from the bed. Charlie thrust her body forward, arms outstretched, trying her best to grab him and pull him back to her. Instead, she fell flat on her face, sobbing and soaking the bed with her tears.

"Little one, tell me why I named you Carlotta," he whispered.

"Charlotte."

"Okay, fair. You changed it to Charlotte when you were in first grade," he acknowledged with a wide grin, his face coming to life. It seemed impossible to her how this man was truly gone.

Charlie lifted her head, straining her neck so she could keep looking at him standing at the edge of her bed. "Because you couldn't name me Wilbur."

He laughed. His deep, rumbling laugh filled the room like the waves of an ocean. "Okay. The second reason."

"Because you said I was special and that I saved you. Why are you changing the subject, Papa? I don't want you to go. Please don't leave me!" Charlie screeched, clawing at the comforter and covering her face with it.

"They say that children who grow up without a parent start out with a broken heart. It takes fortitude to grow up without a mother. That's what you've done. You have it in you. This tenacity, this ability to make do with what you have. Keep that going. Do that for me, okay? Live your life with passion and zest. I will always be watching over you, cheering you on. Oh, and—"

He threw his head back and laughed again, a loud bellow accompanied by his trademark belly rub.

"Dump Lorenzo. There's someone else coming."

And with those words, he was gone. There she was again, all alone in her room. In her life. In her heart. But this time, when she looked around, she saw that things had changed. The sun was shining. The blinds were pulled back. And all around her, surrounding her, was a magnificent abundance of light.

CHAPTER 3

"Dios mio! I am so happy to see you!" Auntie Elma cried, making a sign of the cross before pulling Charlie into her arms. "Carlotta! You scared us. I didn't know whether to send the police to stage an intervention. One month! You didn't return calls, you didn't answer the door. What happened? Are you okay? Maybe you need to get checked at urgent care. Were you sick? What did you eat? Do you need—"

Charlie gently tapped a finger on her cheek. It was only two days since she'd had that dream, or whatever it was. After he'd left, she'd experienced a lightness she hadn't felt since the first time he got sick four years ago. The dust bunnies that had settled on those windowpanes had caused her to have a sneezing fit, so she'd grabbed the hand vac and zapped the living crap out of every single one of them. And then she'd gathered all the wrappers, taken out the garbage, and opened the patio screen doors. Charlie had also thrown away every single moldy pot and pan left on the stove for weeks. She hadn't even realized they were there. She'd lived every day without him in a blur.

Charlie had slept through the rest of winter, but that morning, she'd felt strong enough to leave her apartment.

"I'm okay. I needed time alone."

"Yes, alone, but did you have to refuse my calls?"

"There was nothing to say," Charlie muttered.

Elma led her to one of the chairs by the kitchen table. It dawned on Charlie that she'd never even asked her father how Auntie Elma got so rich. The kitchen table was the third kitchen table in the house, with three separate kitchens. "Sit. Let me get you a drink," Elma said before proceeding to the wall-to-wall fridge and grabbing a can of Fresca from among a variety of a hundred other cans. "Here, I know you like this."

"Thank you."

"Charlie." Elma slumped forward to grab her hands. Charlie saw that they were shaking, so she pressed them stiffly against the table to quiet them down. "Your papa was supposed to give you something, but he never had the chance to. He gave them to me when the cancer returned."

"I know."

"You know?" Elma leaned away from her, eyes wide. "How?"

"He told me."

Tears filled Elma's eyes. Her head tilted to the side, eyes constantly blinking. "What do you mean? When?"

"I had a dream a few days ago. Papa chastised me for shutting off the world, among other things." Charlie chuckled softly. "He told me that my mother wrote him letters and that he planned to give them to me. But, of course, things happened—"

Elma looked away, her silence wistful, her eyes fixed on nothing. "He found a way to tell you," she whispered, shaking her head.

Charlie squeezed Aunt Elma's hands. She wanted to pass on the feeling of peace she'd had after seeing her father. "He looked so good. So youthful and strong. He said he was watching over us and that we should be happy he is at peace."

Elma nodded before reaching for her hankie on the counter and blowing her nose. But then the tears started up again. "He suffered so much in the end. In a way, I'm wracked with guilt that he was all alone in the hospital. But the doctors, they wouldn't let us visit. They only called me in when he was already—"

Charlie circled the table and wrapped her arms tightly around Elma. It was a memory she couldn't shake, a vision that still haunted her every day. Elma had FaceTimed when her father was dying. He'd asked to see Charlie, who, despite driving as fast as she could, pulled over to the side of the freeway when she knew it was too late. Her phone had been their only connection. When his lungs emptied out and he started to gasp for air, Charlie watched helplessly as he tried to lift himself off the bed, struggling to breathe and reaching for something with horror in his eyes. Charlie screamed for him and saw Aunt Elma throw herself on the bed with a high-pitched keen. "Edgar! Edgar! Look at me! Don't look over there, look at me! I love you," she'd screamed. "I love you." And then, without warning, the nurse had ended the call.

It felt good to share these tears with her aunt now. Charlie hadn't cried it out yet, and she knew it was inevitable.

Elma kissed the crook of her arm before tapping on it as a sign to let her go. "I'm going to get those letters," she said, straightening up and collecting herself.

It took a while for Aunt Elma to get back to Charlie. So, she took advantage of the time by using the washroom and walking around the foyer. Charlie always loved looking around Aunt Elma's home, where things were always new and interesting. Every trip to Europe, every souvenir, every memory was proudly displayed. There were pictures of Charlie and her father, some just the two of them, others with the entire family. She didn't know Elma's husband, Joe, that well. He was always traveling, acquiring a company here, setting up a plant there. Charlie never questioned the fact that he was always gone—after all, it became a normal thing for her to see Elma at their house with her father, at her school functions, and on playdates with Justin.

"Sorry, I had to take a minute," Aunt Elma said, coming down the large circular stairway.

Charlie saw that her eyes were swollen and pink. "It's okay," Charlie assured her before taking a seat on the last step and waiting for Elma to sit next to her. Elma handed Charlie a pile of white envelopes neatly held together by a red velvet ribbon. It looked like a perfectly wrapped gift. Charlie laughed to herself. *Are these gifts? What are these, and how will they impact my life?*

"Your mother and I were best friends. Did you know that?"

Charlie shook her head. "I thought you and my papa were best friends in school."

"Well, indirectly, I suppose. I was your mother's best friend and met your father through her. When they separated, I felt the obligation to stay in your father's life so he wouldn't have to raise you by himself." She caught herself immediately. "I mean, obligation is not the right word. I loved you from the day you were born."

Charlie studied the envelopes. They were clean but weathered, the older ones crisp and brittle, their edges somewhat yellowed. Careful not to remove the ribbon, she plucked at each edge with her fingers and counted out loud.

"Every other year on or around your birthday, she would send a letter."

"There's no return address. Do you know where she is now?"

"No, we don't. We know she's in California, running her family's business. But that's all we know."

"There are only fifteen," Charlie declared. "I'm thirty-two."

"I know how old you are," Aunt Elma said with a laugh. "Your mother was twenty when you were born, so she's around fifty-two now. And your father, he was four years older . . . I can't believe he's gone. They were so young when they had you. And yes, the letters stopped coming two years ago. Your father was already sick. Maybe he knew that his time here was limited. He gave them to me one day and told me to keep them safe in case he couldn't give them to you. He did worry when they stopped coming. In many ways, that love of his kept him going. But it also hindered his ability to . . ." She paused before a tear fell down her face. "Love again."

Charlie pulled Elma close, resting her head on Elma's chest, feeling strong and protective over her. "What should I do with them, Aunt Elma?"

"I don't know. I can't tell you what to do with them. All I know is that they are yours now. When they stopped coming, your father changed. And before he died, he asked me to find her. For you. You never really asked about your mother except for about a week after your eighteenth birthday."

"That's because I never really missed having one. My father played both roles so well. And you were always there for me."

"And I will always be here, Charlie. You are our family. We are yours. Always remember that."

Charlie kissed Elma on the forehead and slowly stood up, pulling Elma up along with her. "I'm going to go. Thank you for these." She waved the envelopes in the air. They suddenly weighed like stone, and Charlie's heart felt just as heavy. She didn't want to ruin their visit, so she tried to sound upbeat, even as all this information was suffocating. The air began to thin out, and Charlie couldn't seem to get enough of it.

"Will you read them? What are you going to do?"

"Maybe. Don't know," Charlie managed, turning her back

toward Elma, trying her best to place one foot in front of the other, afraid she would burst into tears.

"Come to dinner on Sunday night. Let's continue that routine, okay? I think your father would love that."

Charlie nodded before grabbing her coat and running out the front door.

CHAPTER 4

This was the house Charlie grew up in, a two-bedroom brownstone in the heart of historic Sunset Park. Once an industrial neighborhood, its warehouses had now been repurposed into renovated stores, and the row of houses a tourist attraction. Sunset Park was named after the public park that offered striking views of the Manhattan skyline, the Statue of Liberty, and the New York Harbor. This neighborhood was known for its diverse mix of ethnic cultures, mostly of Latin and Chinese backgrounds, but lately, it had been a target of the young, hip generation who preferred to live on the outskirts of Manhattan.

"When do you think we can take some pictures?" Mrs. Shebel, the realtor, asked, her stilettos click-clacking on the wooden floors. She was all Tribeca, looking like a model from the Row, black everything, long, lean, and tailored. Charlie had met her at a gallery opening and knew she could bring a new perspective. "We're going to have to clean this up a bit," she said, exhaling loudly at the piles of stuff on the floor. Books, folders, tools—everything Charlie's father had loved, waiting for him to return. It still felt as if he'd just rushed out to the hardware store. He did that all the time, finding things to fix and tinker with around the house, needing this, that, or the other.

He'll be back any minute now, find out he bought the wrong thing, and rush back out again.

"It will only take me a few days," Charlie answered, hesitating when they reached the entrance to her father's bedroom. Mrs. Shebel sped past toward his bed while Charlie stood in the doorway.

"This house has so many interesting elements," she said. "Look at these tin ceilings and built-in mantels. A fireplace in the bedroom. Did your father use this a lot?"

"We did. Almost every night." When he got sick, Charlie would lie on the couch, sleepless and counting the hours until the next alarm went off. He couldn't be off his meds for a second, howling in pain, telling her his hip bones were being crushed, and his nerves were on fire.

"You mean in the winter?"

"No," Charlie responded, turning her head to the red parka neatly folded on the chair by his bed. He was always cold. "Every night."

Mrs. Shebel quickly moved on to the hallway. "And this is your bedroom?" She looked up at Charlie. "Was your bedroom?"

"I moved out three years ago but spent some nights when he got sick."

"I'm sorry," Mrs. Shebel offered, avoiding Charlie's eyes.

She stopped at the doorway, focusing on the built-in shelves that spanned from wall to wall, ending only at a bay window that overlooked the backyard. The pine boards were painted yellow and blue, a cool combination of colors that brightened up the room. Mrs. Shebel grasped the end of one shelf and tried to jiggle it.

"Very solid," she said, her head bobbing up and down, side to side. "There must be at least three hundred books in here!"

"Three hundred seventy-two," Charlie muttered under her breath.

"Did you do this? Color-code them?"

"Indie, traditional, romance, thrillers. By genre and then by color."

She smiled at Charlie. "So, I take it you love books."

"I read a lot," Charlie answered. It had started to feel invasive, to be honest.

She ran her fingers across a set of books, looking at the titles that Charlie had sorted and the colors she had arranged. Charlie didn't want her to think she was this introverted weirdo. She was, but no one had to know it.

"And that whole section," she said, pointing to the furthest part of the shelf, closest to the bed. "Different editions of—"

"*Charlotte's Web.* My dad would read that book to me every night when I was growing up. Let me show you the lower level," Charlie said as Mrs. Shebel attempted to pull another book out. Charlie led her down the hall toward the stairs.

Mrs. Shebel clung to the banister with her life, positioning her feet sideways as she descended the narrow stairs. Charlie found it amusing, thinking of how she'd skipped, hopped, and run up and down those stairs all her life.

"Ah," she said, breathing a sigh of relief. "Here we are." Charlie stood aside as Mrs. Shebel walked around the living room. "Great use of the parlor," she said, glancing up and down at the picture frames that clogged every surface in the room. "I hope you don't mind, but when staging, we will move these pictures out."

"That's fine."

"Love these bay windows. Maybe we can change these curtains and freshen them up a bit. Did you ever have any issues facing the street?"

"No."

"Parking?"

"He had no car," Charlie answered. "He drove a limo for a living, but it wasn't his."

Mrs. Shebel was distracted. She admired the greenery in the living room, pinching the leaves to see if they were real. It was filled with all sorts of indoor plants in face vases, their leaves thick and lush. Some of them were figures with glasses, some with hats, and some were three-dimensional.

"Do you call them Rubin vases?"

"I think so," Charlie answered. "My dad just thought they looked cool."

"The flowers in this room are amazing. What are they?" Mrs. Shebel pointed to the corner of the room.

"Peace lilies, anthuriums. Those pink triangular ones are oxalis."

"And those fuzzy leaves?"

"African violets."

"Ah. Who's the green thumb?"

Charlie shrugged. It had become a habit, hunching her shoulders whenever she feigned nonchalance. "He was."

"So, he did the garden too, I assume. I can imagine what the rear yard would look like in a few weeks," Mrs. Shebel said before proceeding to the next room. "And here's the kitchen." She ran her fingers lightly across the marble counters. "These cupboards are in the process of—"

"Being remodeled, yes."

"We can find someone to finish them," Mrs. Shebel muttered. And, as if to lighten the mood, her tone peaked. "What a nice built-in pantry. And these white subway tiles with black borders are gorgeous. Original, I'm sure."

"Mrs. Shebel," Charlie started, trying her best to quell the guilt from what she was about to say, "would we be able to list everything as is? Meaning I only take what I want and leave the rest for the new owner to sort out?"

"Buyers do that all the time. We can find a buyer to take everything in the house, including any personal effects. I can help find a Goodwill for his clothes and other items you don't need to take with you. In fact, I just did that a month ago. We sold a house in Bushwick where the former owner lost her husband and just walked away from it all."

"Well, I'm not just walking away."

"I'm sorry, I didn't mean it like that. But there are a lot of things here. Things you may not be able to take with you. You have a place in Brooklyn Heights, right? I'm sure it is very nice."

Charlie was no longer interested in the back and forth. It was too much, a stranger picking and prodding through the life her father had built for them. Who gave this stranger the right to touch everything, see only the tangible, when this house meant more than just the mess that was in it? This was where a man had brought up his daughter all on his own. Everything in this house showed that. Charlie tuned her out, making notes in her head of the things she wanted to take with her.

Model cars, maybe his favorite ones, favorite T-shirt, all the pictures. I'll need to buy more banker's boxes.

"Carlotta?"

Mrs. Shebel shoved a form in Charlie's face right before clicking the top of a pen and handing it to her.

"Sorry. Yes?"

"I think I can get you market value. We can start high and know that we'll be willing to compromise at a midpoint. There are a few minor repairs, most of them aesthetic. But the house is well maintained and has good bones. I have no doubt it will sell right away. You'll have to let your tax accountant know, depending on how much this house was bought for. But there's a step up to date of—"

"I don't want any money for the furniture. They can just take everything. They're old and fully depreciated." Charlie realized she was speaking over her, but she just wanted her to leave.

"All right."

"My friend, Rena, is a tax guru. She'll help me. Thank you, Mrs. Shebel. If you give me a few days to clean up, we can start showing the home next week."

"Great. And once again, I am deeply sorry for your loss."

Charlie sat alone in his bedroom, wearing his ratty old parka. Two years ago, when she received her big promotion, Charlie gifted him a personalized coat straight from Paris after one of her work trips. That Parisian coat ended up with Justin. Her father wore it once to appease Charlie and then reverted to his old friend, complaining that the new one was too thick and heavy.

Charlie called it Red. They were inseparable, those two. Once he got sick, he wore Red even when he went to bed. Too proud to tell her he was cold and too frugal to turn up the heat, he'd worn it under the covers. They'd washed and dried it while he was asleep. Frayed at the edges with a hole behind the right pocket, it was soft and flat, almost devoid of any filling. It was one of his most prized possessions. A used jacket purchased from a sidewalk garage sale.

Red was on his deathbed. Charlie wasn't.

Charlie shook her head. Death always brought darkness, and there was nothing good or positive about it, except maybe that he was truly at peace now. Being sick was a tumultuous time for him. He constantly worried about his job, lack of insurance, home, and daughter.

She paused to let out a deep breath and glanced out the window. Maybe it was the starved, and cold air or the snow constantly falling, even in early March, devouring the sun's light.

She moved around the room, picking up things and laying them neatly in piles next to the fireplace. Rena told her to keep his financial records, and there were five banker's boxes filled with papers. He had three guitars, a karaoke machine, and four trophies from local car rallies he'd participated in when she was growing up.

There was extra room in the final box for more papers, so she ran downstairs to the living room, knowing there were pictures she needed to sort through. Rena's mom had suggested she throw the old rusty frames away once she had extricated them.

They're so old, you'd never display those in your home.

One hour and three bandaged cuts later, Charlie had nearly fifty pictures stacked neatly in a folder. Wrestling with the sharp edges and corroded screws had been no fun. She then moved to the fridge door, plastered with dust-ridden Christmas ornaments her father had never taken down. On display were cards with glued-on pasta, drawings, and pictures over twenty years old.

Clink.

Shit. One elbow noodle fell onto the floor.

Clink. Clink, clink, clink.

And then another. And then three more, bouncing off the tile until they all landed inches from her feet. Charlie frantically pulled the drawers open, ruffling through their contents, looking for a bottle of glue. Drawer number two was where he kept his little pig souvenirs. He told her it was because he was born in the Year of the Pig, which also explained why all their kitchen accessories had pigs on them. A plastic pig's tail that doubled as a corkscrew, pig-shaped spoons, ice-cream scoops, measuring cups, and a wooden chest filled with pink pig ornaments of all shapes and sizes. They'd also loved Wilbur from *Charlotte's Web*. That was the very first book they read together, a tradition that continued until Charlie was a teenager.

That's silly. How could a spider weave a web of words, Papa?

Suspend your doubts for a moment, Charlie. The point of the story is that she loved Wilbur so much that, in her short life, she was willing to do anything for him.

And Wilbur?

He lived his life with gratitude to Charlotte, and there was never a day in his long life when he didn't think of her and how she saved him.

What does a pig know about life? He eats and sleeps and eats and sleeps.

Yes, Carlotta, and the memory of her kept him alive and made his life different. Special.

The simplest life can be made extraordinary by just one act of kindness.

Drawer number three was filled with papers—instruction manuals, twenty-year-old warranties, receipts, keychains, toothpicks . . .

She ruffled through the papers until her fingers touched something hard and cold. Slowly, she pulled her hand out with a silver key, a chubby-looking thing with a tube-like end. A cash box key.

Charlie closed her eyes, trying hard to conjure up a memory of where and when she'd seen a cash box. It hit her. A week before he went to the hospital, when he started feeling sick, there was a metal box under his covers. She'd noticed it when she came into the room unannounced. He was already in a weakened state, but Charlie saw him push something aside as soon as she approached his bed. It didn't draw her attention— he was always tinkering with stuff.

Charlie ran back upstairs, skipping steps, breathless by the time she stood in the middle of his room. She crouched down, lifted the skirt, and shone the light of her phone under the bed. It was there. Charlie held the black tin box and opened it with the key. It popped open so easily like it had been waiting to be found.

There were carnival tickets and theater tickets, movie stubs, and little notes. The ink had faded on the notes, but the hand-writing was a feminine cursive in pink ink. Charlie took each note, held them in her fingers, brought them close to her face, and scrutinized every one of them. And when that was done, she clawed at the bottom of the box, finding some pictures. There weren't many, maybe five or six.

One was of her mother holding up a pencil box while her father stood smiling next to her. They wore their high school uniforms. Blue pants, a red sweater for her dad, and a white blouse and plaid skirt for her mother.

Chills ran down her spine when she looked at the next picture. She was staring right into her own face. There she was, a carbon copy. Long brown hair and round chestnut-colored eyes. She had a fine nose and high cheekbones with lips that always felt too big for her face. Charlie had her dimples, thick eyebrows, and slender body, filled at the top, slim in the hips with shapely legs that stretched for miles.

Charlie's heart raced. She began to convulse with anger. How could he do this to her? How did he allow Charlie to live for thirty years without a glimpse of her, the one who gave her away? The pigs. They were an obsession of hers, looking at the rest of the pictures.

Charlie flung the box in the air, sure it caused damage once it hit the wooden floor. Her skin felt hot and prickly. She grabbed at Red, tore it off her, splitting its zipper in the process and throwing it on the bed. She had to get everything her father held dear away from her.

She had always lived with half an identity, always searching, quietly longing. Pushing people away for fear of abandonment, forever waiting for the next best thing. How had her father not seen that? How could he have ignored it? How could he not have cared?

Her mother's spirit was all over this house. Her presence in that box negated everything Charlie had thought to be true.

She was here all along, and I didn't even know it.

CHAPTER 5

"Charlie, this is Dr. Miller," Edgar announced the morning they sat waiting at NYU Langone. Gently, he lifted his daughter from his lap and settled her back on the floor, right in the middle of her tea party. "He was the one taking care of Granny and Grampy." Charlie stared blankly at the tall, thin man.

"Hello, Charlie. May I speak to your father for a moment?" The man struggled to stay standing while a tiny girl behind him wrapped her arms around his long, skinny legs. "Oh, this is my daughter, Serena. We were on the way home from church when I got the call."

The girl ran to the middle of the room, foraged through the toy chest, and pulled out some plastic food. She then took the orange doll and offered it to Charlie. "This one is hungry. She wants this chocolate donut."

Charlie nodded. "You can go feed her."

The two girls played silently, pouring tea and taking turns feeding the dolls. Despite their stark differences in appearance— Charlie, with dark hair and round brown eyes, and the other girl, whose hair shone like spun gold in the light, waif-like and delicate—they spoke without any words, their movements coordinated and in sync. One feeding the doll, the other wiping its chin. One poured the tea, and the other mixed it with a spoon.

"What's your name again?" Charlie finally spoke after the last doll had been fed.

"Serena," she answered. "But you can call me Rena. Because I know we will be friends forever."

"You were supposed to meet me for coffee two weeks ago. We were going to figure out your home sale stuff." Rena stood outside her door, a bag of groceries looped in one arm and a stack of books in the other. Charlie stepped back and waved for her to enter. "Your manager let me in," she said, proceeding directly to the kitchen. "I wasn't sure whether you ran out of town or something, you know, escaped from Brooklyn or—"

When Rena saw Charlie wasn't amused, she stopped, threw the books on the counter, and stepped forward to wrap her friend in her arms, still holding the bag of groceries, a can of corn digging into Charlie's back.

"I'm sorry I didn't call you back. I just needed to be by myself. Everything is slipping through my fingers, and I don't know how to think or what to do. He didn't just leave me. He left me with this whole new life I knew nothing about."

"I know," Rena uttered gently.

Charlie felt lightheaded, clutching her chest at the same time. Her knees buckled, causing her to sink to the floor. She could hear herself sniveling, unable to control the sound that emanated from her lips. It filled the room and echoed across the beams and lofty ceilings. Charlie's arms stiffened as Rena tried to hold her up. But the force of her sobs and uncontrollable heaving caused Rena to drop to the floor as well. Charlie hid in her arms, both of them on the kitchen mat, as Rena steadied Charlie's head against her chest. She was crying, too.

Rena was the only one who truly knew her. She was there through thick and thin, relationships and rebellion. Because of that, Rena was the only one who gave her permission to call out, feel, and surrender to that sorrow.

"She was there in our home all these years! I didn't know, he didn't tell me anything about her. I never asked! Why didn't I ever ask?"

Rena remained silent, stroking Charlie's hair and rocking her back and forth.

"I don't know who I am. I don't know where I came from. Suddenly, it started to make sense to me. The constant running, the need to keep moving, achieving. I had nothing else."

"You had your dad," Rena said.

Charlie lifted her head and swiped her hands across her face, sniffling and wiping the tears that kept coming. They faced each other on the kitchen floor, surrounded by all the expensive appliances Charlie had thought would make her life feel complete.

"Did I? I feel so betrayed by him. He kept things from me, and I'll never know why because I'm such a selfish idiot. I never asked. I was just so focused on moving, moving, moving. That was me!" Charlie raised her voice. "Stupid me. And now I have this ache in my heart. I'm aching for the mother I never knew, the father I lost, the identity I don't have!"

Rena had the grace to allow her to get everything off her chest. So Charlie continued.

"And now, the letters! He wanted me to read them and get to know her! He had to wait to die? When he's not here to explain himself? What a mean trick! What a selfish, egotistical trick!"

Charlie cried until she had no more tears left, her emotions indecisive between anger and sorrow, words deprecating and heartfelt.

Rena offered her a cup of coffee after she ran into the room to fetch the letters. Charlie didn't realize how she'd been holding them. Close to her heart. *What an irony.*

"Are you going to let go of those letters? You've been clutching them to your chest for a while," Rena teased before pressing the button on the Nespresso machine and pouring creamer into the orange designer cup. "Hmmm. This looks new."

"I got it in January at Heathrow."

"That's what I said. New." She pulled a teaspoon out of the drawer and proceeded to stir her coffee. Charlie rolled her eyes at Rena.

"So," she started up again, pointing at the pile of letters now lying on the kitchen counter. They were in great shape, curled around the edges, but now neatly stacked inside a Ziploc bag. "Are you going to read those?"

"Not yet." This wasn't the time to be spontaneous. She knew she'd have to do something once they'd been opened up. Right now, that would probably be like falling into Pandora's box without an escape plan.

"Ah," Rena said, taking the two coffee cups and moving toward the living room with Charlie trailing after her.

Rena sat on the couch. Charlie sat on the floor beside her. The comfortable silence was a relief. After all, Rena was Charlie's oldest friend. She also believed that Rena was an empath with otherworldly abilities. She had always been extremely sensitive to other people's feelings. She absorbed people's energies and experienced people's emotions, sometimes even before they were vocalized or shared. Because of this, Rena disliked crowds and was often overwhelmed in happy or sad situations. She was brutally frank, gruff, and sometimes unfiltered, often letting strangers know how much they annoyed her. Her intuition was so off the charts Charlie often relied on her dreams and predictions. Out of the blue, she would tell Charlie to stay away from something or someone, and most of the time, she was right.

Rena had a quietude that was special. She didn't take her gift seriously, and it was Charlie who kept telling her to recognize these skills.

You're psychic.

Shut up. No, I'm not.

She never pushed her opinions on Charlie or offered any information unless asked. No one knew she was special in this sense, as she often kept these thoughts to herself. In time, Charlie understood how difficult it must have been for her to stay objective about her father's illness.

"You knew he would die, didn't you?"

"Everybody dies, Charlie."

"You know what I mean. I'm not upset or angry that you didn't tell me."

"It wasn't a dream, you know."

"I know."

"I'm sorry for your loss. It was so sudden, so unexpected. We have so many memories with him. He was something else. Always on to our shenanigans."

"He was," Charlie agreed, looking up at Rena.

"Like the time he handed you the cordless phone my mom and dad found on the grass after we pretended to check in from my house before flinging the phone out the car window?"

"Where did we go again?" Charlie asked, her tone growing more animated.

"Meet boys at the Irish bar."

"Shannon McNair. He was so worth it."

Charlie wished she could go back to those times. Life was so simple then. It was never her against the world. He was always there to help her fight.

She mastered a subdued smile. "He bought me a book of 'yo mama' jokes to throw back at the kids in grade school who teased me about him being my mama."

"Yeah, yeah." Rena nodded. "You'd read them and memorize them and then practice them on me."

They both leaned back and let out a sigh. A moment to regret, recall, reminisce. It was Rena who broke through their memories.

"What are you going to do now?"

"I'm thinking of looking for my mother," she said.

Rena placed her drink down on the table. "Wait, what? You don't even know where she is."

"I bet Auntie Elma knows more than what she's letting on."

"Could be. But what about your job, your life here?"

"It'll be temporary. I'll be back. I need more time to think about it, though. Don't worry, I promise I won't hide from you again." Charlie reached under the coffee table and pulled out the metal box. She no longer needed the key. She kept it open as a symbol of her life to come. Things had to come out in the open. Find the truth. Air it out.

"Why? And for whom? For yourself? For your peace of mind?"

"For my father. And maybe partly for myself. Look, there are pictures of her." Charlie handed Rena the one with her surrounded by stuffed animals.

"Holy shit. That's you," Rena said, her eyes wide and her head drawn back. She held one palm up toward Charlie, gesturing to hand her the rest of the pictures. "And look, all the vintage Holly Hobbies and Hello Kitties. Very seventies." Her face froze when she saw Charlie wasn't laughing. Rena shuffled through them, pausing briefly and bringing the images closer to her face. "You're a better version, of course. You got a good mix of her and your dad. And what's with the pigs? Cute, but . . . my god, they were just kids."

41

Charlie nodded.

"What was her name?" Rena asked.

"Celia Ruiz."

"Celia Ruiz. Sounds as pretty as she was," Rena said, shaking her head while grinning from ear to ear. "Holy crap. You have a mother." She flipped through the pictures repeatedly, placing them in order and then rearranging them again.

"I know," Charlie responded. "Would have saved me a lot of angst during our high school days."

"Ha! Like the time Missy Malone invited us to a mother-daughter baking party at her country club. You refused to go, and you refused to take your dad. My mother offered to stand in for him, two daughters and one mom. Do you remember what you said?"

"'That only those with real moms should be going to a mother-daughter event. I was an angry sixteen-year-old, huh?'"

"Not angry. Just sad," Rena answered. "I don't remember why, but you did end up showing up on the day of the event."

"Yeah. The night before, he baked me some salted caramel choc chip cookies to prove to me that he was just as good a baker as any of the moms in our class."

"He was something else, your dad."

Charlie's eyes misted again, a serene smile crossing her face. She pictured her dad in a pink and white apron with *Girl Dad Extraordinaire* emblazoned across his chest. "Yeah. He was."

Rena returned the pictures and watched Charlie slip them back into the box. "I've got my suitcase with the front desk. I don't really feel like taking the train back to Philly at the moment. Mind if I stayed with you for a few days?"

"I would love it," Charlie answered, relieved and craving the company. She reached for Rena's hand and held it, knowing she would've never had the guts to ask.

CHAPTER 6

The air was still cold, but spring was trying its best to break through. Rena ended up at Charlie's for a week. They hardly saw each other during the day—Rena was thick in the middle of tax season, and Charlie spent most days packing up boxes at her father's home—but the fact that she wasn't alone in the evenings was invaluable.

Charlie had made her decision. And now, it was time to tie up loose ends. Once her father's home was up for sale, there were six offers in two days. Charlie held off. She hadn't signed anything yet, feeling the need to slow down her life a bit. The company she worked for just went public, leaving her with a nest egg on a ten multiple. It allowed her to pay off her apartment in full and then some.

Charlie often played trading games in her head. This for that. *My father's life for all the money in the world.*

Remnants of the latest snowstorm were still visible on the ground, covering the roadside with layers of graying, discolored slush. Everyone hoped it would be the last of the season, but she was a little less optimistic.

They had a favorite waterfront bistro blocks away from Charlie's apartment. The sun was blinding that afternoon, its reflection bouncing off the water and beaming colorful rays of light back up to the sky. Charlie shielded her eyes, straining to watch as he approached the restaurant entrance. She used to love looking at him and observing him when they were in client pitches. The way he moved and spoke, the European in him, his accent, his mannerisms, his confidence, those slim-fitting clothes. She'd never believed when he'd said she was beautiful. How could someone so perfect love someone like her?

He saw her and waved. She signaled back with a half-wave and a half-smile. Nervous, she dropped her hands to her side and clenched her fingers. Then she took a deep breath and pushed her shoulders back. "Confidence is rooted in compe-tence," her executive coach used to say. It was the wrong analogy for that day. Love and commitment weren't exactly her strong suits.

He approached her table and kissed Charlie on both cheeks. "Lorenzo. Hi."

He returned her greeting with a slight nod, looking straight at her while taking a seat across the table. His eyes looked empty.

"Thanks for coming"—she cleared her throat—"today." After an awkward pause, "Oh, and of course, to the funeral. I'm sorry I wasn't able to talk to you. People were coming and going, and I—"

He stayed quiet, waving his hand to get the server's attention and asking for a cup of coffee.

"I'm okay. Better, at least," Charlie started again, trying her best to avoid his eyes. She felt it. Not just the heat of his stare but a sudden urge to reach out and touch him. Of course, she didn't, but she wanted to. "I just noticed that the sun is out today. Winter felt like forever this year. I mean, I just remembered. I haven't checked on my car in a while," she rambled on.

He drew a breath and exhaled loudly, impatient. Resentful.

"Why are we here, Charlie?" As if he hadn't heard a word she'd said. Hard to believe these were his first words to her since that day six months ago.

"I just wanted to see you, I guess," she stuttered. *This was a bad idea.* "I've been making a few decisions in the days after . . . well since he left. You were such a big part of my life, and—"

"Nice to know you felt that way about us." He took a sip of his coffee, still keeping his distance with his hands clasped and resting on the edge of the table.

"Lor. That's not fair."

He raised his eyebrows and shrugged. And then he began tapping his fingers on the tabletop.

"I know you're still angry with me. I didn't mean to force you to see me. I just thought I should let you know. I found out my dad had been in touch with my mom. Or at least knew what she'd been up to all these years—"

"What?" he said, visibly surprised, shifting in his seat before leaning forward and reaching across the table for her hand. When he found it, he held on tightly, rubbing his thumb across her wrist. It was a complete change in demeanor. She didn't want his pity, but there it was. He knew better than to offer platitudes. "Oh, Charlie. I'm sorry. What did you find out?"

"That she's still alive, mostly. She wrote him letters. I haven't read them yet. But in time, I suppose I will. I should. Shouldn't I?"

"You should," he said. "It may have the answers you've been looking for."

The server offered Charlie a refill of her iced tea, which she declined.

"Answers," she laughed quietly as the server walked away. "I never even had questions until he died."

"Actually, you did. Maybe you just didn't know it. But you've been searching for something all these years. Something I couldn't give, apparently," he said, using the creamer as an excuse to withdraw his hand.

Charlie felt tension in his voice. She hesitated to bring up old wounds, but she wanted to apologize for everything. That would mean rehashing what she had done and what had happened between them.

"I kept thinking you would leave."

"Why?"

"Just . . . because. Maybe because your mother is this aristocratic Spanish socialite, and I was a motherless girl from Sunset Park."

"First of all, she loved you," he said, a slight smile forming on his lips. Charlie thought she was falling in love with him all over again. Well, as much as she could define that feeling. There'd been quite a bit of talk between her and Rena—that she couldn't love anyone, that she didn't really love him.

Charlie grew pensive, leaning her chin against the palm of her hand while keeping her gaze fixed on the rivulets formed by the melting snow. "She asked me to call her 'mama' the day you brought her to meet me."

"And it was so hard for you to process that," he said.

"I have no right to be anyone's daughter."

"She thought you were the most intelligent girl I'd ever dated, aside from being the most beautiful. That's the thing about all of this. You were like a daughter to her."

Charlie shook her head. "That's because she loved you."

Whoops. They'd had this discussion before, and it always triggered him.

"Oh, come on. What are we talking about? Why are we even here?"

Charlie had lost him again. This time, he had moved away. Pushed his seat back and maintained more of a distance from her.

"Sorry, sorry. I don't want this to be contentious. I really wanted to see you and apologize for everything. We didn't end on the right note, and I take full responsibility for that. I was just so confused. I didn't want to hold you back, hold you down. We had so many dreams and plans, and when my dad got sick, I didn't want you to be burdened with that, too."

"We were together for three years, Charlie. I wanted to marry you. But you used your dad's sickness as an excuse to push me away."

Charlie vehemently shook her head. "No, I did not! He was sick. He needed me."

"And I was right there with you," he said, his voice resigned. "But you kept looking out to the future with one eye wide open. Always thinking something was going to happen."

"You were too good to be true."

"And I felt that way about you. I just wanted to love you."

"I'm sorry." Nothing she could have said could have countered the truth he spoke. "You have good reason to be angry."

Lorenzo sighed loudly. "I'm not angry. I'm extremely hurt. You broke up with me just like that. I quit my job so that we wouldn't be working at the same company together. I saw forever with you, but you didn't see it with me. That's the painful truth."

"I'm sorry," she repeated. There was nothing else she could say.

When he looked at her again, she saw the apprehension in his face, the way it hardened like a sculpture, the lines on his forehead, and the narrowed gap between his eyes carved in cement. *Here was a girl he couldn't fix*, she thought. *Though he tried and he tried and he tried.*

"Your dad was an amazing father. He gave you everything he could. Come to think of it, why open up a can of worms? Maybe you don't need to read those letters. Maybe he kept them from you for a reason. What if you find out that your dad's love was enough? What if you don't really glean anything new from all this? You have a full life, you have a successful career, you have friends, people who love you."

"I don't even know who I am, Lor. Why did I push you away? Why couldn't I just be happy with what we had? I don't want to live a life like you said, always waiting for the other shoe to drop. My dad is gone. There are no more excuses. I wanted to see you today to tell you that I'm going to fix myself. I'm going to read those letters, maybe even find my mother. Maybe after this, I won't—" She stopped mid-sentence, unsure she should say those hurtful words. As hurtful as they were, she realized their relationship was doomed from the start. Not just a case of bad timing but a case of mismatched priorities.

But he egged her on. "Won't what?" He pulled out his wallet and left some cash on the table. Charlie took it as a sign to leave, getting up from her seat and slipping on her coat. He led the way toward the exit.

"And then maybe I won't be so afraid to love someone fully. Maybe I won't be paranoid. Maybe I'll stop sabotaging my relationships. Maybe I can become more courageous. Stop being afraid of everything."

He closed his eyes before bobbing his head up and down. Charlie saw him flinch at her words, taking a step back and trying to keep a steady balance before moving forward again. "You can't love anyone."

"Not the way you wanted me to."

They walked out into the sunshine. Charlie hoped it was a sign of forgiveness when Lorenzo took her hand as they crossed the dock and approached the parking lot. A flock of seagulls flapped their wings above, a sure sign that the weather would be kinder, gentler. When they reached his car, he turned to her and pulled her close. There they were, face to face, that familiar feeling of love and trust sweeping all over her again.

"Where's your car? Did you need me to dig it out of the snow? I can walk home with you."

"The snow should be melting now. I'm going to give it a day or two and then check it out."

"Are you sure?" He rested his forehead on hers, their noses touching. Charlie reveled in the feel of his breath on her face.

"Yes." She pulled away to gaze at him. "I am so sorry, Lor. For everything I put you through."

"You were honest. You did everything out of honesty. I love you, Charlie. I will always love you."

And there it was, that sad acquiescence. Deep breaths, nodding heads, clenched smiles. They were saying goodbye. When he closed his eyes and sighed before pulling her in, she memorized that moment. She had been loved once—she could find love again. This knowledge could carry her through this next phase of her life, at least for a while.

Gently, Lorenzo combed his fingers through her hair and kissed the top of her head. "Be happy, Charlie. Whatever it is you're looking for, don't take what you have here and now for granted. There's nothing out there that you don't already have."

"Thank you," she whispered into his chest.

He held her tightly for a few more seconds, lifted her chin, and kissed her gently. And then, with a sad smile, he let her go.

CHAPTER 7

Holy moly. How did spring sneak up on her like this? The sun was shining, and tourist season was in full swing. Brooklyn was no longer immune to the crowds that swamped Manhattan. The oak trees, once barren and bare, began to bloom again. Parks and gardens slowly turned luxuriant green. The pink and white flowers of the cherry blossoms, now puffed and swollen, traveled with the wind and landed on the sidewalks. People embraced the milder temperatures, shedding their winter coats and storing every reminder of winter. Cafés and restaurants had started offering outdoor seating, and the aroma of freshly brewed coffee filled the air. Brooklyn's cultural scene was coming alive, showcasing new artists and invigorating its sense of community. Roads were blocked for neighborhood markets and outdoor concerts, and street fairs now filled its sidewalks. Spring was always a season of renewal, a brand-new canvas. There were no more excuses for hiding.

Every day brought Charlie a new sense of clarity. She had a plan to close the loop on the open edges of her life. First, there was Lorenzo, and then her extended leave from work. The only item in her father's estate was the home he'd left to her, fully paid and owned. One by one, things were falling into place.

But the biggest quandary remained: would she be reading her mother's letters, and what would she do with what she found out? Although she spent her days in a flurry of activity, mostly winding down her father's affairs and closing down his home, she felt rudderless, lost. She had given everything up, first for her career and then to care for her father. In the end, she was left with only herself. And so, despite everything she had accomplished, she found herself questioning her motives. Was it for her? For him? For whom?

It was a sunny spring day while she sipped a cup of coffee on the banks of the East River, watching people walk through the cobblestoned streets and past the giant boulders anchored on the shore. She decided she was going to get a dog. A dog would not only keep her company, but it would also symbolize a home. You can never leave a dog. You would always have to come back to a dog. A dog could be something she could love unconditionally.

But where would that home be, exactly?

Her father was gone. She'd abandoned Sunset Park for the ritzier Brooklyn Heights. But that wasn't her home either. How could she get a dog if she didn't have a home?

This newfound information that her mother was alive . . . could that be her home?

How would she know if she didn't try to find her?

Surely, there are so many ways of finding a person these days. Heck, she was at the airport for work a few months ago, and the TSA guy who scanned her boarding pass knew she had Global Entry and lived in Brooklyn. It should be easy to trace a person.

Maybe by finding her mother, she would find her home. And herself.

Didn't Auntie Elma say she was in California?

She would take the time off. Drive to California. Get some alone time. Clear her head, cleanse her soul of the pain of losing her father and finding out his secret.

What a brilliant idea.

CHAPTER 8

Nothing at work was ever going to be the same again. Everything had forever changed. The hallways, the lunchroom, the copy room—all the places filled with memories of congregating, gossiping, confiding in your co-workers—were empty. Memories of the team singing made-up songs to describe the stressful projects they led as they shimmied down the halls, laughing, dancing, shuffling across desks MC Hammer-style. Those behaviors, those relationships, were stark memories. Now, it was a younger generation who expected to rise through the ranks without ever meeting in person, confident that their virtual reality was, indeed, reality. For a while, the world had been in disarray. People were kept away from public places, offices were emptied while businesses struggled to keep going. They were run from different parts of a house—the bedroom, the kitchen, the garage.

Even the posh, modern gathering place on twenty-one looked like a wasteland. Where state-of-the-art coffee machines and vending machines offering a variety of food ranging from crappy to healthy once stood, lines of untouched coffee cups and brand-new eating supplies became the focal point of the space. There was excess everywhere, unused and unissued computers

ANNA GOMEZ

on desks that would never be occupied. Under normal circumstances, Charlie would be all over this waste, calling the office operations people to have them haul out, resell, and find a way to get their funds back on all the extra inventory. Budgets would be cut. Spending would be controlled. But these were not ordinary times. Company leaders were still trying to find a happy medium between ensuring their workers were safe and the cost of delaying financial decisions.

The company's hybrid working arrangement required people to come in on Tuesdays and Thursdays. Charlie made it a point to come in on a Wednesday. She knew Derge, the CEO, would be there. He was always there. He tried to set a good example for the leadership team and hoped that if he showed up every day, they would follow. It obviously didn't work. They were the only ones on the executive floor that day.

Charlie entered her office, intent on going through some of the documents she'd left behind months ago. There she was, in her very own career time capsule. The space was littered with things she had taken for granted and never missed all that time. Awards, certificates, and her favorite blue highlighter. Pictures taken during the annual Christmas parties were posted on the corkboard above her desk. Of all the things she'd never had, her career sort of made up for it. A corner office with an art deco desk, paintings from the archives of the building, a couch for when employees turned her into a therapist, throw pillows, blankets, and oh—her Hermès coat. Hanging on the back of her door was that precious coat.

Precious at one time, forgettable that day. She'd forgotten she even owned something like that. Wrapped in their individual bags were shoes tucked away in the bottom drawer, waiting for her. A pair of Louboutins for client meetings, some Burberry flats, and a pair of Gucci loafers. Charlie was that shallow and

54

brand-conscious. She splurged on those things, and for what? To fit into a world she was never really a part of. In the beginning, she'd tried her best to shove her introverted self aside by attending their parties, going on their girl trips, and buying the brands her colleagues coveted. But then she tired of it. She lost interest in keeping up with them and being part of their shallow, useless conversations. She was caring for her father, and there weren't enough hours in a day to accomplish anything more than that.

"Charlie?"

She looked up to find Derge standing by the door. He pinched the bridge of his nose and adjusted his mask.

"Hi, D. I thought I'd come by and see you." Charlie stood up to walk toward him. He hugged her and then settled on her couch while she kept her distance and sat across from him.

"How are you holding up? I know you've had a rough time."

"I'm getting by, thank you. Lots of information to process, things to wrap up, but one day at a time, right? Or step by step, as you like to say."

"Yes, yes."

"If you have a few minutes, I've been thinking about everything that's happened. You know, I took a leave of absence almost four months ago when he got really sick and then assured you I'd be back as he got better. And actually . . ." She paused, remembering how much Derge had invested in her. The patience, the support, everything. "Not just then, but for the past seven years. I want you to know how grateful I am to you and this company."

"Charlie, you helped make us who we are today. A lot of our success has to do with you."

She looked away.

"You've never been good about compliments." He laughed, knees bouncing, constantly fidgety. Because of him, Charlie always believed that successful people were the ones who couldn't sit still and who were enemies of complacency. "But take it as the truth because you are valued here."

"Thank you."

"Are you packing up?" he asked, leaning sideways to look over her shoulder.

"Well, that's what I came to speak to you about. I need more time, I think."

"Of course. You just suffered an incredible loss. There's no doubt that you need more time."

"Well, there's more than that." She looked at Derge, who tilted his head like a puppy straining to hear commands. "I found out that my dad had been in touch with my mother all these years. It's a—"

"Oh," Derge said, lifting his mask in response, his puckered lips suspended momentarily.

"Yes," she continued. "It's a huge revelation to me, and I'm still processing it. But amid all these feelings, I know I'm going to have to find her."

"How?"

"I know she's in California. I thought I might drive there and take some time alone. Life had been moving at lightning speed for a few years, and I'd like to slow it down."

"But . . . drive?"

"Yeah." She smiled sheepishly. "I figured I need time on my own to deal with my situation."

"Makes sense," he said, nodding.

"I don't have to get paid. I've got enough. You've given me enough."

She saw his reaction. Neck slackened, shoulders drooping, weighed down and burdened. "You're not coming back, are you?" She had loaded him enough with her sadness. He didn't deserve it.

"I don't know."

"Will you keep in touch? Let us know how you're doing?"

She nodded, deciding to lighten things up. "Hey, D, do you remember the first year I worked here? I was so shy, I didn't even correct anyone when they placed the wrong nameplate outside my office."

"And everyone started calling you Clarissa. For one year."

Her name is Carlotta! Someone had yelled out in the middle of a meeting.

"Thank God for Linda. She blew my secret identity out into the open." Charlie giggled.

"And look at you now," Derge said, smiling.

"I learned everything I know from you."

"I know." He paused to look directly at her. "I know how difficult it was for you to approach me that day to ask for a limited schedule. You always worked so hard and devoted so many hours, and the fact that you had to slow down to take care of your father was causing you so much turmoil."

Charlie nodded.

"It's just a delay, Charlie," he said, making sure to catch her gaze. "You didn't give anything up. The path has been built. You just had to take a little detour."

Another nod from her. She couldn't disagree. Charlie was resentful about it at first, but as the weeks passed and as she watched her father get weaker, thinner, and more disoriented, she realized that her time with him was going to be limited. What a cruel twist of fate to have him get better from the cancer but die from the treatment.

"How did you know?"

"Hmmm. Well, the first sign was the fact that you were crying so much. It hurt me to watch you that way. But also because I saw you rise through the ranks, driven by your ambition."

"In the end, I don't regret my decision. I'm so glad I got to spend every day of his final year with him."

"You are a force, Charlie. You're honest, ethical, and the best darn revenue officer in our industry. You've always been so closed-up, never really said much or divulged much about yourself. You're an enigma to some, a mystery. After all these years, I still can't say I know you too well."

"And yet..."

"I knew you had so much potential. Something was driving you to succeed. I didn't know what it was, but now I understand more. I know you'll rise above all this pain. But it takes time. And I'm glad you realized that you need the space to recover. Racquel and I wish you all the best. This company will always be here for you. Come back to us when you're ready."

CHAPTER 9

Charlie looked out the window to find her car right where she'd left it six weeks ago. The fact that the car had survived the winter being parked in the alley for over a month was significant. *At least I don't have to dig it out.*

Charlie had drowned in remorse for so long that she figured it was time to get back into the sunshine.

Her mind turned to logistics. How many days would it take to get to California in an electric vehicle? Where would she stop to recharge? Where would she stay for the night?

Rena thought the trip would give her time to read the letters and clear her thoughts.

"I feel so guilty I can't come with you."

"It's tax season, I totally understand."

"Can't you find another time to go? Like after May 15?"

"I may lose my nerve by then. This is something I need to do while I still want to do it."

Without her father, her purpose was gone, but time was suddenly in abundance.

And she didn't know whether to unravel what her father thought was his gift to her. She was just as confused as ever and knew she had quite a bit of untangling to do.

Charlie ended her six-mile run early Sunday morning where her car was parked. It was time to get it serviced and ready for her upcoming trip. The absence of a sound when she pressed her key remote surprised her. She could have sworn she'd locked her car—or maybe not. After all this time, she couldn't remember. When she opened the door and slid into the driver's seat, the inside of the car was warm. It smelled of something . . . something clean and minty. Soap? Toothpaste?

The car shook, and a loud thump came from the back seat.

Charlie screeched, leaping out and onto the sidewalk. She watched as something struggled to emerge from its covering. A blanket, a sleeping bag. She didn't know. A tangled mess of fur stuck out as the car wobbled from side to side.

There's a bear in my car!

The bear wrangled its way out of the bag and sat up. Only it wasn't a bear.

Someone had been sleeping in her car.

A man. A very hairy man.

He grabbed the door handle and yanked it once, twice, three times. Charlie had locked him inside.

The man banged his fist on the window. "Let me out!"

At least, that's what she assumed he said. The glass muffled his voice.

"Not until I call the police! You've been trespassing on my property!" she yelled, shaking her head. She had to think fast. She'd leave him there until the police arrived. Poised to dial 911, she looked up and saw his face. There he sat, looking bereft and hopeless. His breath misted the glass even more. Seemed like the guy's life was already in shambles. She didn't want to ruin it with a criminal record.

Charlie leaned toward the window. "Mister, I'm going to unlock the door. Get out of here before I change my mind and call the police. Put your hands up, and don't try anything dumb."

The man nodded and complied while moving closer to the door. What she saw took her aback. Under the wiry, unruly hair and a full beard that covered most of his face, she saw his eyes. Stark, deep green like the forest, downcast and sad, ridden with melancholy. She began to empathize with the stranger.

Slowly, she unlocked the door and stepped back.

The man jumped out of the car, still holding his hands up where she could see them. Something about his clothes made her think he hadn't been homeless for very long. He wore cargo pants and a sweatshirt, which didn't look worn or dingy. For a brief second, she thought she saw a look of recognition on his face as if he knew her from somewhere. Which, of course, was impossible.

"Miss, I'm—"

"No, no," she said, waving a hand to stop him. "Just go. Before I change my mind and have you arrested."

Keeping his head down, the man nodded and started to walk away. When she saw him turn the corner, Charlie heaved a sigh of relief. She slid into the driver's seat, locked all the doors, and stepped on the brake.

Nothing.

After multiple tries, it dawned on her. Not even the dashboard was coming to life. Her car was completely dead. Why should she be surprised when she'd left it in the cold and snow for so long? Charlie got out and stood on the sidewalk, searching her phone. She knew the closest charging station was five miles away. All she had to do was call for a tow truck. Or so she thought. Charlie paced back and forth in frustration. Several calls to different companies, and no answer.

"Is everything okay?" Startled by the interruption, she turned to find the same man standing a few feet away.

"Yes," she said, her voice raised in annoyance. "Everything is fine. I thought I told you to go away." Surprisingly, she wasn't afraid of him. She just wanted to figure out her next steps without the unnecessary intervention.

"Doesn't look like everything is fine." He pointed at her car. "Must be completely drained."

"I'm getting a tow truck."

"Okay, then." He shrugged, clutching the handles of his backpack before turning away.

Charlie looked around. There was no one else in sight. The entire neighborhood was asleep. Maybe this guy could help. "Wait!" she called out and was surprised that he spun around so quickly, as if he expected her to change her mind. "The truth is, I haven't been able to reach anyone."

"Well, it's early in the morning on a Sunday. Some 24/7 services don't apply to the weekends."

She was so out of her element. "Is there any way to charge this car so I can get it going? My dad used to handle these things . . ."

The man stared at something in front of him. At first, she thought he was scoping her apartment, which was across the alley.

"What are you thinking?" she asked, trying not to act suspicious.

He stayed quiet for a few more seconds. "I see an outlet in the wall down there."

Charlie chastised herself. She'd been watching too many episodes of *The First 48*. How on earth would he even know where she lived?

"We'll need a few extension cords. Do you have any industrial ones?" he asked.

"What's the difference?"

"Sorry," he said. "The thicker, heavy-duty ones. For outdoors mostly."

"Actually, I may have. My dad—" she stopped. The memory of him lit up her face, and she gave the stranger a cautious smile. "Let me go get them."

Charlie was back in a few minutes, holding some thick orange cords and some smaller green cords. The man nodded as she handed them to him. "Now what?" she asked.

Slowly, the stranger began connecting one extension cord to the other. Charlie helped him unravel them. He attached the prongs to the rear of the car and headed across the street to her apartment building. Charlie watched while he lifted the metal casing built into the brick wall and plugged in the cord.

"There we go," he declared, smiling. "It's Sunday, so hopefully, the alley traffic won't be too bad."

"Thank you," Charlie said, showing her relief by wiping her brow before sitting on the curb and leaning against the wall. "How long do you think it will take?"

The man remained standing. She noticed he was quite tall and lean.

"Well, we just plugged it into an ordinary 110-volt outlet. It will take 24 hours to fully charge your car."

"What?" Charlie reacted, her voice an octave higher than normal. "No! Obviously, we can't hook it up for 24 hours." She calmed down, reminding herself that he had nothing to do with her negligence. "How much time will it take for a partial charge? I think all I need is about 10% to drive it to the charging station."

"Three hours, maybe?" he guessed.

Charlie glanced at her Garmin and pressed some buttons to check the time. Three hours would get her charged by lunch. Enough time to get to Auntie Elma's for an early dinner. "Much better, but oh gosh, what a pain."

"I can watch it for you if you want to just leave me here."

"Oh no, I can't do that to you. It's my car, and this is my fault."

The man shrugged. "It's not like I have anywhere to be."

"First, I have a question. How did you even get into my car?" Charlie asked, her tone biting and her hands gesturing all over the place.

"It wasn't locked. It was the only car that was open."

She couldn't argue that point. Who knows what happened almost two months ago? She could hardly remember even parking her car. And what did it matter? He was there, helping her out.

Charlie saw his embarrassment by the forced grin on his face. She turned away to avoid the awkwardness of it all. She also didn't know this man and was careful not to say anything that might trigger him. He didn't seem agitated, though. In fact, his eyes remained kind, and his demeanor tranquil.

"May I sit with you then?" he asked.

"I guess."

The man made an effort to keep his distance, taking his place on the ground a few feet from her. He sat with his knees up against his chest while she stretched her legs and crossed them at the ankles. Charlie took her phone out and began to scroll. As they sat in silence, she focused her attention on texting Rena.

I've got a story for you. You won't believe what happened this morning.

Tell me!

Busy right now, but I'll call later.

And then her cousin, Justin.

Yo, Jus. What do you think your mom's making for lunch today?

"Great job finding the extension cords," the man said, interrupting her texting spree. "Did you just happen to have them lying around?"

She smiled at him. "Sort of. I'm packing to leave, so I just had them in a box."

"I probably shouldn't ask where you're going," he said matter of fact.

"Probably not."

"You said something about your dad. Is he out of town or something?"

"Something," she answered curtly before turning away.

This stranger was relentless. He stared at her as if he understood, and he looked like he, too, had lost something. She could tell he was trying to make small talk, but neither of them knew what to say.

"Well, I'd buy you a coffee if I could," he finally said, trying hard to break the ice.

"Ha!" she exclaimed, her laughter breaking the barrier between them. He laughed, too.

"Wait right here," she instructed. It was the least she could do for the help he was giving her. "I'll get us some. Americano okay?"

By the time Charlie got back, one charging hour had passed. "What's that?" she asked, handing him his coffee.

He dropped a pamphlet he'd been reading to the ground. "I've been going to the library lately. It's their schedule. I can never figure out their hours. They're closed some days this month and have odd hours when they are open."

Charlie decided she would name him Bear Man. Though his beard covered his face, his eyes were expressive, giving her a sense of his depth of character and experience.

They sipped their coffee in silence for a while. Bear Man continued to read his pamphlet. Charlie felt guilty about being so short with him. Despite the way they had met, he was there helping her when he didn't have to. Even if he seemed down and out, he was bestowing her with an act of kindness. He wasn't

65

angry or resentful. He didn't rant about the ills of society or ply her with sad tales of his misfortune. In fact, he was quiet and pleasant.

"I'm sorry you had to change your plans today," she said, her gaze still fixed on her stalled car. *Stalled, just like her life.* And then she caught herself. "I mean, whatever you were going to do after you—" *Woke up?*

"Nah," he interrupted, looking at the ground. "I have no plans."

"No plans for today? Or no plans at all?" she asked, curious about his world.

"I'm still wandering, I guess."

"Listen," she said, turning to face him. "I'm sorry about being so short with you. The truth is my father passed away last winter. He was obsessed with—" she paused to snicker. "With the Christmas holidays. He used to help me put up my Christmas lights and turn them into this whole complicated production. I had flashing lights out my window and dancing reindeer on the roof of my building." She realized he was staring at her, trying to understand her range of emotions by listening to her voice. She tried hard to be on an even keel, but it wasn't exactly working. She could tell by the way he looked at her. But she missed her dad at that moment, and the flood of her emotions threatened to overflow.

"I'm so sorry for your loss. I know how that kind of loss upends one's entire life."

She pulled her knees to her chest and nodded. "Well, no one's more sorry than I am. Upended. Definitely."

A handful of cars driving down the street gave them time to sit and watch in silence. Charlie thought about how this man expertly found her car's charge port, which was concealed behind a door beside a rear taillight.

"I'm assuming you've had some experience with this type of EV," she commented.

"In another life."

Charlie cringed every time a car ran over the cords, but she tried to conceal the apprehension on her face and any sign of tension. With every thud, she worried that one of the wires would pull apart. Once in a while, Bear Man would catch her gaze and smile, assuring her that everything was okay. In between the humps and bumps and the rolling of cars, she stayed on her phone, swiping on articles in the *New York Times*, while he went across the street to check on the charge. All around them, the city's slumber was over. Life was buzzing once again. People were walking their dogs, and families were heading to church in their Sunday best. Charlie and Bear Man didn't need to speak. They didn't have to mask the silence with their words. The city had come alive and was doing it for them.

Over two charging hours later, Charlie yelled over to Bear Man.

"How much of a charge does it have now?"

"Seven percent," he yelled back after peeking into the driver's window.

Charlie headed over to her car. "I think I can make it five miles on seven percent."

"Okay." He didn't argue with her. Instead, he unplugged the cords from the building outlet, rolled them up, and placed them in her trunk.

"How can I thank you for your help?" she asked, closing the trunk of her car. "Can I pay you for your time, at least?"

"Oh no, I'm the one who should be paying you."

She looked at him quizzically. Had she already forgotten? He was sleeping in her car.

"Oh!" she answered. "It's okay. You helped me so much today." And then she slipped into the driver's seat, pressed on the brake, and clapped happily when the car started. "I'd better go get this charged before it drains again. Thank you for all your help. Good luck."

And with that, Charlie waved at Bear Man and drove away.

CHAPTER 10

Charlie was unnerved by the encounter with the stranger. She was torn between her gratitude and being incensed by his actions. Those eyes haunted her for a few days. She was familiar with the look of loss. She'd been wearing it for as long as she could remember. What was it he said about wandering through life? If only he knew that she'd been meandering longer than both of them combined.

Two days later, Charlie got her car cleaned and detailed. The interior wasn't damaged. All she found were two Mentos wrappers. Charlie felt guilty about her overreaction.

"I truly thought it was an animal," she told Rena. "Haven't you heard about bears entering people's cars on those camping grounds?"

"Yes, but in New York?"

"We have zoo animals, Rena."

"Animal or man, you did the right thing. Animals have evolved. They now know how to unlock car doors. And there are so many crazy people out there, too."

"He wasn't crazy, though. He seemed pretty normal."

"Did you get to ask him why he was in your car? What was he doing there?"

"No. He was being so kind to me, and he was obviously homeless. I didn't want to push it any further."

Charlie tried to focus on her upcoming trip. She thought about those letters every single day, grappled with her decision to read them, relentlessly questioning Auntie Elma to divulge what she knew.

"You're what? Why?" Auntie Elma had asked, unable to hide her astonishment.

"My father wanted me to get to know her. What better way?" And when she saw Aunt Elma deep in thought, she added. "I know you know more. I even think you know where she is. Please tell me."

"Oh, Charlie. That's not my story to tell."

"Why not?"

"Because if your father wanted to tell you, he would have told you years ago."

"So, you do know," Charlie said, throwing her hands up in the air in exasperation.

"Oh, Charlie."

"Will you at least help me find her?"

"Of course. But it may take a while. I can help by contacting friends of friends. We can see what we come up with. So, you should just wait a few—"

"I can't wait. I have to do it now. While I have the guts."

Her life's decisions would be based on this new discovery. Her sense of self, of belonging somewhere to someone, depended on it. She had to move quickly. It wasn't a comfortable place for her to be, not knowing, not seeing, not having a plan.

Sutter's Grocery was full of nosy tourists, lookie-loos picking up items and then putting them back. Charlie walked around the store, recyclable bag on her arm, picking up toiletries and snacks from every aisle. Even buying groceries was a step forward for her. She was extremely proud of herself. Tourists swamped the walkways, ambling around with their kids, undecided and confused about so many choices. Charlie enjoyed overhearing their conversations. They reminded her of the times her father would walk her to the little store to get a prize every time she aced a test.

From across the street, she could see a man standing by the entrance of her condo. She didn't think anything of it, walking toward him just like any other stranger on any other day.

"Excuse me, miss?" the man said when he approached her.

"Can I help you?"

He sputtered an uneasy laugh before nervously running a hand through his hair. "You don't recognize me cleaned up."

This man had wavy brown hair, a five o'clock shadow . . . and those vivid green eyes.

Still, Charlie wasn't sure. There was a world of difference between that day and now. She squinted and shook her head.

"I'm Graham. I slept in your car."

"Oh," she said, hugging her grocery bag to her chest.

"This is for the use of your car," he said, handing her two one-hundred-dollar bills.

Charlie backed away, waving her hand in refusal. "Where did you get that money?"

"From my bank."

"From your bank," she repeated. "You have a bank account but no place to sleep?"

"Long story. I'm sure you don't care to hear it."

"You're right, I don't." Charlie turned her back on him and shielded the security keypad with one hand. As an after-thought, she turned around and faced him. "Can I ask you something?"

"Yes."

"How long were you sleeping in my car?"

"Since March."

"March? As in for a month?"

"I'd go to the warming shelters on most nights, but once in a while, I just needed to be alone, so I'd sleep in odd places here and there. One night, I got caught in a bad rainstorm, and your car was open. I didn't expect to keep coming back, but I noticed the car sitting in the same spot for weeks, unlocked."

"I was a little preoccupied." Heat rushed to her cheeks.

"I figured its owner was on an extended trip out of town," Graham added. "It was the perfect hiding place for me. Brooklyn Heights is not exactly known for . . . people like me."

"Huh," Charlie said, curious. "Interesting. Are you hiding from the law? Was it drugs that did you in? Did you steal from someone?"

"None of the above. As I said, it's a long story. I'm just trying to make my way home."

"Where's that?"

"Oregon."

Charlie saw how discomfited he was, looking down with his shoulders hunched. The thing was, his posture didn't change the fact that she was fascinated by his eyes. They were piercing and soulful, messy yet mysterious, like the way moss covers the cracks in a stone. And the rest of his face wasn't bad either. In fact, he was quite handsome. She was excited to tell Rena her theory—that he was an ex-model who fell on tough times.

"You're right. We all have our long stories. Too many stories, not enough time." She caught herself mid-sentence, feeling guilty for being so harsh. She softened her tone a bit. "Listen, keep your money. You need it more than I do. I'm sorry for being so short. I've just got so much going on, and I'm preparing for a trip."

"Don't apologize. I was a squatter in your car."

Charlie nodded and shielded the keypad again to type in her code. "I have to go. I really hope everything works out for you."

CHAPTER 11

Charlie was leaving in two days. She was packed and ready to go. Her condo was fully cleaned, and the service would take care of her mail and water her plants. She wanted to get one more run in, visit Auntie Elma, and have dinner with Rena. Until then, there was no itinerary, just a Google Map of the places she'd have to stop to refuel and a list of hotels she could stay in along the way.

Spring was in full swing. People were everywhere, and shorts became a thing. The annual Cherry Blossom Festival brought people from all over the world to admire the delicate pink and white petals covering the landscape. Her father once told her that cherry blossoms symbolized life—its brevity, impermanence, and unique but fleeting beauty.

Papa, people live longer than two weeks.

Ah, but when you get older, time will fly so fast it will feel like you only lived for two weeks.

That recollection brought her sadness, placed a permanent knot in her belly, and addled her with regret.

While she was cleaning out her fridge, her phone rang. It was Auntie Elma.

"Hi, Auntie," she greeted.

"Charlie, darling girl, when are you leaving?"

"Friday. The day after tomorrow. I'm just having dinner with Rena tonight and making sure I get everything closed up before I go."

"Uncle Joe's dad fell ill, and we have to take a plane to Chicago in a few hours. I'm sorry, but I won't be able to see you before you go. Can you delay your trip a little bit?"

Charlie paused for a second, taking a bite of a cheese puff she'd found while cleaning out the cupboard. "I've been delaying this. I think I'm just going to have to get started. No need to see me, Auntie. I promise I'll call every day, check in with you, and see what you've found out."

"I've been reaching out to her family to see whether anyone knows where your mother is. I'm sure I'll find out shortly. Why don't we keep in touch? I'll send you what I have as soon as I can. Where are you staying when you get to Los Angeles?"

"Is she in LA? Is that for sure?"

That made Auntie Elma chuckle. "Oh, Charlie. You're leaving, and we're not even sure where she is. Just plan on LA for now. I heard she is somewhere in Malibu."

At that point, she was wolfing down some crackers. "I want to be close to where she is, so once I know, I can book a place."

"And where would you go if we don't find her?" Auntie Elma was beginning to sound concerned. Her tone had changed, the lilt in her voice disappearing. "It's just not like you to have no plan."

"I'm trying a different way. Maybe this will help me live in the moment and learn to listen to what's happening around me for once. I wasted so much time trying to get somewhere, and I don't even remember what my destination was."

"Nothing was your fault, Charlie. And we have to keep going through this loss. Hopefully, we can turn all this added information into something positive."

"I hope so." Charlie paused. "Auntie Elma?"

"Yes?"

"Did you ever read those letters?"

"No," Auntie Elma answered. "But not for the reasons you may think. I was selfishly trying to protect myself and my memories of your mother. I loved your father, and I thought that knowing how much he loved her would hurt me more."

That just confirmed what Charlie had known all along. "You were in love with him."

"Yes. But Uncle Joe—"

"Uncle Joe is good for you."

"Yes." Auntie Elma began to cry. "Life doesn't work out how you want it to, but it always works out for the best. Remember that, Charlie."

"I love you, Auntie Elma."

"I love you, my little Carlotta. Travel safe, and make sure you check in with me every day. Or else Uncle Joe has connections in every police department in the country."

Charlie's giggle prompted Auntie Elma to do the same.

"Oh no, seriously? You're now officially stalking me?" Charlie yelled out when she saw Graham standing beside her car. "Maybe I need to call the police this time."

"Where are you traveling to?" he asked, ignoring her perturbed stance, hands on hips, and a cold, steely glare.

"I'm a black belt in karate." Liar. It was Krav Maga, but that took more explaining. Who cared?

"Where are you traveling to?" he asked again.

"Please move," Charlie said, trying to get past him. "I'm serious, and I'm going to call the police."

"Please!" Graham yelped. "Hear me out. I just need to make my way home to Oregon, and when you mentioned you were going on a road trip, I thought I could pay you to give me a ride. I could keep you company." He stepped aside to let her through.

"Pay me?"

"When I get access to my money in Oregon."

"No thanks. You do know this all sounds so weird. Like, why would I ride in a car with a stranger?"

"Technically, I'm not a stranger. I lived in your car."

Charlie had to laugh. This was ridiculous. Why would he ever assume she would ride with someone she met one week ago, let alone someone who illegally trespassed on her property?

"Case in point. You're kind of a criminal. Or a trespasser, at least."

"Come on, I have no criminal record. I've just had a hard time lately and need a ride back home."

"I'm sorry," she said, tugging on the car door. "I can't. I know I owe you for helping me out with my car. I'm grateful. I really am. But this idea. It's insane." She tugged on her car door again. This time, he stepped aside. "Use the money to buy yourself a bus ticket."

"It's more than that," he whispered.

Graham lightly touched her arm. Charlie felt a warm, tingly, familiar spark run through her body. She had no idea why and forced herself not to dwell on it. Did she know him from somewhere? Why didn't she feel threatened by him?

"Please—" He stopped abruptly and caught her eye. "I don't even know your name."

"Precisely!"

"Please," he said again, visibly shrinking, retreating into himself but keeping his eyes on her.

She let out an exasperated breath. "Charlie."

"Please, Charlie. I swear, I'm not going to harm you. I just need to make my way home," he said, pleading with her. "I lost everything."

I have no one. What a pair we are.

Her disposition shifted at that moment. What else was there to lose? She felt drawn to this man, maybe out of pity, maybe because so many times the community had stepped in to help her father. He had helped her when she needed it. He kept her company for almost three hours, and nothing about him made her feel unsafe. Maybe she wanted to pay it forward. Or maybe— she didn't want to admit this—but she'd seen him before, at the food pantry. She was certain of it now that she'd had a chance to see his face clearly. He was the man with the pained expression, the one whose eyes wouldn't meet hers, or anybody's, for that matter. He was the man whose sadness emanated like a dark cloud. His presence was heavy, a grim cloak of gloom hovering as he waited his turn. But then his eyes. When he'd finally addressed her, she'd seen the turmoil in them. They'd matched her own. Hence, the extra muffins.

"Wait a minute." She grabbed her phone and typed out a message, then pointed to a large bench under a maple tree on the sidewalk a few feet away from them. "Let's sit there and talk about this."

When they were seated, she said, "I'm not driving straight through. I'm taking my time to see the country on the way to California."

"Please don't take this the wrong way, but you can't drive straight through," Graham said, pointing to the car. "You have an electric vehicle."

"I know what my vehicle is! Which is why I said I am going to stop each day," Charlie huffed. "Do you have money for a hotel room? We are definitely not rooming together."

"I can write you a document with my social security number and anything else you need, and I will pay you back as soon as I get to Oregon."

"Hmmm." Charlie didn't know what to think. How in the world could she be sure this guy was even legit? And then a little voice in her head said, *You'll either be murdered or swindled. Lose, lose, whatever it is. But at least you won't do the drive alone.*

What kind of logic was that? She laughed to herself. "Dear Lord, this is going to take forever, isn't it? What, twelve days?"

"An EV charges about every 230 miles. So, yes. Ten to twelve stops," Graham said.

"So, what happens when I get to where I'm going?"

"Where are you going, exactly?"

"I don't know. I'll know in a few days."

Now it was Graham's turn to look at her like she was crazy. "Huh. So, you're a fly-by-the-seat-of-your-pants kind of girl."

"Anyway," she said hastily, trying not to react to what he just said. "How are you going to get to Oregon from California?"

"It will be close enough. I can get a friend to pick me up or get me a bus ticket home," he offered before walking back his words. "Come to think of it, that friend is gone too."

When Charlie stood and began to walk toward her car, Graham remained on the bench.

"I haven't decided yet," she said, turning to him and taking a few steps backward. "But before anything, there's something we're going to have to do."

CHAPTER 12

"My god! Are you okay? What's the emergency?" Rena arrived in disarray, her hair in a clipped bun, and she was wearing sweatpants and a tank top. "Good thing I was at the flower market fifteen minutes away."

"Shhh, not so loud," Charlie hushed, pointing with her lips to Graham sitting on the bench.

"Who's that?" Rena asked, looking over. "Oh. Woah."

"Shhh!" Charlie said again.

"That's the—"

"Homeless guy," Charlie confirmed. "Okay, so, now he's offered to go on the drive to California with me. Says he needs to get to Oregon, and California is close enough."

"He def does not look like a criminal, Charlie. He's actually quite hot."

"He looked like a bear two weeks ago, Rena. Don't let the shaved hair cloud your judgment."

They both glanced at Graham, still sitting on the bench, fingers clasped together as he leaned forward.

"Oh," Rena said, snapping her fingers in Charlie's face. "I knew it! He looks like the guy in *The Time Traveler's Wife*. The Theo guy. He was naked a lot. His lips, look at his lips."

"Shhh!" Charlie commanded, shaking her head.

"Okay, fine. So, what did you need me to rush here for?" Rena asked.

Charlie guided her farther away from the sidewalk, still convinced they weren't out of earshot.

"You know things. You feel things. I want you to talk to him and see what vibe you're getting."

"Charlie, you're giving me more credit than—"

"Please?"

Rena grudgingly complied, dragging her feet on the asphalt in an exaggerated manner as she made her way to Graham. Charlie smiled as she watched Rena take a seat next to him.

"Wait a minute. Hey, you're—" Rena exclaimed rather loudly.

Charlie watched as Graham slightly shook his head. And then he pulled out his wallet while Rena looked on. They continued to speak in hushed tones as Charlie stood by impatiently, shifting her weight from one foot to the other and folding her arms across her chest.

When they were done talking, Graham remained seated while Rena quickly shuffled over to her. Charlie pulled her to the other side of the car.

"Well?"

"I think he's legit, Charlie. I don't have any negative thoughts coming through. I'd honestly feel that you'd be safer if he did the drive with you."

"What if he takes a detour and murders me at some national park?" Charlie pressed. "I mean, I don't know why, but I feel like I need to help him out."

"Charlie, you were alone in an alleyway with him for hours when the entire city was asleep. He didn't try anything, did he?"

"No, but—"

Rena came closer and placed two fingers on Charlie's head.

"Ow! What are you doing?"

"There. Here's a lock of your hair. Let's make sure we plant it on the front seat so I can identify you, okay? And stamp that car with your fingerprints like there's no tomorrow."

"Not funny." She took Rena's hand and pulled her toward Graham. "Come with me. I have more questions."

Graham looked up to find the two women flanking him.

"So, what's the real story, Graham?" Charlie began.

"I just need a ride back home," he answered.

"Are people looking for you? Is the government spending millions of dollars for a phony kidnapping of some sort?" Rena chimed in.

"No, no. I decided to go off the grid. Needed to balance my well-being. I swear, my mom knows I'm okay and safe. I just had to get away from everything. Give up what I had so I could start over." Graham looked away when he said that.

Okay, so this guy has a mom and is close to her. Maybe he's not as crazy as we think.

His point wasn't lost on Charlie. But apparently, it didn't affect Rena. "By sleeping in someone else's car?"

Rena's sarcasm was met with silence. And then, in a sudden change of direction, Charlie sensed him pulling away. She didn't know why she was so attuned to his reactions, but she was. He no longer seemed despondent. His desperation just faded. This guy had pride, and she somehow pushed a button.

"Listen, I know how crazy I sound to you both, how this all looks so unusual. I'm sorry I even asked. I promise not to come by again." He stood and offered a hand to Rena, who shook it firmly. And then to Charlie. "It was nice to meet you both. Thanks again."

Charlie glared at Rena before chasing after him. "Wait, no, Graham. We didn't mean anything by those questions. Maybe we can work something out."

"I've already got his driver's license information on my phone. We're good from that end," Rena assured her.

"You mean, you may allow me to ride with you?" he asked, relief in his voice.

"I guess," she answered, turning to Rena for some kind of affirmation.

Rena nodded in response.

"Thank you," he said, smiling. "Like I said, every expense incurred will be reimbursed. You have my word."

Like she had her father's? Or Auntie Elma? She still felt really queasy about the situation, but her inner voice told her it would be good to have company, someone to douse the quiet when it got too loud.

"And that's my cue. I'm going to leave you two to work out your . . . uh . . . logistics," Rena said, kissing Charlie on both cheeks. After taking a few steps away, Rena turned around. "Hey, Charlie! You know those tech stocks I've been trying to get you to invest in?"

Charlie nodded, wondering about the smirk on Rena's face.

"Not a good idea at the moment."

CHAPTER 13

HARRISBURG

"Jus," Charlie greeted, placing him on speakerphone while she picked up the last of her things and stuffed them in her handbag. *Wallet, keys, sunglasses, contact solution, Global Entry card . . .*

Global Entry? *Not this time.*

"Hey, Char. What's going on?"

"Well, I'm laughing to myself about needing my Global Entry . . . never mind." She let out a chuckle but immediately caught herself. "How is your grandpa doing?" she asked.

"He's fine. A bad case of heartburn, we're told."

"Oh, thank goodness! Please send him my love. I'll try to visit when I get back. You know, I'm getting ready to leave."

"That's why I'm calling. You know I love you, right?"

"And I love you too," Charlie responded, her head flicking from side to side as she checked every room.

"It's just that . . . well, this is not like you. Being impulsive like this. Taking a road trip with someone you don't know, trying to find someone you've never known all your life."

Charlie stopped moving around and stood in the middle of her living room. "Who told you?"

"Rena. Who else?"

"Justin, this does not reach your mom. Promise me."

"What are you going to do if this doesn't pan out? It will hurt you more. You're already suffering a great loss."

"Justin," she said, choking back tears. The pain she hid in the busyness of her trip slowly rose to the surface. "She's already left me. How much worse can it be? I've already been rejected for thirty years. What else can she do? Die on me? Papa already did that."

"Charlie, I didn't mean to—"

"I know, I know." Charlie began to move again. This time, she fiddled with the thermostat to ensure the heater was turned off. "I love you, Justin. It will be fine. I'll be back if it doesn't work out. I'll be careful."

She heard Justin grunt in acceptance. It made her smile.

"Call me if you want me to come get you."

"You and Rena," Charlie laughed. "And Justin. The guy. Your mom. Promise me."

"Fine. I promise."

Charlie slipped the phone into her purse and walked toward the knock on the door.

"Good morning." Graham stood at her front door with a bright smile on his face.

Already, all Charlie's concerns seemed to melt away. "Hi. Come in."

"What a great place you have," he said before handing her a caramel macchiato. "I hope I got it right—tall, non-fat."

"It's perfect," she answered, taking a few sips and then putting it on the counter. "I'm all packed, and I was just about to take these boxes down to the car."

"Let me take them for you. I'll just set my stuff up in your car if you don't mind. And then I'll be back up for your boxes."

Charlie handed him her keys. He didn't look homeless anymore. He wore branded sweatpants and a Moncler sweatshirt. Granted, they looked worn and washed, but she noticed how well he carried his clothes.

"Just want you to know I took a shower at the Y after my morning run." He forced another laugh.

Homeless guys probably don't have the inclination to run. She knew he was someone who had just recently had a stroke of bad luck, and it made her feel safer because she had also just had a stroke of bad luck. *Misery will surely love company.*

She waited for him by her car as he rolled the dolly piled with boxes to the street. Once he started packing them in the tiny trunk, she motioned for him to stop. "Wait, sorry. I need to get these." Charlie pulled the batch of letters out of the box and held them close to her chest. "I'll take these in the front with me."

"Did you want these books in the back seat so you have easy access?" he asked, pointing to one of the boxes.

Charlie could see him trying to make out what they were. "Yes, that's fine. It's better to have them close to me."

"Looks like different editions of *Charlotte's Web*. Is that your favorite book?"

"Mine and my mother's."

"Are these Wilbur?" Graham was referencing the pink stuffed pigs in the open box.

"I figured I'd bring them for my mom in case she needs proof that it's me." She stopped short and chuckled when a vision of her holding up a stuffed pig flashed through her mind. "*Hi, Mom, it's me, Charlotte.*"

Nevertheless, Graham looked at her and nodded.

She was sure he didn't understand what she meant, and she

appreciated the fact that he pretended to. She noticed he had one leather suitcase, the size of the ones you're allowed to carry on the plane with you. "Is that all you have?"

"Basically," he confirmed. "It's not even mine. Father Matt from the church mission gave it to me. Everything else is gone. Would it be okay for you if I drive?"

"Be my guest," Charlie answered. It would be nice not to take charge of anything for once.

There was one more thing Charlie wanted in the back seat: a gold-wrapped spiral book. She saw Graham fix his gaze on it as she lay it on top of the box of books.

"Photo album," she said. "Pictures of me and my dad."

Once the car had been packed up, they sat for a while, looking at their maps. The silence between them was a sign that they were both deep in thought.

Graham spoke first. "I figured we would be stopping twelve times to get to Los Angeles. We charge up every 230 miles, and we're about 2,200 miles away."

For once, Charlie didn't have to take the lead. She welcomed this new role. "Okay. Where's our first stop?"

"Harrisburg. I'm sure there's a hotel chain we can stop at."

"Great," Charlie said. "I'm not making any reservations until we know where we want to stop. That way, we're not held to stopping if we want to go farther."

They were quiet until they reached a cruising speed on US22 West.

"How are you feeling?" Graham asked, keeping his eyes on the road. "About leaving, I mean."

"A little scared, I guess. I haven't been away since school. It's weird, but I never thought I'd be leaving Sunset Park this soon. I'd still be there taking care of my dad if none of this had happened," she reflected. "And you? First thoughts?"

"I'll be going home."

"Good thought," Charlie answered.

"Can I ask what's in that pouch? You've been gripping it rather tightly for the past hour."

"Letters."

"Are you going to read them?" Graham asked, his fingers pressing buttons on the navigation system.

"I was, but now you're here and . . ."

"All the more reason you should read them. I'll be driving. You've got time."

"We'll see."

"Who are they from?"

"My mom." Charlie offered nothing more. She turned to look out the window, hoping it stopped there.

"Where is she?"

"I don't know. That's why we're in this car."

He turned to her and briefly caught her eye in the process. "We're going to a place you don't know. How does that work?"

"You're the one who asked to hitch a ride with a stranger. How does that work?" Charlie said, laughing.

Graham chuckled, too. "Well, there's one thing I know."

"And that is?" Charlie asked light-heartedly, her disposition changing.

"We are two very lost people."

After driving for a few miles, Charlie offered him more information. "They're letters written to my dad."

"You should really read them."

"I think I should, too. I was afraid to find out more about what happened between them, and I lived my life in oblivion, you know? But now that he's gone, I want to know more."

"Then, read them. Read one or two or three a day. We'll be on the road for twelve days. Even them out or read them at random."

"And on some days, let's not read one at all," Charlie said.

Graham smiled. "You don't have to tell me what she says or what you read. But I'll be around, just in case you need someone to talk to." And when Charlie didn't answer, he followed up. "You okay?"

"Yeah. Just observing the landscape and how it's been changing between here and Brooklyn," she offered, the tone of her voice rid of its earlier pensiveness. "This medley we're used to, that of the urban energy of skylines and cityscapes and bustling vibrant streets, turning into rolling hills and farmlands. The colors change from brown and orange to bright green and yellow, and the sunlight just seems to be brighter among the fields. Did you notice any of that at all?"

"Not as vividly as you just described," he said with a chuckle.

Once they chose a hotel, Charlie checked them into separate rooms. She was embarrassed when the receptionist asked whether they preferred adjoining rooms.

"He can be on a separate floor, whatever you have," she answered without giving Graham a chance to respond.

"May I have a copy of the receipt?" Graham requested as soon as they walked away with their keys.

Charlie nodded.

"Did you want to get dinner?" he asked despite Charlie having already pressed the button to summon the elevator.

"No, it's fine. For some reason, I am so tired. I'd like to just chill in my room if you don't mind."

"You sure you don't want to look around, get to know Harrisburg?" he teased.

Charlie shook her head. "Maybe tomorrow."

"Okay," Graham answered as Charlie stepped into the elevator. "The car is in a charging station right now, so I'll wait for it to load, and then I'll park it closer to our rooms."

"You sure?"

"Yes," he said.

"Okay, well . . . thank you. And goodnight." Charlie waved as the elevator doors closed.

CHAPTER 14

COLUMBUS

Sleep had never been a friend to Charlie. Since she was a little girl, sleep was only a few hours of respite from the ruckus in her head. When she wasn't thinking about people and things and work strategies, she was planning what to wear, where to go, and how to get there. Her mind was an internal planner with dates and numbers spinning around in an endless cycle. Her doctor had prescribed some pills, which she took on occasion, specifically during overseas trips. But those times aside, Charlie's brain just never shut off.

The previous day's trip was on her mind.

As soon as they'd taken that first turn out of Brooklyn, her world had become unmoored. Now she was in adjoining hotel rooms with a man she didn't know. Aside from those eyes, the only thing going for him was his kindness. His plan? His motives? It hadn't occurred to her to ask him. Would he even tell her?

Rena had assured her she'd check in via Life360 and that she'd track Charlie a few times a day to ensure they were on their way per the plan. The trip to Harrisburg was relatively short. Charlie had been glad to get out of the car after four hours. It was nerve-wracking that day. Her back hurt from sitting straight up for all that time. She'd wanted to be ready to sprint, clutching the car door handle the entire way in case she needed to jump out. She also had an extra remote if she needed to unlock the door.

Charlie stared out the window now. Despite the lingering chill in the air, she saw spring in the blooms of the trees and the green of the pastures. She made mental notes to visit the Hershey Chocolate Factory sometime in the future, was intrigued by the Gettysburg Museum, and wished they could stop to explore the Amish markets and shops they passed on a winding road of rolling pastures.

They used to have a rule, Charlie and her dad. Whoever was driving got their pick of music. Since Graham had offered to drive, she'd helped him hook up his playlist to the car's sound system. She was surprised at this choice—a seventies mix of songs ranging from The Beatles to The Rolling Stones.

"May I ask a question?" Graham said, turning to her for a second.

"Sure." Charlie appreciated his gesture. *Who does that these days? Ask you if they can ask you a question?*

"Did you get to read one of your mom's letters?"

"I'd like to go a little farther today, maybe stop to recharge, and then keep going," she replied.

"Sure."

"Should we stop now?" Charlie swiped a finger on her phone. "I can find a charging station."

"We have about one hundred miles left on the charge."

"I know, but I kinda want to make sure we don't stop in the middle of the highway. Who knows if that's an accurate reading?"

"I think we're okay to go a little farther?" It was a question, not a statement.

Charlie shrugged. "I'd rather not take the chance. My dad was always pushing the limits. My Auntie Elma would remind him on long road trips that we were already at the empty line. He'd say that meant we had thirty more miles," she said. "Then, one day, we ended up stuck in the middle of I90. I was so young, I had to stay in the back seat as cars zipped by while my dad walked a mile out to the nearest gas station."

"He left you in the car?"

"With my aunt. The speed of the cars caused our car to rock back and forth. I was so afraid, I threw up."

Graham slowed and veered right toward the nearest exit. "It's about time to reload."

Charlie responded with a smile.

Charlie found she was no longer clutching the door handle. She still had the key fob on her lap but felt more relaxed. She was also beginning to get into Graham's music. He sang along with Air Supply, and Charlie couldn't help but join in.

"Where are we headed today?" she asked. They were on ABBA by now, and "Dancing Queen" was up next. She saw Graham smile when she was swaying to the song.

"We should be in Columbus in an hour," he said. "What hotel should we choose for the night?"

"Hmmm," she said, her tone playful. "How about the second exit in town?"

"Sounds like a plan."

Charlie was warming up to him, and he no longer seemed so scary. It might be time to ask for more of his story. After all, they had a long way to go, and the drive was still a bit awkward between seventies hits, quiet stretches, and distant conversation.

"I think I'm going to start reading those letters tonight."

"That's good," he answered.

"Yeah."

Silence while he focused on staying on the left lane as they approached a fork in the highway.

"What's your story, Graham? How did you end up on the streets? Are you a veteran?"

"Not a veteran. I was in a business, a tech start-up. It was . . . it was just too much. I had a nervous breakdown." He kept a firm eye on the road. "I walked away. I just wanted to disappear for a while."

"Don't you have friends or family that could have helped you?"

"I do."

Charlie waited.

"There was nothing they could do. They tried to help, but . . . I guess I was too stubborn. I kept going until I had nothing left in me."

"What's your family like?"

"Normal. I have a mom, a dad, and a sister." As he spoke, Charlie noticed his brows furrow and his jaw grow tight.

"I bet you miss them a lot," she said.

"Yeah."

"I miss my dad so much," she said, surprising herself. The letters, the trip, and the uncertainties facing her made her feel so vulnerable. She wished Rena was there.

Graham nodded.

"Can I ask—"

"Graham, you don't have to ask me if you can ask me." She laughed.

"Why now? Why is it just now that you're searching for your mother?"

Charlie paused before responding. "'Cause my dad died?"

That sounded harsh, so it deserved a follow-up. "I knew I had a mother," she said, sensing the bizarreness of that comment. "I mean, obviously. Everyone has a mother. My dad said she was so young, and her parents took her away. I didn't know that my dad had been communicating with her."

"But you never asked more questions? Never wanted to find her?"

She shrugged. "I thought about her, wondered about her, but I was afraid I'd hurt my dad's feelings if I brought it up. I missed having a mother, even though my Auntie Elma stepped into that role. I didn't want to hurt her feelings either. You know, where I grew up, it was one big family. The community took my father in, and they were all involved in my life—grandparents, neighbors, his work friends."

Graham stayed silent. Charlie felt like she hadn't explained herself well enough. "It's different now. I just lost my father. And I guess what I'm craving is the love of a parent. I have another one. I may as well try to find her."

"That makes total sense," Graham said, glancing at the map before slowing the car down. "You were being considerate with what you were given. That's admirable."

"Still, I know it's hard for people to understand. But thank you."

"On another note, guess what?"

"What?"

"We're here," Graham announced as he entered the hotel parking lot.

Letter #1 Year 1992

My Eddie,

I don't know if you've forgiven me yet, and I don't blame your silence. I know it's been a whirlwind of pain for you. She's two today,

95

my Charlotte. I wonder if she's talking yet—if she's as clever as I think she is. I bet she's full of words. She's probably been cursed with my father's brains and blessed with your tenacity. First and foremost, will you give her a kiss for me? Don't tell her it's from me, though. I know she won't know I exist. And that's so fair. So fair. But I miss her. And you. And I thought I'd write you this letter to tell you how sorry I am, not just for what I'd done but for leaving Charlotte with a motherless future. Everyone convinced me that it was for the best. It took a while for me to realize that. The day I left, or was it the day you told me to leave? I don't remember it anymore. How can I not remember those days two years ago? I am only twenty-two, but I feel way beyond those years. Like my mind is already so exhausted from feeling, crying, hating, and laughing. I'm tired.

I want to escape from here, I do. I do. But then there are times when I doubt myself. I doubt my ability to stay and be a good mother. After all, what I did . . .

I want to write this all down because I usually don't remember. But you know what I do remember? You. Your mother was a teacher at our high school. I was a junior at cheerleading practice. And one day, you were there to pick her up after school. I ran into you, and you looked at me like I was just a lost child you wanted to save. But I knew then. I knew we'd be friends. I knew I'd fall in love with you. Who in their right mind wouldn't? You and your torn-up jean jacket and aviator sunglasses, that lopsided smirk that made you too cool for all of us.

When my parents found out we were seeing each other, they took me away. My father was always so sure that money could make anything happen. When we moved to California, I thought I'd never see you again. But you didn't give up. They tried to separate us by sending me to boarding school in Switzerland. I'm still ever so grateful that your parents helped you get to me. You were my knight in shining armor, saving me from the clutches of the evil king who tried to break us apart. They told me I was too young. But all I wanted to do was be with you. I don't remember how you got the money to fly us back to the States, but when we eloped, we figured we would settle as far away from California as we could. You said your parents would take us in, and well, they were as far away from California, all right. We got married in front of Elma and Rob. Everything was perfect. Seemed perfect. Until I had her. The baby I always wanted to give you, our little Charlotte. We said we'd do the Spanish version and call her Carlotta. But you know why we named her. She was going to make me a better person. She was going to save me like Charlotte saved Wilbur in our story.

But I was broken from the first day we met. And even before that day. I always knew I was going to lose you both. But I did it anyway. The desolation, despair, and self-loathing I felt once I gave birth to our baby was just so overpowering. I couldn't live another second with the thoughts in my head. And so when you found her alone in our home after ten hours, I gave her up so willingly. I gave her up because I loved her.

Please, Eddie. Give me that, at least. I loved her.

Charlie spent the night sitting on the side of her bed, staring at the blue and orange carpet checkered with lines that edged up against the wall. She hardly moved, feet solidly planted on the floor, her mother's first letter in her hands. It was about seven in the morning when she decided to take a walk.

Downtown Columbus was just coming to life. Charlie walked past shops, restaurants, and cafés, most of which were still closed. After grabbing a cup of coffee, she continued walking down Broad Street past the Rhodes Tower and the Palace Theater. The sun was up by then, slowly peeking out of clouds that were losing their fight to stay. There were signs of life everywhere around her. People bustled about in work clothes, suits, dresses, joggers, and jeans, their voices, conversations, and laughter transmitting through the air. Life was clearly in full force, while hers had reached a standstill.

I don't know if you've forgiven me yet. It's been a whirlwind of pain for you. She's two today, my Charlotte.

She was running late but needed more time to collect herself.

CHARLIE: I need about an hour more. I'll return to the hotel soon, and then we can head out.

GRAHAM: Where are you?

CHARLIE: I found a park by the river, and I just sat for a bit.

GRAHAM: Wait, right there. I'll come find you.

She walked farther, stopping to sit on a bench overlooking a body of water. Once settled, she pulled out her phone to find a location. She had reached the Scioto Mile, a public park with a promenade lined with bike racks and fountains running along the river. She marveled at the art installations and large stone sculptures surrounding her, aware of the swish of the paddles and the muffled voices of the kayakers in front of her. While looking for her location on the map, Charlie read that the name "Scioto" meant "deer" in Shawnee and that this river served as one of the main transportation routes for the Native American tribes and the early European settlers.

Graham showed up exactly fifteen minutes later.

"Hi."

He waited for her to nod before he sat beside her.

She didn't expect him to show up so soon, to see her with her face red from all that crying.

"You okay?" he asked, leaning forward with a look of concern. He pointed to the book clutched under her arm.

"One of my dad's *Charlotte's Web* editions," she said, feigning nonchalance. "Just want him near, I guess."

"I get it."

Charlie stared out in front of her, focusing on a branch floating on the river.

"Listen, I don't think I can do this. I think I'm going to turn back and go home. You can drive with me, we're only about ten hours away. Or I can drop you off at the nearest airport and buy you a ticket to fly directly to Oregon. You seem to know what you want to do, so don't let this stop you."

He shook his head. "No. Why? What happened?"

Charlie started to cry. "I'm just at the first letter, and it has already broken me. I don't think I can take it." She tried to save face, quell her emotions, took deep breaths, and wiped her tears with the sleeve of her sweatshirt. "I can't," she repeated. "I need to be back with the people close to me."

"I'm here." Graham's tone was terse, like she'd insulted him.

"Graham, you're a complete stranger," she said between hiccups. The tears kept flowing. She thought back to the day her father died. It was almost the same pain, except that it was a hollowing of her heart then. She figured it was more from resentment now.

"And I suppose you don't want to talk about it?"

"Not yet. I can't even believe I'm crying in front of you."

Graham shifted in his seat, his knees tilted slightly toward hers. "Charlie. You are doing such a brave thing. I wished I was half as brave as you. I ran away from everything and couldn't even face what I was going through. And look at you, running toward it."

She laughed, feeling the tears running down her cheeks and seeping through her lips. "Driving, you mean."

He smiled. "The best thing about being homeless and jobless is time is the only thing I have on my hands. I want to take this journey with you, Charlie. Take your time. We can slow down the drive. You can stop reading those letters, or you can keep reading them at your own pace. You can share them with me or keep them from me. Anything. But I feel like we would both be giving up if we returned to where we were." He looked directly at her. "You decide, though."

Charlie exhaled loudly, a part of her resigned, another part resolute. She didn't know what she agreed to, but what he said was true. Besides, she felt a little responsible for his journey home. Maybe all she needed was the voice of someone familiar. She made a plan to call Rena later on. "Where to next?"

"Circle City. Racing Capital of the World."

"Ah, Indy," she said, feeling the sun's warmth on her face.

He offered her his hand, and she took it. With their fingers tightly wound together, they stared out into the blue sky, watching the world go by without them.

She was certain they'd catch up eventually.

Just maybe not that day.

CHAPTER 15

INDIANA

They were on the road before noon.

"What's there to see in Indy?" Charlie asked about an hour into the drive. So far, she'd seen nothing but the long stretch of road that was Interstate 70.

"We can stop by the racetrack," Graham offered.

Charlie felt a slight tinge of pain upon hearing that. Her father dreamed of racing cars and go-karts. She'd fulfilled his dream five years ago by gifting him VIP tickets to the Indy500. He went with Uncle Joe, who wasn't really interested in cars. And when she picked him up after the races, he was all decked out in memorabilia—hat, jacket, belt, and all. He'd thanked her for the tickets, effusive about having met his heroes—Andretti and Sato—and getting the once-in-a-lifetime chance of watching them do warm-up laps.

She had to fight through all these memories if she was going to make new ones. "That sounds like fun," she answered.

* * *

The track was quiet. Charlie and Graham snuck in with a tour group that was completing their walkthrough. Charlie had never been there, but Graham had. He showed her around, explaining the significance of the control tower called the Pagoda, the victory podium, and the garages in Gasoline Alley. They got to walk on the Yard of Bricks before deciding to sit in the stands for a few minutes.

"I have a picture of my dad standing right there!" she exclaimed. "It's in that photo album I brought with me."

Except for a sprinkling of maintenance crews, they were quite alone. Charlie felt a cool breeze brush past her before wrapping her in a warm embrace. She was inundated with a fevered sense of peace, and her heart was full and complete. A man in a red jacket appeared, brushed past the maintenance crew on the open field, and disappeared just as quickly as he had come.

"I think I'm going to read more letters tonight," Charlie announced. "Being here today, remembering what this place meant to him, I want to honor my dad's memory. He asked me to read them. I have to stay strong. Find the beauty in their story, no matter how ugly it may turn out to be. But the first one . . ."

Graham said nothing. She loved that he didn't press her or offer opinions. He just listened and waited.

"The first one was written in 1992. She was twenty-two, and I had just turned two. It was mostly an apology letter. She talked about her regret for giving me a motherless future. She wrote about how they met. But she didn't talk about why she left. My dad never told me he met her while she was in high school. He was a few years older. Her parents tried to separate them, and he followed her to Switzerland, where they eloped. They moved to Brooklyn, where my father's parents lived, and got married in front of Auntie Elma and another friend."

"She was only twenty, huh?"

"Yeah. I don't know why, but I'm relieved to learn they were married. That I was a product of two people who loved each other, I guess."

"Do you think you carried that with you all this time?"

"Oh, for sure!" Charlie said emphatically. "Lorenzo—" She paused before continuing. "My ex. He came from a perfect family with no drama, no intrigue. His parents had been married for ages and held hands when they walked around. I felt . . . unworthy." She caught herself. She was saying this to a stranger! "Oh gosh, scrap that. I don't mean to be a drama queen. All this stuff with my mother . . ."

"We all have our thing, Charlie," Graham countered. "What's her name, your mom?"

"Celia. Celia Ruiz. And his love for *Charlotte's Web* apparently came from her."

Charlie was in quite a rush to be alone. As soon as they arrived at the hotel, she hurriedly bade Graham good night, told him she would just order in, and settled in the room to read more of her mother's letters. She was nervous—every telling would divulge a secret she wasn't sure she could accept—but knowing she wasn't alone helped her tremendously. She had Graham on speed dial. He'd insisted on it.

Little did she know that she would take him up on it as soon as she climbed into bed.

Graham picked up the phone on the first ring. "Is everything okay, Charlie?"

"Yes, yes. Sorry to bother you. I just wanted to say thank you for taking me around the track today. I'm about to read my mom's letters but wanted to call you first." What she didn't tell him was that she just needed to hear his voice and know that he was nearby.

"It was my pleasure. I had fun," he said.

"I really felt like my dad was with us."

"I'm sure he was," Graham responded.

"Do you believe in stuff like that, Graham?"

"Yes, I do."

She believed him, leaning into that feeling of kinship that had been growing since they'd left New York. "Okay. I'll see you in the morning."

"See you in the morning."

She opened her mother's second letter, dated 1994.

Letter #2 1994

She's four! My Carlotta is four! Is she talking, walking, running? Is she the most capricious girl you've ever met? Is she in preschool? Who is watching her while you work? Are her grandparents thrilled to have this little bundle of smarts running around their home? And how is Elma? Is she helping you, raising this little girl as if she were her own? That's what I am hoping for, Eddie. All those things.

I'm free! I met some people at a party, and we all decided to take the bus to Minnesota. Here I am, in the heat of the summer. Our trailer is not so bad. We're living in a campground called Stony. How apt! Life is good. I never knew how the luxuries of my life had held me hostage all this time! I always feared I could not survive without my father's money. And now look at me! Living on our own here, doing what I want to do, free of all the pressures of being the daughter of a Ruiz. What does that mean anyway? Names on buildings, on land, on businesses? What does that all mean, Eddie?

Come to think of it, nothing means anything without you and my little girl. But I'll take this for now. The mountains are soaring above the endless blue skies, and all my cares are awash in a sea of nothingness.

Charlie held the letter in her hands, reading everything her mother had to say and feeling every word. The words came to life, jumped off the page, and spoke to her. Although the second letter was short, Charlie spent time putting the pieces together. She re-read the first one and connected it with the second one, and, like chapters in a book, they were chronological and connected.

When her phone rang, she pressed the speaker button with one eye struggling to stay open.

"Hey!" It was Rena.

"Hi, there. How are you?"

"I was calling to ask how things were going."

"You know it's past ten, right?" Charlie sank deeper under the comforter until only her head was exposed.

"As if you sleep anyway. And why do you sound like a chipmunk? Have you been crying?"

"I have my moments."

"Are you still taking your meds? You know what happens when you don't get to sleep. It's not good for you."

"No, I haven't since we got on the road. I'm learning things about my mom that's making me wary of sleeping pills." Charlie shifted to her side and leaned her head on one elbow. "By the way, what's with the little heart emojis you keep sending me on Life360?"

"To tell you I love you while I'm tracking you." Rena laughed. "All good with your travel buddy? I checked him out, by the way. He has a story, that boy, but he's legit."

"And you're going to leave it at that, right?"

"He's right there, chica. You can just ask him yourself. I'm going to let you go. Just wanted to hear your voice. Call me once every other day, like a good friend."

"Ha!" She wanted to say, "You're worse than my dad," but really, nothing was worse than not having her dad.

CHAPTER 16

ST LOUIS

She lied and told Graham she had slept well. The truth was that she'd been up since three, so she was ready to go when she greeted him by the car at their allotted time.

"Where to, now?" Charlie asked, rubbing her hands together excitedly.

"St. Louis!"

"And what's to see there?"

"Well, I was thinking we should drive straight through and maybe check out The Hill for some really authentic Italian food."

"Don't forget, we should be recharging once we're down to one hundred miles," she said, smiling. "You know, just in case."

"Oh, I know." He smiled back. "Don't you worry about that."

Traffic turned the four-hour drive into five. They had now fallen into a comfortable rhythm, with small talk at times and silence at others. There was also a lot of singing along. Charlie had forced him to listen to her playlist, which included sad songs, mostly about betrayal and heartbreak. They left Indianapolis and ventured onto the country roads of Indiana. The scenery

106

didn't change much. Rolling plains, windmills, and corn fields flanked single-lane highways during most of their drive.

"Letter number two was interesting," Charlie began about three hours into the drive. She fell asleep a few times, which felt odd. "It was written in 1994, and she was twenty-four. She mentioned me a lot."

Graham nodded but kept his eyes on the road. "That says something, doesn't it?"

"So, I think she grew up in an uber-wealthy family because she kept on mentioning how she hated her father and his money. Even in the first letter, it seemed like all she wanted to do was run away from all that. Oh, and did I tell you she called him Eddie?"

"Eddie and Celia. Now we have names. Go on," Graham prodded.

"Celia meets people at this party and runs away to Minnesota with them. They live in this trailer. I think she's in some sort of commune."

"A commune? As in, growing their own shit?"

"I'm not sure. The letter ends there. Just telling Eddie she feels free."

"I can't wait to hear more about Eddie and Celia," Graham said. "But for now, look over to the right. There it is!" He pointed to the Gateway Arch, soaring in the distance. "The gateway to the west, symbolizing the westward expansion of the U.S., starting with the Lewis and Clark expedition."

"Oh, you will. We have thirteen more letters to go. And dude, you sound like an encyclopedia."

They located the hill and parallel parked on a downward slope along a row of residential structures. Italian flags in green, red, and white lined the roads. Streetlights, fire hydrants, and the overhangs attached to each building bore the same colors. The Italian influence was difficult to miss. A heavy cultural mist wrapped around the area, reminding Charlie of Sunset Park.

Sally Grotto's was first on Graham's list. It was a quaint place occupying a two-story flat's first and second floors, complete with a front porch and a garage. Yellow tablecloths and white metal chairs gave one the feel of being in someone's mismatched dining room. They sat at a table for two with a view from a large bay window.

"What would you like to drink?" Graham asked, raising his hand for the server.

"I don't really drink. Water is good."

"Hey, I got this dinner. I do have some cash, so it's my treat," Graham said.

"Oh. Where have you been hiding all the money? In your backpack?" Charlie teased. "Which leads me to my question—"

Graham gently raised a finger to signal a pause. "Let's order first."

Once they ordered—pasta with squid ink for him, meatballs for her—he leaned forward, indicating she had his full attention. "You were saying?"

"I hardly know anything about you. Can we shift gears and talk about you?" Charlie sipped her water and broke a piece of bread.

"Hit me," he said, taking a swig of his Old Fashioned. The way he said it—the moistening of his lips, the steady eye contact— wait a minute. Was he flirting with her?

Nevertheless, it made her feel . . . well, it made her *feel*.

"Who are you?"

He considered her question for a moment before answering. "Right now? I'm not sure. But I used to work at Power One."

"The tech company that just went public? I worked with

them a few years ago. I mean, they were a client of ours. Man, that sold for way above its present value."

He nodded, then let out a laugh. "I like this businesswoman side of you."

"That's my job. I do a lot of due diligence for acquisitions."

He closed his eyes and clutched his chest. "My heart."

Charlie glossed over that comment. "And you left? Quit? Were fired?"

The conversation stopped once the server popped up to lay their orders on the table. She watched Graham devour the pasta and ask for a second glass of liquor. She liked the way he was so human, so ordinary. Until that moment, he was really so controlled, always trying to be quiet, a listener, a fly on the wall who was just there for the ride. She was enjoying his company, and he seemed to relax in hers.

"I left. It was more than just the need for a break. I had broken down mentally. I couldn't bear to go to my condo and couldn't stand the life that came with all that. I just wanted to shed everything."

"So you were in senior leadership?"

"Something like that," he admitted.

"Which is why—"

"Exactly," he interrupted. "Which is why I had to get off the grid. Sell my condo and get rid of all the fluff. I had planned to go home to my family, but just . . . got derailed a bit. I'm still not mentally clear on what I will do, and I don't want my family to get lost in the whirl I'm currently in."

"Why do you think now is the time to head home?"

"You."

"Ha. Me?" She felt that same flutter again and pinched her thigh in an effort to ground herself. "You mean you want your thoughts to get screwed up even more by dealing with someone like me?"

"No. I mean, you had a car."

Charlie giggled in response. She nervously picked at her meatball. It was exactly as Derge had said: she wasn't good at praise or compliments.

Graham didn't want it to end there. "I think we were meant to meet. I think you coming into the picture was a sign. It's time for me to go home."

Maybe he doesn't think I'm crazy after all. Maybe this was serendipity. Life becomes easier to accept when you believe in happenstance. And she could appreciate someone looking to find their way back.

"To going home," Charlie said, raising her glass to him.

CHAPTER 17

KANSAS CITY

Driving for 250 miles through the Missouri countryside was uneventful and filled with comfortable chatter. They stopped at a diner in Sedalia and found a charging station at a mall before reaching downtown Kansas City. Somehow, Charlie avoided speaking about her father. She kept the conversations light—favorite movies (anything Julia Roberts for her, *Mad Max* and *Trainspotting* for him), where they shopped (Bergdorf for her, wherever there was a bargain for him), what they loved to read (non-fiction for him, thrillers for her).

"Oh, look!" Charlie tapped on the window as they turned into Grand Boulevard. "There's the Hallmark Visitors Center. I wonder if we can tour sets and see famous people? I would stay an extra day for that."

Graham slowed down so she could look out the window. "Looks like the greeting card products."

"Oh," Charlie said, leaning back into her seat. "I was hoping it was the TV shows." She giggled.

"You like watching those movies?"

"Auntie Elma, not me. I was thinking I could take pictures for her."

Graham smiled. That was Charlie's favorite part about him. His eyes would crinkle at the corners, and his lips would spread across that strong jaw to reveal those perfect teeth. He was handsome, that was for sure. Very different from her normal propensity toward exotic-looking men with dark hair and dark eyes. And yet, those eyes seemed to change colors so often, clear under the sun and dark when the stars were out. They kept her wanting to discover more about him, peel back the layers a little more each day. They spun stories in her head of days he spent roaming the streets and of the days before that. She saw kindness, compassion, and empathy in them but also pain and darkness. Sometimes, those eyes shone bright like jewels, and other times, they were a dark barrier. There was so much to learn about him, and she figured that although their time together was short, she had surely gained a friend.

"Learning about how greeting cards are made could be quite interesting," he said.

The streets were busy. Parked cars dominated every open space, and hordes of people blocked the crosswalks.

When they finally reached the hotel they'd planned to stay at, the lobby was cordoned off by lines of people, little pop-up booths, and photographers roaming the area. People wore costumes, some with capes and others wearing masks and headdresses. Charlie and Graham stood in line for fifteen minutes. When they finally reached the front desk, Charlie handed the cheery receptionist her driver's license.

"Thank you for your patience, Mr. and Mrs. Hastings. We have your room ready. Would you like two keys?"

Charlie pursed her lips before vehemently shaking her head. "No, no. I reserved two rooms."

"What's the name of the other reservation?"

Charlie shot Graham a look. "Both under Hastings."

"No. Uh-uh," the lady said. "We have one double reserved. Actually, the last room left."

"Must be a mistake," Charlie argued. "We need two rooms. Will you just refund my deposit, and we can look for another hotel?"

"Ma'am," the lady said, twirling her hand, "look around you. I don't think you will find availability in the entire city. We are having a gaming convention this week."

That piqued Graham's interest. He looked away as if trying to remember something. The reception lady had already been batting her eyes at him, but now that he'd leaned over and placed his elbows on the counter, she was in attack mode.

"So you're not a Mr. and Mrs.?" the receptionist purred.

Charlie managed not to roll her eyes.

"It's April! Holy shit! Is it Neptune Con?" He suddenly looked like a little kid at Christmas. He whipped his head from side to side excitedly, looking around.

"I think I can give you free passes to the auditorium. The interactive gaming event is this evening. Dwight Walker will be there," she added.

"No way! I thought he just got married?"

"Ahem." Charlie faked a cough in an attempt to reel him back in. "Graham, we have a problem here."

"Just a second, please," Graham told the attendant. He pulled Charlie to the side of the counter. "Listen, it doesn't look like we have a choice. Let's ask if the room has a couch. I can sleep there tonight. Or on the floor."

"What? I'm not sleeping in the same room as you."

"Okay, that's fine," Graham said. "You stay here, and I'll sleep in the car. Or find another hotel. It may be easier to find a room if it's just one of us looking."

Charlie nodded and rushed back to the reception lady, afraid she would lose her place in line. "I'll take the room."

As they walked toward the elevator, she felt a pang of guilt. At least that's what she would explain it as, but in truth, she felt uneasy about not having him close to her. Somehow, she was nervous about being alone. Despite being in different rooms, just knowing he was there gave her some comfort. Plus, sleeping in the car! She didn't want him to relive that experience.

Why do I care so much?

When she glanced at the key card, her heart sank. More than ever, she didn't want to be alone.

"Listen," she began, "there's no reason for you to find another place to stay. I mean, we've been traveling together—you would have killed me by now if that was your intention." She handed him one of the keys. "I guess we're in room 906, which is a double. You can take one bed, and I'll take the other. Just don't think this is my way of making a pass at you."

Graham laughed. "It's been you and me and the open road for nearly a week. And I've never felt unsafe with you."

His words were meaningless, but the pleasure she derived from his slow drawl, which matched the length of time his eyes drilled into hers, was unsettling.

Charlie chuckled, trying to figure out her feelings. For the first time since her father died, she didn't feel alone. Like someone was with her, on the front lines, fighting to make sense of everything. "Funny."

"I do think I'm going to take that lady up on her offer if that's okay with you. Look around the hotel, see who's here, listen to some of the discussions."

"Of course." Charlie nodded, stretching out her arm and offering to take his bag from him.

She proceeded ahead to the room, tired and hungry. It had taken so long for them to weave through the traffic that they hadn't thought of stopping for dinner. Once she let herself in, she had a big decision to make: which bed should she stake her claim on? The one by the bathroom, so she could go freely in the middle of the night, or the one closer to the balcony door, so she could jump out in case of danger?

She laughed to herself. *Gosh, girl, you are so dramatic.* Nonetheless, she took the bed nearest the balcony, leaving Graham's bag on the other.

Then she raided the mini bar and found some potato chips and a bottle of ginger beer.

Letter #3 1996

First, I'd like to send you all my love and condolences for your loss. Losing one's parents is unimaginable. Especially parents like yours, who have loved and supported you through everything in your life. You were so loved by them, Eddie. And I am sorry that our daughter will miss the opportunity to grow up in their love. I only knew them through you, but that was enough time to know they will be sincerely missed. I am sending you and our daughter kisses, hugs, and so much love.

I spoke too soon! Six months after I got lost in Minnesota, my father's goons found me. I don't really remember how it went down, but here I am. It's not so bad here, to be honest. Except it's always like this for me—the time warp of withdrawals, sobriety, therapy. How many times have we done this rodeo before? For my parents' sake, they now have answers. My psychiatrist, Dr. Luna, has just diagnosed me with bipolar disorder, explaining my manic periods of depression and impulsive behavior. I asked her what that had to do with the drugs, the uppers and downers, the coke, the meth. (Did you even know I took all of those things?) She said the two go hand in hand and are both direct risks to each other. I do drugs to ease the effects of my bipolar disorder, and my weirdness gets worse because I do drugs.

By the way, I guess they now have categorized the severity of this disorder. I am Bipolar II—I think the manic episodes are less, but the depression is just as bad. All I know is that if I am not the most severe case, I have a chance of getting better.

Carlotta is six now! I am sure she is in first grade. Did Elma help pick out her first Communion dress? I hate Elma so much. Sometimes, I feel like she's stolen my family away from me. Can you imagine it? I'd been with you for three years, and Elma has been with you for six years now. It makes me angry to think about it. But I know we did the right thing. When I think about all the fights we had and how I'd lash out at you for no reason, hit you, punch you. You never did anything to hurt me back. If that was any indication that you genuinely loved me, then I know you did.

I guess I always had this thing in me, even when I was younger. I'd have these dark thoughts in my head. I'd lie in bed, wide awake for hours, thinking of the end of the world, of death, of earthquakes and calamities. And then panic would often set in, leaving me so breathless that I would have to hurt myself to make those thoughts subside. No one knew except Ruby, but she was so much younger than me that she didn't understand what she saw. And then I met you, and I thought you had scared all those evil monsters away.

Dr. Luna says that the disorder surfaced back up after I had my baby. Now, that's a little bit of an irony, considering she would save me. I have more medicines than any old person you've ever seen. My grandpa used to have those daily pillboxes that bunched pills together on a given day. Imagine three of those. That's what I have. I just hope they make me better.

Give me twenty years to get better. Oh, I don't know how much time it will take. But it feels hopeful to have an end date. At least it's not life without parole or even death. That would be so hopeless to die before I get better. I imagine it's a long process. And I heard my doctor tell my parents that some people just never get better, either. So, give it time.

And after that, come find me. I'll be ready for you.

Two hours later, she heard the swipe of the key at the door. Charlie turned and faced the opposite way, embarrassed that she'd been crying for an hour or so. She turned her pillow over, hoping the other side had dried. And then she pulled the comforter up to her chin. She heard Graham ruffle through his bag and enter the bathroom before hearing his quiet footsteps coming closer.

And then, his voice was barely a whisper. "Charlie, you still awake?"

Charlie kept her position, facing away from him and mumbling into her pillow. "Yes."

"It was amazing," Graham gushed. His tone was still quiet but seemingly elated. "The lady, Jill, got me into one of the discussions. This is huge in the tech industry because, remember, we're all a bunch of gaming geeks. I watched a tournament and checked out some interactive gaming tents."

"Okay," Charlie responded. Except it sounded more like "pay." She couldn't breathe through her nose and tried desperately to stifle a sneeze.

Silence filled the room. She thought it was over, that she could will herself to sleep. But then she felt his presence, and strangely enough, she knew. She pictured him standing right at her bedside, looking down at her ridiculousness, a head sticking out of a tightly balled comforter.

"Are you all right? Did you read the letters?"

The floodgates finally broke open. Three months of trying to make sense of her loss, of cleaning up the remnants of the life she'd had with her father, of being unable to figure out who she was and what her life would be like without him. Grief was first hidden in the everyday trivialities of life and was now straining to break free. She turned to see Graham hovering over her. He wore shorts and a T-shirt and looked so sympathetic she thought he would cry, too.

"Yes!" she exclaimed, sobbing, her cries turning to a high-pitched squeak that pinged against the walls. She didn't know what caused her to do it, but she scooted her body to the side of her bed and lifted the blanket, signaling for him to climb into bed with her.

He didn't even hesitate.

Quietly, he rested her head on his shoulder and draped the other arm across her chest.

"I know," he whispered. "Let it go, Charlie. I'm here. I'm here for you."

"I'm sorry, I'm sorry," she cried. "It's just too much!"

"Shhh," he said, stroking her hair and pressing his lips on her forehead.

He smelled really good, like the fresh spring air and soap, maybe sandalwood. What did Lorenzo smell like? She couldn't remember. All that mattered was that she hadn't been this close to anyone in so long.

"It's been a long day. Let's talk tomorrow. Try to go to sleep. I'll be here."

She woke in his arms, listening to the peaceful rhythm of his snoring. What had she done, asking him to hold her, a stranger who could have taken advantage of the situation? Except she knew that he wouldn't. Why she had so much trust in this person was confounding. Charlie smiled when she realized she hadn't slept this soundly in months. She decided to take advantage of the situation, closed her eyes, and fell right back to sleep.

It was ten o'clock by the time she opened her eyes again.

She grinned when she saw the sun in his eyes. Somehow, they'd shifted their positions. Now, they faced each other, Graham with one arm bent under his head and Charlie with her head on the pillow, her hair partially shadowing her face. She wasn't self-conscious, even when she knew he'd been watching her. It felt natural, like she'd known him for a million years. The intimacy of the moment was marked by the quiet rise and fall of their chests.

"Good morning," Charlie murmured. "I am so sorry about last night. And I'm sorry I overslept."

"Don't be sorry. I needed that, too."

"I feel so dramatic all the time."

"That's not true," he said, still whispering. "You've been pretty normal despite everything you've been through."

"Thank you."

"I just had a thought, actually. Since it's already late in the morning, do you want to stay an extra day so we can check out the Hallmark Museum today?"

"Is that because you'd like to stay one more day for the convention?" she teased.

"Kinda." Graham reached out to tuck a strand of hair behind her ears. "I'm kidding. I want to spend another day with you here."

"Okay," she said. And then an afterthought. "Graham, how old are you?"

"I'm thirty-five. You?"

"I just turned thirty-two. I'd really like to learn more about you." She felt bolder, like a barrier between them had been broken, and she was eager to make this a two-way friendship.

"Okay," he said. "But first, did you want to tell me about the letters?"

"Maybe over breakfast. I had chips for dinner."

"Ah, I was at a buffet."

Charlie laughed while swinging her legs off the edge of the bed. "Let's go. I'm starving."

"Is it okay if I step into the shower first?" he asked, sitting up on the bed.

Charlie thought it would be the perfect chance for her to read another letter before they left. For some reason, she felt stronger. "Sounds good," she said, reaching over to the night table to grab another one.

Letter #4 1998

Who even discusses a lobotomy these days? That was outlawed in the seventies! But I heard my parents asking about it at today's session. I was like . . . woah? What? You'd remove a lobe of my brain at the risk of incapacitating me forever? I researched it, obviously. In the end, they were stopped, and it was shushed, and my mom cried in relief. They told her I would just have to be medicated all my life. As in, forever and ever. I don't know, Eddie. How does one accept that?

I know that my parents have been in touch with you. I found out, yes, eight years later, that they had been checking in on Carlotta. What do you guys call her anyway? Carlie? Carol? Lotta? Charlie? I think I like Charlie. I bet that's what she named herself. She's a Charlie. The perfume girl was lanky and no-nonsense with high heels in a black men's suit. Remember that, Eddie? A strong, resilient little girl.

Anyway, I think I have a plan to get out of here. I'm twenty-eight years old now, and I think I met someone who can get me out of here. I won't tell you anything about that now. But wish me luck!

They sat in a diner and ordered breakfast—she, French toast with a side of bacon, him, an acai bowl.

"Geez, I feel like a pig eating next to you."

"That Chinese buffet is sitting like a rock in my stomach." He chuckled. "Otherwise, I'd be ordering the eggs Benedict. By the way." He dug into his pocket and pulled out two hundred-dollar bills. "This is for my share of the room, and breakfast is on me."

"Graham, I feel like an ATM after all your cash payments to me. Can you just list everything down as an IOU and write me a check at the end of this trip? Or PayPal me when you get home. I think by now I know you won't ditch me."

"If that's what you want." Graham shrugged.

Their silence was filled with a symphony of sounds—the clinking of cutlery against the plates, the rustle of napkins, and the gentle clatter of dishes being laid on the tables. They focused on their food for a while, sipping their coffee and listening to the rumble of conversations around them.

"Can I ask you," Graham began, after taking a swig of his water, "are you in a serious relationship?"

"Not now. I was, but we broke up after my dad got sick. You?"

"I was, but not now either. I was actually engaged to someone last year."

"What happened?" Charlie asked, leaning forward.

"The pressure to conform, get engaged, have a family, while my career was blowing up . . . it was intense. I met this girl from New Jersey. My parents loved her. I wanted to please everybody. And in doing that, I realized how miserable I was."

"Didn't you love her? You know, they say that love should conquer everything."

"Do you really believe that?"

"Yes and no. Don't you notice how a love story isn't great until it ends in tragedy? It's not a sweeping saga unless someone leaves or dies," she said with a smirk, her tone riddled with sarcasm. "But I'm not being cynical when I say that. I do believe that love can be transformative. I've seen people sacrifice their lives for love. I think my dad fell into that category. He devoted his life to raising a daughter. I never saw him date or even want to meet women." She sipped her coffee. "You?"

"I thought I loved her. But in the end, I realized I loved the idea of her. The idea of having a family and a successful business. But she wasn't the one."

"It was the sex, wasn't it?" she teased, feeling her cheeks flush.

"Ha!" he barked. "That too!" And then he turned pensive, swirling his finger around the edge of his glass. "But now that I think about it, it was all physical. There was no connection."

"I don't even know what that means," Charlie said. "I guess I've never had it, really. Maybe it would have been different if we had taken the time to revel in certain moments. But life was so noisy, so busy. I feel bad because I stayed with Lorenzo for three years and knew from the start that he wasn't the one for me either."

"How so?"

"Oh, I don't know." She hesitated, picking at her fingers to avoid looking at him. "I guess I'd been reading too many romance novels. Expectations can be quite high," she said with a giggle.

He locked eyes with her and nodded.

To ease the tension, Charlie pointed to her plate. "Hey, did you want my bacon?"

"Sure," he said, using his fork and knife to fish the bacon from her plate. "Thank you."

"Look at us, huh? Such losers."

"Don't worry, whatever it is we're looking for, I think we'll find it." He laughed. "Eventually."

Servers moved quickly around them, and one server poured more coffee while another set the dessert menu on their table.

"Dessert after breakfast?"

"Anything to get you talking," Graham said, smiling.

"So, my mom." Charlie cleared her throat. "Celia. It was such a shock for me to read more about her. She was depressed. I think that's why she left me and my dad. I guess when she ran away to Minnesota, her dad found her and brought her home. They had her diagnosed and concluded she was bipolar. She said she wasn't surprised, that she'd always had these dark thoughts in her head. She was prescribed quite a lot of medication."

"How do you feel about finding that out?" Graham asked, stirring his coffee.

"It's weird how there's so much of my personality in those letters. She writes pretty straightforwardly but with a lot of color in her tone. She's sarcastic but also full of anger. She was mad at Auntie Elma for taking her place with me. But in that letter, she said the doctor thinks her sickness flared up when she had me."

Graham nodded. "How many letters did you read?"

"Two more. That was the third one. The fourth one was really sad, Graham. She was twenty-eight years old. She said her parents were discussing a lobotomy with the doctor."

"Wait a minute," he interrupted. "What?"

"Yeah, I googled it. It's a huge operation where they remove a part of your brain, so you're desensitized or something like that."

"That was outlawed," he said. "WTF?"

"Well, they didn't do it or anything. But I think it was her way of telling Eddie how desperate her parents were to make her get better. It was a really short letter, but in the end, she said she'd met someone."

"A man?"

"I assume so." She motioned to the server for the check.

Graham studied her carefully before speaking again. "Why did you cry last night, Charlie? What made you so sad?" Graham reached for her hand. He held it across the table.

"She's sick. I think she left because she was sick. All I kept thinking was how sad her life had become without her family. Without me, without her. I kept wondering why my father had given up on her. We could have remained close, even if she was sick. Why would he abandon her, especially when she also mentioned that her parents were in touch with my father in her letter? I was so confused and angry. I'm getting answers, but each answer gives rise to double the questions."

"It's not that easy to remain with someone who is sick. Maybe he was protecting you."

"Maybe," she agreed. "But it's also not like my dad to walk away from a challenge."

"I guess you'll have to keep reading the letters," Graham said.

"I guess so."

They returned briefly to the hotel, where Graham sought out Jill, the front desk lady, to extend their stay by one more night. There were still no rooms, but she spent ten minutes trying to find a second one until he said it wasn't necessary. Then she gave him the stink-eye, which he didn't notice, all of which amused Charlie greatly.

At the Hallmark Visitors Center, they learned about the

history of the card company, viewed some vintage cards, and checked out the art collection, which featured artists such as Norman Rockwell and Thomas Kinkade. They especially enjoyed watching the manufacturing process, where cards were printed, embossed, and carefully crafted. It was then that Charlie, in a wistful moment, turned to Graham and said, "This was my dream, you know. To own a store filled from wall-to-wall with books and greeting cards."

Charlie was feeling the pinch when they arrived back at the hotel. She desperately needed time alone, time away from Graham, to figure out what was happening and the myriad of feelings bombarding her heart and mind. "Why don't you go and check out more of the convention? I'm going to order room service. I'm exhausted." She didn't know why, but she started to feel an attachment to the letters. She began to identify with them and placed herself squarely in the middle of her mother's story. After all, every letter started with her—she was mentioned at the start of each one, her age highlighted as her mother narrated the events in her life. It was as if their lives ran parallel, separated in time by twenty years. The letters no longer felt distant. She felt protective about the information in those letters. And there itself was her dilemma. She was so open about them with this stranger. And the guy she'd only known for a few days but trusted enough to find comfort in his presence. In fact, she'd often forget his newness. It was like he'd always been in her life.

"You sure? I'd like to check things out a bit more. I'll be back early. I know we have to leave first thing in the morning."

"Take your time. I'll see you later."

Charlie settled in the room and ordered room service. Then she sat on the couch, folded her legs in, and dialed Rena's number.

"Hey, stranger. How are things? I tracked you today. Did you extend your stay in KC?"

"We did," Charlie acknowledged.

Rena made a whooping sound. "Why?"

"We thought we'd tour the Hallmark Card place."

"Sounds like my Charlie. Was it fun?"

"Yes, it was. I started to think about that bookstore dream seriously," she said, laughing.

"So, everything is fine?"

"Yes. I guess I just had to hear your voice. I feel . . . so different. First, I have now accepted the fact that I have a mother. And that she's a living, breathing person. It's like she's always been there. I didn't wake up one day and have her. She's been there the whole time."

"And the letters?" Rena asked.

Charlie felt a kink in her knee and stretched her legs out. "Holy crap. I've only gotten through four of them, but woah. Even when they are more superficial conversations, like where she ended up or that she ran away from home, I feel them. I feel every word. She's troubled for sure. Maybe that's why Papa left or stayed away. Maybe that's why I'm like this—"

"Like what?" Rena's tone turned argumentative. "Like nothing. You're fine."

"Well, I'm kind of a ghoster. I can't hold relationships, and I don't like people."

Rena chuckled. "Who isn't? And who doesn't?" And then, after a brief pause, "And the guy?"

"He's so kind. Too good to be true, you know?"

"Is he in his room now?"

"Well . . . not exactly. The hotel had no rooms available. There's some sort of gamers convention going on. He's like a kid in a candy store. He's there, exploring, looking around."

"Answer the room question, please."

"We're sharing a double."

Another whoop. And then a shriek. And then a knock on the door.

"It's not like that. I'll explain later. Don't worry, everything is good."

"Charlie! What the fudge!"

"Gotta go! The room service guy is here! Love you and all good. I promise!"

Charlie woke at three a.m. and found she had slept through Graham's return. She tried not to wake him with her constant movement and the swishing of the sheets. But soon, she realized it wasn't her. In the stillness of the room, she heard him. First, it was a quiet mumble, a toss here, a turn there. And then it began. One leg first, and then both legs, pushing themselves against the heaviness of the comforter, bouncing on the mattress, accompanied by words Charlie could not discern.

"Graham?"

The thrashing continued. Arms in the air, legs kicking off the sheets.

"Graham!"

"Mmm?" he answered, lifting his head to look at her.

"Are you okay?"

"Yes, why?"

"You seemed like you were having a bad dream."

Silence. Then, "I'm sorry I woke you up. Please go back to sleep."

CHAPTER 18

OMAHA

At a rest stop in the middle of the two-hundred-seventy-five-mile drive to Omaha, Charlie thought she'd bring it up. "Hey, G. Are you okay? Were you having a bad dream?"

"Yeah, all fine. Sorry about that. The reason why two separate rooms work better," he said, ruffling his hand through his hair.

"Not a big deal at all. I was awake."

"Still. I'm kind of embarrassed," he countered with a grimace. "I swear, it doesn't happen often."

"All those video games. You were probably just so hyped up last night. All the geeks coming together."

"Maybe." Graham adjusted the rearview mirror and placed the car in reverse. "Ready to go?"

One hundred miles into the drive, Charlie turned to him and asked, "Want to listen to the audiobook of *Charlotte's Web*? I have the annotated version."

"Hmmm," Graham teased. "Not sure I can stay awake if that's what we're listening to."

She playfully tapped him on his shoulder. "Stop it. It's a beautiful story. I was named after her, you know."

Graham turned to her again, this time with that signature smile. Right there and then, she reminded herself to call Rena. Her heart may have fluttered a little. She may have been a teeny bit smitten. "I'll tell you what. Since I'd rather listen to your lovely voice, just tell me the story. I'm all ears."

She turned her body sideways to face him, her left knee crossed against her right leg. "Okay. Ready? Here we go. So, there's so much more symbolism in what a lot of people think is a children's story. It's initially sad and morbid because Wilbur's future has been planned for him. But my dad told me the story in terms of the lessons in them. For example, my mother named me Charlotte because she said I would save her life. Like Charlotte, the spider began writing these web messages to save Wilbur from being slaughtered."

Graham reached for her hand and rested both his and hers on her knee. Charlie turned her palm up so she could clasp his fingers. She had to admit his touch was invigorating. "Keep going."

"I think my mom's messages are going to be related to these lessons. I can just feel it. Friendship, sacrifice, compassion, life and death, and the power of words. When my dad got sick, he was so at peace with it, as if it was an expected event. And I kept telling him to fight because he was all I had."

Graham remained silent. Charlie could tell he was thinking about what she'd said. She knew there was a connection, that he was hurting about something.

"Hey, did you ever read any of the Mother Goose rhymes? Since you're into classic children's books."

"Just one book." She chuckled. "Why?"

"My sister loved 'Hey Diddle Diddle.' You know, the cat jumping over the moon thing."

"I have that book somewhere in storage," she said, her brain going in different directions. "Oh, random! But I have some photos of my dad reading the book to me. Hold, please," she said, unbuckling herself and bending over to reach into the back seat. She suddenly realized how that must have looked, so she pulled the edges of her shorts down to ensure nothing unsavory was sticking out. She let out a tiny grunt as she reached as far as she could to pull out one particular photo album.

"I want to show you some pictures. We have so many of these. My dad used to go to Walgreens at least three times a week to get pictures printed. I kept asking him why when he had them on his phone and computer, but he said he liked hard copies better."

She sat back down and buckled herself in. Then, she began flipping through the pages. "Funny, some of the ones I know he had developed aren't in here. But there's enough. So, these are pictures of every age. I want to relate them to my mom's letters when she actually calls out my age."

Graham nodded, turning the music down.

"See, look." She held the album sideways so Graham could see. "Here's so many of me reading *Charlotte's Web* with and without my dad." Indeed, about ten pictures of Charlie were on the couch, on the floor, on her bed, in the car, reading her favorite book.

"Tell you what," Graham offered, veering to the right lane and exiting toward a truck stop. "Why don't we drive through somewhere for food? And then take a break and look at the pictures together?"

Charlie faced forward and folded the album on her lap. "Sounds great. I need to pee, too."

They parked at the truck stop between a McDonald's and a Panera Bread, holding a cup of soup in their hands.

"I just love this, don't you? Their butternut squash soup." Charlie closed her eyes, her lips curved upward in a smile.

"Great rec. It's really good." Graham rested his cup in its holder and reached for the photo album. "May I?"

Charlie nodded.

"Your dad was quite a looker," he said, looking at a page full of Edgar's pictures.

"He was. My friends would always call him the 'Hot Dad.' And they always wondered why he never had girlfriends. Even Auntie Elma. When I think about it now, she was always there. Always."

"It's obvious he carried a torch for your mom. Sometimes . . ." He paused and fixed his eyes on Charlie. She caught his gaze and self-consciously looked at her knees. "There's just that one person. No one else comes close."

Charlie was speechless. Was that her cue to admit she was slightly attracted to this stranger? She didn't know what to say. Good thing he covered it up rather quickly.

"Wanna see my family?" he asked.

She nodded, exaggerating the movement of her head.

Graham fished into his back pocket and removed his wallet. He pulled out a picture from the side flap, weathered and torn, pieces of the wallet stuck on the glossy paper. His mother looked like Princess Grace, elegant and coiffed, and his father was the guy in the original James Bond movies. Between them was a young girl with flawless skin and striking features, a perfect combination of his parents. Charlie saw parts of Graham in her.

"What are their names?"

"My mom is Cassandra, and my father is William. That amazing angel over there?" He gently traced a finger over her face. "My sister, Madison."

"What do they do?" Charlie asked, seeing the difference between her humble upbringing and the opulence surrounding that one single picture.

"My dad ran many businesses for his family. My mom was a corporate lawyer."

"Wow. And your sister?" Charlie asked, trying her best not to reflect her deflated ego through her tone.

"A violinist for the New York Philharmonic Orchestra."

"Very bougie," she commented.

"And your family? Did you have a large one?"

"My dad was my only family. He was a limo driver who drove to and from the airport for years. He also did odd jobs around Brooklyn, from fixing guitars to rehabbing a home. I was raised by people from our church and community. He was a single father, and so many of the older generation took him in. Until he was able to get on his feet and buy us a home in Sunset Park. My Auntie Elma was his best friend forever. She married a wealthy man in pharma sales, and they have a really awesome son named Justin. That's basically my extended family." She noticed he wasn't finishing his soup. "Hey, do you want your soup? I can finish it for you."

"I don't know where all of that goes," Graham said, laughing. "But yes, help yourself." He handed her a new spoon, still wrapped in plastic. "Anyway, do you think that's why you never really questioned not having a mom?"

"No, I think . . . I had always wished I had a mom. In fact, I understand now why I lived the way I did. Why was I so closed up and afraid to become attached to anyone? I was afraid they'd leave, just like my dad did in the end. So, I did wish I had a mom, but I didn't miss having one because my Auntie Elma played that role."

Charlie proceeded to lap up her soup while Graham looked at maps on his phone.

"How much farther are we from Casper?"

"About five hours," he answered, still swiping and typing.

"What do you say we try to drive straight through? Charge up now and then charge up again on the way?"

"You won't be afraid of running out of charge? I'm shocked," he ribbed. "You know that means we'll be driving through the night."

"Hey, I know you won't let me down," she teased. "Let's just plan to rest a bit in Casper, stay an extra night or something. I hear they have a variety of museums." She turned up the volume and got lost in the music.

CHAPTER 19

CASPER

It must have been a satellite glitch, or at least that's how they both explained the gross miscalculation in the distance. Casper, Wyoming, ended up being 450 miles away. They had to find a charging station in the middle of the night, take a thirty-minute nap at another rest area, and fill the car with Mentos Starburst wrappers and Red Bull cans to survive the drive. By the time they arrived at their hotel, it was late in the morning. Once they were checked in, Charlie turned to him in the elevator. "How about we meet for dinner this evening? I'll see you in the lobby. We can just relax and take a nap now for a few hours." The truth was, she also needed to catch up on her mother's letters.

It was four p.m. by the time she woke up, rested and refreshed. After a quick shower, Charlie wrapped herself in a hotel bathrobe, feeling clean and luxurious. She lay on her stomach, dangling her feet over the edge of the bed. She wondered what Graham was doing. They'd only been separated for five hours, and she was already looking forward to seeing him again. She had a couple of hours, though. It was time to continue her mother's story.

Letter #5 2000

Happy Y2K!

I'm thirty years old, and my Charlie is ten. I am told that little girls grow up quickly these days. Is that true? Tell me, Eddie, what do you tell her when she asks about her mother? I hope you told her I've died because, in a lot of ways, that's what has happened to me. When I was ten, I remember my nanny telling me that the fairy living outside my window would always be there to protect me. She asked me why I was always afraid, and I told her about all the awful dreams I was having about dying. I was deathly afraid of dying. I kept thinking about it, and I even lost sleep. Anyway, I guess I don't fear it anymore. I've died over and over again. Losing you, my daughter, and now this.

I thought this man loved me, so I ran away with him. It turns out he thought I had money, given the care I was receiving from my parents. When he discovered I had none, he threw me out of his apartment. We were in Phoenix! So I ended up doing what I do best: befriending a doctor who got me access to everything I wanted. He said I was so beautiful no one could refuse my requests. The day I was picked up passed out on the sidewalk was the day I called my mother. She flew on one of our planes and found me in a jail cell in Central City.

I am home now. And I don't think I can ever leave.

Letter #6 2002

Char-lotita is twelve! I have great news! I work for my dad in his office. I record his appointments and set up his meetings. I also work with his secretary, Gina, and help with filing and banking. I write up the deposit slips and take the checks to the bank. I feel so useful and so needed. Maybe I can do this for our little business when I return home. I think I can come back.

Is my pre-teen acting up like a teen? What is she into? Elma has been sending me pictures of her—thank you for letting her do that. She is so beautiful. Elma thinks she looks just like me, but I think she is prettier. She has the light highlights in her hair that come from you and the nice, fine nose that comes from your family. I like her hair long like that.

Oh my, I'm so happy. I think I may be getting better.

Letter #7 2004

I'm surprised it took them this long to do this. Our daughter is now fourteen! But they did, and I'm glad they lost. I'm sorry they tried to claim legal custody of our daughter. I think they figured they should try before she turned eighteen. They have two granddaughters from Ruby, so why did they need a third? I don't know.

Nevertheless, I knew the judge would not find you an incompetent parent. In fact, I know that our daughter is in the best place she could ever be. Mom told me they are impressed with the care you've given our daughter and your involvement in her life. I also know they halted their action when they found out they'd have to call Charlie in as a witness. I'm beginning to think they're not that bad, Eddie. They did do the right thing after all was said and done.

Congrats, Lover!

Charlie cheered her mother on, relieved that things were working out for her. She also began to feel an affinity toward her grandparents. They recognized her as theirs and tried to fight for her, although she wished they'd done it differently. They were always there for Celia, picking up the pieces whenever needed. Her mood had lifted, and the dread of reading more letters diminished.

Charlie decided she would focus on her evening with Graham, tell him about the letters, and have some fun getting to know him more. There was no way to define how she felt about him, but he intrigued her. So she texted him, asking him to meet her at the bar by the hotel called Curiosity. It was supposed to be a popular dive bar with drinks, junk food, live music, and a dance floor. It had been a while since she'd danced. And she was going to take her time getting dressed. After all, she hadn't really paid attention to her looks lately. In fact, she'd kind of let herself go. It would be nice to reconnect with herself, her heart, mind, and even her body.

Charlie saw Graham's reaction when she walked into the bar, careful not to slip or get her heels caught between the grooves on the soft wooden floor. He'd only ever seen her in jeans, shorts, and T-shirts. She'd done her hair, loosened the curls so they cascaded down her shoulders, and wore a hot pink halter top and a short black skirt. She was an hour late, but the band was just getting set up. Graham had a big grin on his face as she slid into the booth opposite him.

"Hey. I hope this place is okay."

"It's perfect. And it's empty, just the way I like it."

"It's a Tuesday night," Charlie reasoned. "I'm sure it's packed on weekends."

"Let me get you a drink. What would you like?"

"Can you see if they have a Moscato? That's really all I drink. If not, maybe a cider?" Charlie grabbed the menu and started leafing through it. "I'm more hungry than anything."

Graham laughed. She laughed, too, rolling her eyes at the same time. "I know. I'm always starving."

When he returned with the drink of her choice, she was happy. They ordered their food and leaned back just as the band began to play. Charlie was surprised when Graham started to hum with the band. He had changed after they shared a room. He was more talkative and more relaxed. More himself.

"You know their songs?" she asked, simultaneously putting a french fry in her mouth. In front of them were shared plates of Parmesan garlic fries, mini tacos, and chicken wings.

"They're doing a cover for an indie band I really like."

Charlie smiled at him. He smiled back.

"I have to tell you something," Graham began. "I don't want you to get the wrong impression. I really believe that most of the time you only get one chance, one shot in life. And I don't want to regret not telling you this."

Oh no, Charlie thought. *He's going to tell me that he's married with five children or that he's into guys. Or that I'm not his type. Or he just wants to be friends.* Her jaw dropped, eyes once again fixed on something on the table so she could avoid his. She took a deep breath. "Tell me."

"I have never seen anyone as beautiful as you are tonight."

"Thank you." Charlie exhaled in relief, one hand self-consciously smoothing her hair back. She really should stop thinking the worst of everything all the time. "You don't look so bad yourself. And you didn't even try." She giggled.

After sharing that moment, Charlie tried to change the subject. "I read three more letters this afternoon. And can't wait to read another one tonight."

"Anything you'd like to share?"

"Her family is definitely well-to-do. She ended up running away with a man who used her for her money, and she ended up in jail. Her mother picked her up in Arizona and took her back home. She said something in that letter that really stuck out to me. She said, 'I don't think I can ever leave' when referring to being home. Why does she hate being with her family so much?"

"Maybe she was trying to assert her independence. Maybe her father was controlling, or she was just that type of child."

"I think we're all that type of child," Charlie reasoned. "Anyway, the next letter was quite nice. She tells him she is now working for her father and settling in at home. It sounds like she just wanted to be needed, and working for her family makes her feel that way."

Graham tilted his head, interested to hear more. "That's great."

"Oh wait, and then! Apparently, my grandparents filed for custody of me and lost! She didn't mention more than just saying she knew my dad was a great parent and they wouldn't be able to take me away from him."

"Sheesh. It's like a rollercoaster ride."

"Totally."

"But how do you feel about that?" Graham asked.

In a way, she knew he would. He was always interested in how she reacted to her mother's words.

"Loved. Wanted. I felt that way from the first letter. She would say, 'Oh, my daughter is two, four, six, eight, ten . . .' Every letter would start with me. Graham, she loved me."

Two drinks later, Charlie came rushing out of the bathroom, trying to maintain her balance while making her way back to their booth. She slid in next to Graham.

"Oh my gosh, Graham! Look at this!" Charlie slammed her phone on the table.

"What happened? Is everything okay?"

"Yes! I was peeing in one of the stalls, and look at what I saw! Right in front of me. It's a sign! I know it is!"

He hovered over her, his head almost on her shoulder as she swiped her phone and showed him a picture. "It says 'Celia + Edgar,' carved right on the door."

Graham took the phone from her and held it in front of his face. He turned the phone horizontally, using his fingers to zoom in. "The lighting is bad. I can see Celia but not Edgar."

"I swear that's what it said! I just couldn't get the flash to work!"

"I believe you, Charlie. And yes, I think—"

"No, no! You have to see it for yourself. You have to come with me!" she shrieked, sliding away and pulling him to stand.

"You want me to go to the ladies' room with you?" Graham asked, amused. He looked around tentatively, smirking.

She looked around, too. There were only two other couples in the entire place.

"The ladies' room? Are you sure you're not—"

"Yes! I mean, no! I'm not drunk!" she argued. "No one goes in there. You have to see it! Remember what we talked about, all this symbolism, you only get one shot, blah blah! You have to see this. How many people are named Celia?"

She grabbed his hand and pulled him after her. First, she was in a frenzy until she realized she needed to slow it down. "You have to act cool," she whispered in a complete turnaround.

"Uh-huh."

When she reached the door, she looked left and right before pulling him along the hall and into the stall. There they stood, shoulder to shoulder, facing the inside of the stall door, with only an inch or two of room between them.

"You see?" she said in a hushed tone, tracing her hand across the names deeply carved onto the wooden door.

Celia + Edgar ♥

Just then, someone else entered the bathroom.

* * *

Charlie turned to Graham, panicked. She placed a finger on his lips, urging him to be quiet. Graham responded differently, looking into her eyes and drawing his face closer until their noses touched. What was he going to do? Did she want this? She had never felt this way about anyone. This closeness. This friendship. This attraction. It pulled at her from so many directions, and now that his lips were so close to hers, she wanted to feel them on her so badly. She felt the jolt of pins and needles coursing through her body, closing her eyes while allowing Graham to trace the tip of her nose with his finger. Charlie held her breath when his thumb skimmed the outline of her lips as he drew close and closer.

So, did she want this?

Yes.

She did. She wanted that first kiss. She couldn't remember anything feeling so right. So right, that to let it slip by would be her biggest mistake.

Flush.

Charlie drew her face back and smiled. They waited for the faucet to turn on, and then the hand dryer went off.

"Let's go!" she said, running out of the stall with him following right behind her. In a dizzying fit of laughter, they ran down the narrow hall, composing themselves as soon they reached the common area. They were like teenagers with a secret, strutting to the bar as if nothing happened.

The band was coming back from a break. Graham walked over to them while Charlie waited in the middle of the dance floor.

"This one is for Charlie. From Graham," the band leader announced over the microphone as Graham sauntered toward her, his eyes never leaving hers. When he got to her, he drew her close, resting one hand on the small of her back and holding her hand with the other. The tips of his fingers grazed her skin, sending a torrent of heat down her body.

"Dance with me, Charlie."

Slowly, the lights began to dim, and music flowed across the room. Mirrored balls dropped from the ceiling, producing infinite sparks amidst a kaleidoscope of colors and shapes swirling across the floor. She felt a contradiction arise within her, fully present at the moment, feeling his touch, the rise and fall of his chest. And yet, she was floating, flying through the air, dazed with excitement, desperate to ground herself in the uncertainties that lie ahead. She didn't know the song he requested, but somehow, its words became hers when he whispered them in her ear.

If you would be my lover
I swear I'd do this over
Cry all the tears, embrace all my fears
As long as I know you're here
I'll walk with you through every storm
Hold you close, keep you warm
Together, we'll face whatever comes our way
Because I'll never leave, I'm here to stay.
I was lost, but now I'm found
You've picked my heart up off the ground
I would suffer the pain and carry life's load
For as long as I know you're waiting
Waiting for me at the end of this long, lost road.

"I saw you that night," he whispered in her ear. "At the food pantry. I couldn't get you out of my mind after that. And when I ended up in your car—"

Gently, she lowered his head so her lips could touch his ear. "I saw you too."

Charlie wanted so badly to burst into tears, to release everything she'd been feeling since she started on this trip. There she was, falling in love with a stranger right after losing her father and gaining a mother on a road trip that was soon coming to an end. She didn't even know what she was going to do in California. But despite those worries, she had to relish this moment. Because right there and then, she learned what falling in love was all about. Her heart was leaping, running through a meadow filled with daffodils, looking up at the sun.

And she wasn't going to let this chance slip by.

This was what her father meant when he came to her that night. Life was so unpredictable, but she couldn't keep living in the past. She didn't know what the future held for her, but this was the present. Letting this moment slip by would be the biggest mistake of her life.

As the song ended, Charlie and Graham clung to each other, swaying slowly to the silence in the room. "Stay with me tonight, Graham," she whispered back.

Graham knocked on her door a few minutes after they returned to the hotel. Charlie had freshened up and dressed for bed. She opened the door to him while holding on to letter number eight.

Letter #8 2006

Eddie, Eddie, before you hear it from anyone else, let me tell you what really happened. I swear, I was going to pay it all back once I got a real job, not this pity job my father gave me. I was borrowing money from the deposits for a short amount of time. I needed to get my medicines, you know. And then, when they found out and took that job away from me, I didn't think she'd miss the jewelry she kept in her safe. I mean, she has so much! All these diamonds and Tiffany jewels. Useless things, she can't even wear them all. I'm her daughter. And it's just me and Ruby. So it would have gone to us anyway.

I hate them. They raised me with these standards, and then they took it all away from me! Like how am I supposed to live? I'm a Ruiz. They need to honor that. We own most of the buildings in downtown San Francisco, so why am I not entitled to any of that? Eddie, I want you to ensure that Carlotta gets her fair share from these bastards.

"I'm sorry. I can come back later," he said, backing away from the door.

"No, no. Come in. Is it okay to read it while you're here with me?"

"Definitely."

Graham sat on the couch facing Charlie, and she sat on the edge of the bed. She held the letter in both hands and pored over it.

"Charlie? What's going on?" Graham stood abruptly and went to her side as tears cascaded down her cheeks.

"What if I turn out to be like her? She's hot and cold, hot and cold. She does things so out of character, and then maybe not. Mental illness is hereditary, isn't it?" She sobbed, handing him the letter to read. He scanned it, then lay it gently on the nightstand.

They sat on the bed, facing each other.

"Charlie. I can't imagine how anyone would ever think you'd turn out to be like her. First, she's a wonderful woman, intelligent and intuitive. She's conflicted, but what she's doing isn't really her fault. It's beyond her control."

"What if it's hereditary? What if I am destined to inherit that from her? Is that why my dad kept her away from me?"

Graham held her face in his hands, skimming his thumb on her cheek to wipe her tears away. "I haven't seen any of it. In fact, all I see is a beautiful, intelligent woman who's scared shitless of losing the people she loves," he said. "We're all afraid, Charlie. But none of what happened with your parents had anything to do with you."

"I don't know that," she cried.

"I do. Your mom missed out on having you as a daughter. Think of all the great times you had with your dad and how proud he was of you. You are not her, okay?"

"Okay." She sniffed.

"Okay," he whispered in her ear, starting there and then trailing tiny kisses on her forehead and the tip of her nose before brushing his lips against her cheeks. She tilted her head up and aligned her lips with his.

And then he kissed her.

"Our first kiss," she said, locking eyes with him.

"The last first one," he whispered before increasing the intensity. He took her top lip between his and outlined it with his tongue, exploring her mouth as if it were some valuable treasure. He was so gentle and careful, pausing at each moment to look at her and ask for her permission to go further.

She tugged at the hem of his shirt, prodding him to lift it up over his head. In response, she unbuttoned her top and pulled him to her as she lay on the bed. His eyes were on fire, staring at her as she showed herself to him.

"My beautiful, magnificent girl."

They moved slowly, languidly, as if savoring every touch, every feel of their bodies together. And when he entered her, she couldn't help but think, *We fit each other so perfectly.*

The moment was cathartic. She trusted him, a trust she'd never bestowed on anyone but her father. This man was touching her in so many different ways. His skin felt like fire on hers, his lips gently pleased her, and his body professed love, loyalty, and truth.

Lorenzo was wrong. I can love. I can love.

"I can love," she caught herself blurting out loud.

Graham stopped in his tracks, catching her gaze with tenderness in his eyes. Holding her head in place with both hands, he pushed himself deeply into her and kissed her so profoundly she felt her heart coming out of her chest and heard promises spoken even when none were made.

"Love only me," he breathed. "Love only me, Charlie."

They woke up in the middle of the day, tired but rested, hungry but sated. The two of them spent the night with their arms, legs, and bodies intertwined, voices hushed, speaking slowly, laughing loudly between moments of tenderness and rapture.

Charlie eventually sat up and glanced at the clock by the bedside. "It's eleven o'clock. What did you want to do today?"

Graham pulled her back down, lifted her up, and sat her right on top of him. "This."

She played along, clasping his fingers and holding his hands above his head. She spread her legs and straddled him. "Surely there's still a lot more to see in Wyoming," she whispered, lowering herself onto him until they were one.

"This," he groaned, thrusting upward to meet her, "is all I want to do all day long."

CHAPTER 20

SALT LAKE CITY

They left early the next morning, knowing they'd have to stop and recharge on their way to Salt Lake City. The drive was longer than normal, with 402 miles to cover. Everything seemed different to Charlie. After spending two nights together, they shared an understanding. Charlie didn't know how to define it, nor did she want to talk about it. They were a couple in every sense of the word—the way they moved together in and out of bed, the touches, the smiles, and the whispers. But the reality was that they had only a few days left together. She tried to figure out how many more days they had but then pushed the thought away.

They drove along the natural landscape of Wyoming, the vast open plains, and the rolling hills that sat among the colorful mountain ranges in the distance. They stopped once, recharged the vehicle for another two hundred fifty miles, and then proceeded along Interstate 80 toward the Utah state line in comfortable silence. Charlie could tell when Graham was deep in thought, his eyes watching the road in front of him, but his brows rumpled and hands wrapped tightly around the steering wheel. She reached over to stroke his cheek, just to take his attention away from whatever it was that worried him.

"Hey, I was just thinking." Graham rested his hand on her lap.

Charlie covered his hand with hers. "Tell me."

He turned to her with a sheepish grin, the corners of his mouth pulled back slightly. "Is it safe to assume we're staying in one room now?"

"Very safe," she assured him. "How much longer do we have?"

"Four hours if we drive straight through."

Charlie unwrapped a new roll of Mentos. He opened his mouth so she could pop one in, which she did. "Is it okay if I open my mom's letters?"

"How far have we got?" Graham asked.

"We're almost done. I'm going to be on number nine, and it goes until number fifteen."

"We'd better get going, then."

"Here goes," she said, pulling the letters out and sorting them until she found the right one.

"I'll read it to you."

Letter #9 2008

This is going to be a long one.

I am here for good or until I'm better, whichever comes first.

After my mom and dad learned about the jewelry, my mother bought them all back from the pawn shop. I don't know what made me do it. I felt like I had lost face. I couldn't be trusted. I can't raise a child, can't hold on to a lover, can't even do something as simple as deposits. What am I good for?

Charlie stopped reading. Graham turned to her, and she looked at him with tears in her eyes. "Is it okay if I stop reading out loud?" She was more embarrassed than anything, opening up about her mother. She should be more discreet. What if this was an indirect reflection of who she was or who she would be in the years to come?

"Of course," he assured her. She leaned back in her seat and continued to read the letter.

They found two empty bottles of Seconal and me lying face down in the pool. They drained my lungs, pumped out my stomach, and here I am.

It's not bad, actually. I guess I'm in what you can call a Permanent or Long-Term Mental Health Facility. Something about organized living is really hitting a stride with me. I just got here three months ago, but it was the help I wanted. Help I needed. So I'm not fighting it.

I am still undergoing withdrawal therapy, with really large doses of counseling. So far, I've made one friend. Her name is Nina, and she's the daughter of a French socialite.

There are days when clarity begets darkness and regret. I now understand the implications of my actions. Wherever they stem from, they are mine, and I have to own them. I can now visualize that day I lost you and our daughter.

You had to go on a two-day trip to check out a job prospect in Chicago. A high school friend was starting a catering business there, and you thought you'd borrow some money from our parents to invest in it. Here we were in our twenties, with no jobs and a one-month-old daughter. You didn't want to go, but I insisted you do it. Selfishly, I wanted this to work out, to prove to my parents that we could make it on our own. I assured you I would be okay. I told your mother not to come until the evening because I'd be fine with her. All she did was sleep and eat. I'd handled that for one month, and I knew what to expect and what to do.

But as soon as those doors closed behind you, as soon as you were a few feet away from us, I was overcome with panic. I didn't know why, but I started thinking about getting out of the confines of our apartment. I felt strangled, like the walls were closing in on me. I was suffocating. As I looked around me at our little baby sleeping in the cot next to our bed, I was filled with such animosity toward her I knew that another moment alone with her would end tragically. And so, I dialed my old dealer's phone number. "No, we can't do it in that house," he said. "Meet me under the tree right on the corner of Hoyt and Bond."

The next thing I remember is you crying, sobbing, holding onto our daughter while an ambulance took me away. I was screaming, clawing at you, telling you that I was only gone for a few minutes. When, in fact, it had been two days.

Mothers are supposed to give their children life. Protect them from harm. Not put their life at risk with reckless acts and selfish motives. It was just like yesterday—I could feel her skin against my fingers, her breath on my face when I held it close to mine. "Remember, I love you, Carlotta." Those were my last words to our daughter. And I often wonder, after all these years, do you think she heard me?

In between those dark memories are periods of lightness, thankfulness, and gratitude for still being alive.

Am I angry that you chose our daughter over me? That you walked away that day with our daughter in your arms, and I never saw you again?

Oh, Eddie, I broke my own heart. You made the only choice. They were going to take her away and put her in foster care. This is why you stood up for her and raised her on your own.

To this day, I can't explain why I do the things I do, why I don't have impulse control, or why I say things I often regret and think that the world is always out to get me.

To this day, I don't know why I did what I did.

Malibu is gorgeous, and the sunrise is stunning and poetic. My everyday view is one that needs to be immortalized in a song or a painting. I want to learn how to paint it someday. On some days, I still get very upset about how I got here. On others, I am accepting. I think this will be how the rest of my life will be. I'm thirty-eight years old. Gonna be an old lady soon! Someone here said that with the kind of lifestyle I've lived, I'd be lucky to make it to forty. So, I guess from here on, every day I'm around will be a blessing. It also means you're going to surpass me in years! And how is time just flying by? Our daughter is . . . oh my, eighteen! When I was that age, I had so much unnecessary anger and angst—I hope our Carlotie is experiencing the best years of her life. Elma says you are an amazing father and that you were awarded Mom of the Year at her school! I'm sad I couldn't play that role, but I am so blessed that you are her father.

This time, she could hear her mother's voice speaking to her father, all the fervor and pain. These were the words that shed light on her leaving—that it was her father who left.

As she read more, Charlie let out an audible gasp, covering her mouth and closing her eyes to shield her from every upcoming word. Graham reacted by caressing her shoulder. It was all he could do to comfort her, and she knew it was best for him to keep driving.

It was too much. Just too much. Her mother was committed to a psychiatric facility. She stole money and used it to buy drugs. And now she was accepting of the fact that she would forever be living within the walls of a hospital. She was resigned to the fact that she would never be coming home.

"I'm sorry," Charlie said, squeezing Graham's hand. "It just caught me by surprise."

"It's okay," Graham answered. "Look, we're almost in Utah. I'll find a place to stop."

As they approached the state line, the terrain began to change. Rock formations sprouted in view as they drove through the breathtaking desert filled with towering cliffs and deep canyons. Charlie took a moment to admire the expansive views while Graham kept driving. During that time, she read letter number ten.

Letter #10 2010

Why did you come to see me, Eddie?

I'm doing so well, forgetting the life I left behind. I didn't need to be reminded of it! I couldn't believe my ears when they told me you were here for a visit. I just couldn't. The shock of finding out you haven't forgotten about me was too much for me to bear. It pushed the reality of what I'd done in my face.

Since I was living in a blur for some days, I thought at first that I had dreamed all of it. And then I saw your name on the sign-in sheet and knew it was real. Your handwriting, with the way you cross your T's—it was you.

What did you come for, E? Surely not to take me away because you know that what I have is incurable. You know that I'm capable of hurting myself, and when I had our baby, I almost hurt her. I'm no good, a broken mess. Don't you ever come to see me again.

"Oh, Graham!" she cried, this time in a high-pitched tone. "He went to see her! She refused to see him and turned him away, but still! He tried to see her!" Charlie did not expect this feverish onslaught of events—the highs, the lows, and the highs once again.

Graham turned to her and smiled. "Woah."

"Over there," Charlie said, pointing out the window. "Are we in Snowbird? I think that's where we're staying."

"One room, right?" Graham teased as he turned into the parking lot.

"One room."

Letter #11 2012

Ah, my love. I am so thankful that you didn't give up on me. I am so thankful to the doctors at this facility for allowing me to spend one night with you. My heart stopped when I saw you at the door.

You have a beard! And you are so handsome. You look like the man I fell in love with twenty-five years ago. Your eyes are still bright, like the sun, bluer than the sea in front of me.

You ran to me when my knees gave way at the sight of you. Held me in your big, strong arms. In an instant, I was that seventeen-year-old girl again, in search of herself and instead finding this beautiful man who would love her like nothing else mattered. We cried together for a while, and when you gently touched my face to rid me of my tears, I said no. These tears don't hurt anymore. Not this time. I need to soak in them and wash all my wounds away.

Charlie is twenty-two now, and her pictures—wow! She looks like a beauty queen. A beauty queen graduating from Harvard! Where did she get that resolve, that resilience? Surely not from me. I give up on everything.

I'm sorry, but I was upset when you told me she knew nothing about me.

But I understand now how things must be.

Eddie, we looked like two lovers who couldn't get enough of each other. When you held me close all throughout dinner, you told me that I was the only one you've ever loved, the only one you will ever love. You made me feel like I was the most beautiful creature in the world. The way you held me whispered to me how much you love me and how there had been no one else in your life but me. When you kissed every scar on my arm, every cut and slice on my skin, you told me there would never be any more pain. What on earth have I done to deserve this? To deserve your love? The gentle way you made love to me, the nervousness of not having been with any other woman since me. How? How could I ever repay that?

That night, you gave me the one thing I never had in my whole forty-two years on this earth. Peace. I no longer need to prove anything or fight for anything. You have calmed me down, given me my peace. Thank you, Eddie. Your love is putting all my broken pieces back together.

Once they checked in, Graham suggested they enjoy the outdoors while the sun was still up. Charlie agreed. She needed the fresh air, just like she needed this new perspective about her parents. The ski lodge they'd chosen was nestled at the foot of a mountain, surrounded by giant evergreens and the ice-capped peaks of Mount Superior. The architecture was inspired by the natural beauty of the area: wide open and panoramic, each room overlooking Little Cottonwood Canyon. Right behind the lobby was the heated outdoor pool. They settled on the deck chairs lining the pool and directly in view of the ski lifts going up and down the mountain. Spring was in full swing, so there was no longer snow on the ground. The landscape had now transformed into an abundant countryside, alpine meadows littered with wildflowers expanded in all directions. The contrast between the rugged mountain tops and the vibrant greenery was mesmerizing.

"I was a little embarrassed, crying like that in the car," she started. "I mean, just opening up my family's secrets in front of you." She caught herself. "I mean, I don't want to scare you off or anything. You hardly know me."

"Whatever your parents' story is, it has only made you who you are now. And you are something else, Charlie," he said, taking her hand.

"Okay. Well, I'm excited to tell you what happened next," she said, excited. "He went to visit, and she turned him away. But, sometime later, he came again, and they reunited! Love wins, Graham! She writes about their reunion, how they both fell to the ground and held each other. Oh, it was so beautiful. She was forty-two, and I was twenty-two. He brought pictures of me, and she raved about how pretty I was."

"I'd rave about how pretty you are, too."

She giggled and blushed.

He motioned for her to come to him, so she took her place between his legs and leaned on his chest.

"Now that I think about it, my dad went on these overnight trips when I was older. I didn't live at home, but he would call and tell me he was going ice fishing with so and so, or to Vegas to watch a boxing match, or that he had to drive clients on cross-country overnight trips. Once, I remember seeing his car parked at a long-term parking lot a few blocks from his house. His car was easily identifiable, with a Yankee license plate and a huge sticker on the windshield with his driver number, 0707. I wondered about it for a while. And then I figured they must have switched cars on him."

"All the while, he was having sexy times with your mom," Graham said. "So she must be irresistible, just like her daughter."

"I'm so happy," she said, glossing over his comment. "I know I should be feeling left out. You know, their reunion should have somehow included me, but . . . I feel like this is their happy ending, and they had to figure themselves out before bringing me into the picture. I'm nervous about reading the next few letters. I would have been satisfied ending with this one. Their reunion."

Graham wrapped his arms around her and nuzzled her neck. She giggled, pulled his arms in tighter, and closed her eyes in bliss.

Seconds later, they noticed a crowd gathering around the pool and looking up at the sky. Just then, the loud rumbling of a crop plane flying low, its wings almost touching the tips of the trees, overshadowed the drone of voices all around them. The plane flew directly in front of them, a banner flapping in the sky.

"Wait. Is that. . . ?"

Graham tipped his head up, looking straight up. The clouds seemed to move out of the way, slowly floating, evaporating so that all that was left was a clear blue sky. *Marry Me, Celia.*

Charlie tugged at Graham's sleeve while shielding her eyes from the sun. "Do you see that? Does that say Celia?" And then she turned to the others who were just as interested in watching the plane streak through the air. "Does anybody else see that? Or is it just me?"

Two people from behind the crowd yelled, "We see it. Are you Celia?"

Graham looked ahead. He craned his neck forward, peeking through his fingers to ensure he saw the same thing. "Holy cow! It does."

Just then, a woman shrieked. The crowd started to clap.

Charlie didn't bother looking at the Celia of that day. "You see?" Charlie said, her heart swelling with joy. "First the bathroom door and now this. He's here, G. I can feel his presence everywhere. He's watching over us, telling us we're on the right track."

CHAPTER 21

SNOWBIRD

Things felt different when Charlie woke up the next day. For one, there she was, lying next to a very handsome man whose arms were wrapped around her body. She could get used to that. Second, she couldn't help but smile when she thought of her parents and the secret they'd shared. It was like an undercover operation her father had pulled off all those years. He was happy, she was sure. He loved and was loved, and that was important to her. For years, she was overcome with guilt that he had no life but her. Now, she was so excited to get to know the woman who couldn't keep her father away.

Eddie, we were like lovers who couldn't get enough of each other.

Graham stirred, turned to his side, and wrapped one leg around hers.

"You had another bad dream last night."

"Mmm," he muttered into her neck. "I did?"

"Yeah. For a second, I didn't know whether or not to wake you. But you seemed to quiet down after a while. After I held you."

"You see, that's all I needed," he said.

"I was thinking we could spend the day up on the mountain. Take the ski lift and go for a hike." She felt him come to life and wrapped her legs around him when he rolled over on top of her. This man was insatiable and had awakened this part of her that she never knew existed. To be touched, consumed, loved. She dreaded the day it would have to end. "I read a sign in the lobby that said there's a band playing at the lodge in the evenings. And then another—"

"Charlie."

"What?"

"I need you right now."

"Okay," she said, catching her breath from the pleasure of his touch. "But later—"

"Yes, later."

The tram to the top was filled with all sorts of people. Parents, grandparents, children. Lovers, siblings, tourists. Charlie was enamored with the panoramic view of the sky, the snow, and the towering trees, but her attention was stolen by the families next to her. The loving mothers held their children close as the cable car lifted them higher toward the clouds. Auntie Elma had taken on that role in her life. She was there for every milestone important in a girl's life. But it was a guest role, one that was filled on an as-needed basis. There was nothing organic about it. Auntie Elma was always there whenever a woman's perspective was required, but Charlie came home after school every day to an empty house.

"Alex!" Charlie's thoughts were disrupted by the mother calling attention to her son, who had decided to roll on the floor.

Graham whipped his head in their direction as if he knew the little boy before he looked away.

"For a second there, I thought you knew him."

"Who? That little boy? No, I don't," he said too quickly.

"And that man?" Charlie tried to tease. She nudged him in the direction of a man wearing a trench coat, squeezing between the poles to stand next to them.

Graham turned his head briefly. "No idea."

They trudged through the rugged mountain path, the sound of crackling branches and crunching snow in a steady rhythm masking the silence that lingered between them. This time, the clouds were in full force, the skies gray, and the fog heavy in the air. Graham seemed deep in thought, his head drooping down, his shoulders hunched as he led her through the woods.

"A penny for your thoughts?" she said in a sing-song voice, trying to lighten the somber mood.

Graham did not respond. He turned to her with a half-smile but just kept walking.

When they got to the clubhouse, they sat in front of a grand fireplace that spanned from wall to wall, two stories tall. Charlie ordered a hot chocolate, and Graham ordered a bourbon.

"Isn't it a little early for that?" she asked, catching herself again, not wanting to sound like his mother.

"Nah," he said, taking two swigs of his glass before motioning the server for another.

He must be having a bad morning. Everyone's entitled to that.

"I've been thinking," she began.

"You seem to be doing a lot of that," he answered. His tone was curt, and he wouldn't look at her.

"Seeing all the families around us today. I kinda wished I had a sibling."

Graham shrugged, staring at the flickering fire without a response.

"You're lucky you have a sister. I was thinking that I'd love to meet her someday. Maybe when we get to California, she can come get you, and I can meet her?"

Charlie observed an immediate change in demeanor. His face looked pained, a slight grimace crossing his lips before he quickly guzzled what was left of his drink. "Yeah, sure."

"Really?" She was a little disappointed at his reaction. Not necessarily because she wanted to meet his sister but because she had hinted at something in the future beyond their drive to California. "I studied piano for twelve years, and my Auntie Elma was adamant that I should learn a musical instrument. We have that in com—"

"Charlie, please, can we figure that out later?"

She had never seen him like that before. He kept flinching and looking around like the last thing he wanted was to be sitting there with her.

He tugged at the zipper of his jacket before adopting a posture so rigid Charlie could see him straining his neck.

"Sure," she said. "Are you okay?"

"Yup. I'd really like another drink, though." He waved at the server for his third glass.

Charlie watched him down that third drink and tried to find other things to talk about. Her thoughts were on Madison for some reason. The families she observed on the way up the mountain—the closeness, the protectiveness—got her thinking of siblings. Rena had three, and they were all bonded by unbreakable loyalty. But Graham's elusiveness piqued her curiosity. His family meant everything to him, so why was he being so avoidant? "Hey, can I see that picture of your family again?"

"Can we just . . ." he stammered, ". . . can we talk about something else? Or maybe not talk about anything at all?"

Something was wrong.

She noticed how much he was struggling all morning. Even in bed, his actions were urgent, as if he was trying to tell her something he just couldn't find the words for. Was he wanting to say goodbye? Did he want to cut the trip short?

"Graham, something's wrong. Tell me what's bothering you. Is it because I've been so nosy, asking about your sister? It doesn't make sense. We've been . . . well, we've opened up quite a bit, and I didn't think I was overstepping." She looked at him. "If I was, I apologize."

Graham inhaled sharply. "Charlie . . ." She braced herself for what was coming. "She's gone."

Charlie frowned. "What do you mean? When did you last talk to her? We still have a few days. You can call her when we arrive. We can meet her if she's already left."

"She's gone. She's gone," he said, banging his fist on the table. "And I don't want to talk about it. Today is her . . ." His chest heaved like he was running out of air. "Today is the first anniversary of the day we lost her. She's gone, Charlie. Madison is dead."

"What? What do you mean, Graham? Oh my god. I am so sorry, I am so sorry. Come here." She pulled him to her. "Why didn't you tell me?"

Graham leaned back and gently pushed her away. "I was supposed to be there that night. It was my fault. I canceled on her for some damn deal that needed some last-minute changes. She died because I wasn't there to protect her."

"I'm sure that isn't true."

He ran his fingers through his hair and faced away from her. "I just . . . I just need time alone. Is that okay? Would you mind taking the tram back to the hotel? I'll see you in a couple of hours."

"Of course," Charlie said, her heart heavy with sadness. "Don't worry about me."

"Thank you," he said, reaching his feet quickly and walking away from her.

He took a few steps forward before immediately turning around and approaching her again. Graham knelt and took her hands in his. "I'm not leaving you, Charlie. I just need some time to myself right now. I am *not* abandoning you. I'll see you tonight at the hotel, okay?"

She nodded, still in shock from what he had told her.

And then he walked away.

Charlie was alone on the tram ride from the mountain. Well, almost. Directly opposite her, facing out the other corner toward the mountain, was a well-dressed woman with short, gray hair. She wore a white designer ski outfit adorned with a green and red stripe running down its side. Her coat was the latest from a ski collection that Charlie was eyeing for the season. In both hands was a red velvet pouch with a jar inside it. Charlie could only see her from the side but watched silently as the elegant woman's shoulders began to shudder.

"Excuse me," Charlie called her attention. "Are you all right? Can I help you with anything?"

The lady kept her back to Charlie and shook her head.

"Here," Charlie said, walking over to her and guiding her toward the seats in the middle of the car. "Maybe it will be better if you sat for a little while."

The lady leaned on Charlie, clutching the vase and resting it on her lap. "Thank you." When she noticed Charlie admiring the vase, she added, "It was given to me by my husband during an auction at Sotheby's. A Viennese antique vase from centuries ago. You may think I'm a crazy old woman who is going up the mountain carrying a vase," she said, laughing.

"Not at all," Charlie assured her. But she was curious.

"I'm sorry you had to see me like that. It took me a full year to find the strength to scatter my husband's ashes on the mountain he loved so much. We used to have a place up by the lodge. He was a skier who had trained for the Olympics. Last year, I lost him suddenly. He was perfectly healthy. Had a cut on his foot, which never healed. And then an amputation happened, followed by an infection."

"I am so sorry to hear that."

"Oh no, don't be. We had fifty glorious years and three beautiful children. We never wasted any time making memories. Said I love you many times a day. We lived knowing life was short and never regretted a single moment. I'm just missing him today more than most days." She looked up at Charlie, who was holding onto the rail directly in front of her. "What about you? Are you on your honeymoon? I saw you with a gentleman earlier. I could tell by how he looked at you that you were a couple."

Charlie forced a smile. "Not really. I'm driving to California to see my mother. I lost my dad four months ago. I, too, am still dealing. That man is just a friend."

"What is your name?" the lady asked.

"Charlotte. Charlotte Hastings."

"Nice to meet you, Charlotte. My name is Margaret Zuckerman. Maggie for short."

Charlotte hoped she heard it right. *Zuckerman. Wilbur's farmer.* She was speechless. What a coincidence. When she couldn't get a word out, Maggie did it for her.

"I'm so sorry to hear about your father. But whatever pain you are suffering from losing him, think about how at peace he must be right now. Death is peace for those who believe, Charlotte. But instead of talking about death, let's focus on life because it is truly very short. Grab it by the horns and ride it like there's no tomorrow." She let out a giggle. "Literally and figuratively. When you have had something good, you have every right to want it again. Don't hide from life because every single moment is a part of the journey that has been planned for you."

"My father used to say that all the time. He used to say that life is never a coincidence. That the universe has a plan for each of us," Charlie added. "I feel like just meeting you here is a sign."

"Don't hide from the signs," Maggie said. "They are everywhere. I see Homer in everything and hear his voice when I'm lonely and confused. Not in a crazy way, but I watch now. I watch for little signs that show he is with me."

Charlie's heart stopped. "What did you say your husband's name was?"

"Homer." She looked at Charlie, who tried hard to mask the shock by pasting a smile on her lips. Homer was Wilbur's owner. "I know. An unsuitable name for such a glamorous man." And when she saw Charlie hang on tightly to the post for balance, she added, "I'm sorry, did I say something wrong?"

"No, no. Nothing." Charlie regained her composure. "What you said today has really made me believe. And to think that I was about to comfort you! And here you are, comforting me."

The car came to a stop, and the doors to the platform swung open.

"I sense that you need it more than I do, Charlotte. Keep the faith and be happy."

Life had always been a contradiction of sorts for Charlie. While inspired by Margaret's words and all the coincidences they carried, the sudden change in Graham's demeanor scared her. Of all people, she knew firsthand how life could take a turn. How every time she tried to walk life in a straight line, something would happen to change everything. She thought about her grandparents and how they had simply disappeared one day while they slept. Or when doctors told her that Edgar was in remission. Or even now, finding out she had a mother. What glorious news! Only to be caveated by the fact that she was mentally ill. Something for something. There was always something. A trade-off, a price to be paid.

Back at the hotel, Charlie stopped by the front desk before heading to the room. She couldn't help but place Graham in that category now. He told her he wasn't leaving, and yet she was spiraling. How stupid of her to let someone new in. How ridiculous this twelve-day fling was. What had she done wrong? Was this her fault? She should be used to it by now, people coming and going. None of them ever stayed. All because she didn't love enough, focus enough, laugh enough. Nothing she did was ever enough. She couldn't even take care of her father enough to save him.

Why was she still thinking of Graham? He was gone. He probably wouldn't even continue the drive with her. She saw how the women at the lodge were eyeing him. He could get a ride anywhere, anytime.

She climbed into bed and read the next letter.

Letter #12 2014

Hello, lovah! You've been coming quite often. Now that Charlie has a life of her own (and a boyfriend, you told me!), you've been seeing me what, once every two months? There's no longer a need for these letters, I guess. But I like writing them to you. It helps me remember our moments. We've had quite a few in the past two years. Quiet ones by the moonlight, crazy ones in our bed, sad ones when we've had to part, and tearful ones when you tell me all about Charlie living a life without me.

I threw a plate at you. I know. And a couple of glasses. I woke up that morning adamant that I was going to meet my daughter. That you couldn't leave without promising me you'd bring her here to see me. You nodded while avoiding my gaze. I knew you didn't mean it, so I had to prove my point. You stand amid these outbursts and look at me without fear or judgment. Each and every time, you would look at me with your laughing eyes, the sun, and see clear and apparent in an instant before gently taking my face in your hands and wiping away my tears. You make me understand in so many words why we have to wait for the right time. I know we have to wait. That the proper time will come. I know.

I love our little apartment. The one you rented a few miles from here. Sometimes, between visits, I look out my window and can see the speck on a little hill a few miles away. That speck is my home, my refuge. It's where we both are living other lives outside of our current lives. Does that make sense? I've been watching these movies lately, you know, the action-hero movies. I think they call it multiverses. You and I are in one multiverse. When we're together, we live in that one world where nothing can hurt us. In our world, we have a perfect daughter named Carlotta, and she loves her mom more than anything else in this world.

She couldn't get Margaret's words out of her head. Her parents had found a way to see each other despite her mother's confinement. They had done what Margaret had talked about—they had taken every minute of every moment to live. And then she wondered—what if she hadn't existed? Would he have moved and lived with her full-time instead of dividing himself in two? But then it struck her—he'd had lived two lives, two adversely different lives. He'd protected them both from each other. No one could live a life like that except Edgar.

By the time her phone rang, Charlie had dozed off. She reached for her phone in the dark, ready to give Rena a hard time for calling in the middle of the night.

"Charlie?"

"Hi," she mumbled.

"The front desk texted me that I have a new room."

"Yeah, I figured you probably want to get the heck away from me."

"Why? Why would you think that?" His voice was an octave higher, tainted with incredulity.

"Because that's what always happens."

"That is not going to happen between us, Charlie. I don't want another room. I'm standing right outside. Please let me in."

Charlie kicked the covers off her and ran to the door. Graham rushed in and took her in his arms. For a while, they stood together, her head buried in his chest, their bodies crushed together. When Charlie stepped back, she noticed how unhinged he looked. He looked like the day she found him in his car, except now he had no beard. She kept a hold of his hand and led him to the bed. Slowly, she climbed in, lifting the covers to allow him to slip in. He shed his clothes before sliding in next to her. The room was dark, their faces illuminated only by the light streaming in through the window. Charlie reached out to trace the contours of his face, her touch gentle yet unmistakably filled with longing. Graham leaned into her caress.

"I'm so sorry, Charlie. I didn't mean to be so abrupt."

"It's okay."

"No, I should have told you this from the beginning. When I lost her . . . I lost my mind. I lost the most important person in the world to me. She had so much life ahead of her, cut short by one random act, a mistake that never should have happened."

She turned her back to him, inviting him to press himself against her so close that there was nothing left between them. He lay on his side and wrapped himself around her.

"How? What—"

"An accident," he said. "She was trying to fit in and act cool at a party. She took something that was laced. It was fatal."

"I am so sorry, Graham," Charlie whispered, afraid she would break down. There's the death that makes sense, like relief or respite after a long sickness or prolonged suffering. And then there's this, the one that defies logic. The incomprehensible one. The one that uproots your faith. Causes you to lose it.

"I hid behind your grief, made it mine. Walked through your sadness with you and thought that if I absorbed yours, it would make mine go away. I now know that I have to face it separately. I called my mother and told her I was coming home."

Charlie said nothing. She knew he had more to say. Gently, she reached a hand behind her and held the back of his head.

"Do you know what?" His breath on her neck felt good. "In all this, today, in all my anguish, you were the hope, the bright light that made me see things clearly. How different life would have been if you had been there with me? For me?"

"I'm here now," she said. She wanted to promise the future but knew it was too soon. Here and now was good enough.

"Show me."

Slowly, Charlie undressed, fixing her gaze on his as she unhurriedly peeled her clothes off, reveling in the heavy air of anticipation. She kissed him lightly at first, her excitement heightening as he responded to the movement of her body on him. She teased him with her lips, trailing her kisses from his neck to his chest, lower and lower, until he began to writhe in pleasure.

"I love you," he rasped. "I love you."

She lifted her head in surprise. "You don't have to say anything."

Gently, he cradled her face in his hands and guided her upward until her mouth was aligned with his. "Just feel this," he groaned, kissing her deeply, caressing her mouth with his tongue, and pulling on her top lip with his teeth before gently flipping her on her stomach. "Do you feel it like I do, Charlie? That you and I—"

Charlie sensed his hesitation when she no longer felt his weight on her. He tipped back on his legs while using his hands to touch every part of her body. She shuddered from a longing so deep she thought she would die if he stopped.

"I feel it," she gasped. "I've been waiting for you."

As he joined her from behind, she moaned loudly, encouraging him to go deeper, to bury his sadness in hers. This act, this pain, this pleasure healed her heart, joined them together, and bonded them in their grief.

CHAPTER 22

ELKO

They squeezed into a booth together at the Blossom Lodge for breakfast, looking every bit like lovers. A kiss after every joke, a touch of the hand, her head on his shoulder. Charlie had never felt so sure about anything in her life. She knew she loved this man. As a friend, as a confidante. As a lover. But she also knew more than anyone that life's plan was inescapable. No one gets to choose what happens next.

"Where to next?" she asked him over pancakes and sausages.

This time, he skipped the acai breakfast and ordered steak and eggs. "Well, I thought we would charge up in Elko and then end up in Reno for the night."

"How many days do we have left?" Based on the hotels she needed to look up, she knew the answer, but she asked him anyway. She wanted to cling to every word, every indication that he, too, may want to extend their time together.

"As long as you want," he said, smiling.

"Let's never go home, then," she flirted back.

"I like it," he answered, leaning into her for another kiss.

It seemed like they both had nothing to say after that. Charlie returned to buttering the last piece of her pancake while Graham guzzled his coffee. There were no words of comfort at this point. Time would pass, life would go on, and soon, she would have to let him go. She looked at him sadly, her eyes narrowing and her tone flat. "But you know, we need to get started on our lives," she said before sitting up straight and laying her hand on his. "We have to do this. Find our lives, find ourselves."

"I know."

Charlie glanced around the diner and noticed a man standing behind the cake display counter, positioning his camera directly at them—well, no, directly at Graham.

Where was it that she'd seen this man before? *Oh yes, he stood close to us on the lift up the mountain.* In fact, she felt odd about him being so near, listening in on their conversation, but the tram was so cramped. It wasn't like he could have stood anywhere else. She also wondered why he wasn't dressed for the snowy conditions. He was still wearing the same dress pants, trench coat, and shiny black shoes.

She nudged him with her elbow. "Strange," she said. "I think that man is trying to take your picture."

Graham looked up, slapped a hundred-dollar bill on the table, and grabbed her arm. "Let's go."

"Did you know that guy?" Charlie asked.

As soon as she strapped herself in, Graham pulled out of the parking lot. He didn't seem frazzled, like it was no big deal to him that someone was aiming a camera at him.

"No, not at all."

"Hmmm. He was on the lift with us yesterday."

Graham reached out to take her hand. "A professional photographer, maybe. He was probably taking pictures of the

171

display case or something and just pointed the camera toward the window. I might have overreacted."

In normal circumstances, she would have prodded him. His answer wasn't good enough. But she was so ensconced in her own woes that she didn't want to waste time on reasoning. "Oh well," she said with a shrug. "Better safe than sorry."

A few miles into their drive, Charlie tapped him on the shoulder. "Hey, do you want me to read letter number thirteen out loud to you?"

Graham nodded. His grin was genuinely playful, and the corners of his eyes always sent ripples of delight. He turned the music off and listened intently, with only her mother's words and the sound of her voice filling the space between them.

Letter #13 2016

My love, how did you like the picture book I made of our daughter? I took the chance and had it mailed to you . . . I assumed there was no risk of Charlie finding it since she's moved out. I put it together as a vision board for my painting lesson. I'm supposed to be painting images that bring me joy, so I'm learning the difficult task of portraiture. At the end of all this, I want to be able to paint a picture of our daughter and how I see her. It is not just her physical beauty but conveying who she is as a person and a woman, expressed through art, I suppose.

You just left a few days ago, and already I am feeling so empty. We always joke about you staying inside me for as long as possible, but it's true! Not just in the physical sense, but what I have of you stays with me and helps me navigate an otherwise aimless life. I mean, now that I've seen how hard you work, I want to be able to contribute to our daughter's support in some shape or form. But how can I do that when all I do is spend my days in this resort, unskilled and inexperienced? How frustrating!

Mom, Dad, and Ruby came to visit me today. They asked how you were doing, and I told them you are running a thriving limo business. I plumped my feathers and stuck my chest out when I told them that Carlotta would soon graduate from Harvard student loan-free! I saw Dad nod and smile when he heard that. Ruby said I looked content. And then she corrected herself and said content was probably not the word I wanted to hear. So she said, "You're serene, calm. Peaceful."

I feel so . . . I said, "Easy. Easy to love."

My mom said, "Celia, you've always been easy to love."

I liked hearing that.

My dad said that Dr. Luna reported how your visits and our time away from the facility have done me some good. He knows there are tough times, times I still grapple with these voices in my head, but Dr. Luna says I'm living in my present most days. I thought it was a suitable time to ask him about Charlie and how to make sure she is considered one of us, a Ruiz. He told me not to worry about it. Everything due to her as a granddaughter will be set aside for her. I guess it's good that they will keep those funds separate. I'm still learning to control my spending when you're not around. I see something, and I want it, and I get it. And then, as you know, I forget why I wanted it in the first place!

I feel loved, E. Loved despite all the mess I caused in my life. Would Carlottita ever love me just like you do? If Dr. Luna gives her approval, would you be able to bring her here to meet me? Ever?

Charlie choked back her tears as she read that line. Seeing the playful banter between her parents through her mother's eyes warmed her heart. But she also knew that their end would be inevitable. Edgar, the love of Celia's life, was gone.

"You could be an audiobook reader," Graham said, bringing her hand to his lips for a kiss. She knew he was trying to lighten the mood, but her mind was elsewhere.

"Graham, what would you have done if you didn't end up in my car? Do you think you'd still be there?"

"I don't know. Probably. My head wasn't on straight. I needed more perspective."

"Some perspective these past ten days have given you." She laughed.

"Oh, but they have."

"How?"

"I learned that other people have pain that's greater than mine. In agonizing over my loss, I forgot about the twenty-five years I had as her brother. The love and laughter that some people have never known in their lives. What about you?"

"Well, I learned that my mother and father loved each other. Which is epic." She leaned over to kiss his cheek. "Considering I didn't have a mother six months ago."

Charlie's attention shifted to the view outside her window. To the right of the winding drive was a glacier-carved canyon filled with dense vegetation and topped with snow-capped mountains. They passed hiking trails, campgrounds, bright yellow wildflower fields, and cascading waterfalls.

"Look at those mountains. Are those mountains? They look more like rocks jutting out of the ground. Giant rock formations."

"The Ruby Mountains," Graham noted.

"Ooh, was that because it has rubies?"

"The early prospectors did find red stones, but they were garnets, not rubies."

Charlie squeezed his thigh. "I have a sexy walking encyclopedia."

Graham seemed lost in thought, his eyes fixed on the road in front of him. When Charlie changed the music, he was oblivious to it. It wasn't like him not to sing along, ask what song it was, or rag her about changing his playlist. She found out soon enough that he still had things to say.

"You know, you made me think of something. People knock that kind of life, where you have nothing to worry about but yourself. I know there were dangers every night, the risks that are apparent when you're living on the streets. But there is also some kind of peace that comes with that. No possessions, not having to deal with people who go behind your back or cheat you. You're fighting for a meal, not a promotion. You're keeping one eye open at night to ensure you're safe from strangers, not people you trust who suddenly turn on you."

"Oh, Graham." Charlie didn't know what to say. She'd been so focused on her grief all this time she'd never looked at life that way. "You had a lot of hurt in your past."

"So, yeah. I guess I'm trying to say that meeting you has changed my life."

Charlie wanted to tell him that he changed hers, too. But she didn't want to tie him down. They were both on the road for a reason. "Well, if I hadn't met you, I would probably have given up after two days and flown to Malibu instead."

They both laughed.

"Sounds about right," he said.

"How much longer until we stop? I'm feeling a little bit needy at the moment." Charlie held a mischievous grin while hiking her legs up on the dashboard as he reached in to touch her. She closed her eyes as the heat of his fingers burned inside.

Graham swerved into the nearest exit, a man on a mission. "We have an emergency situation here. I say we stop right now."

They found a charging station by a small enclave of shops along Main Street. Once parked, they walked through the tiny downtown area, holding hands and peeking into the shop windows. They spent an hour there before heading on to Reno.

"Oh, a bookstore! Can we stop in?" Graham pointed to a sign that said *Biblio Antique Books*. He quickened his steps and walked ahead of her, then stopped and turned around when he heard her call to him.

"G, come here, look!"

Charlie was standing by a bus shelter with advertising billboards on both sides. She stood with her hands up in the air, pointing at the billboard in front of her. An insurance company sign with hands clasped together, palms up in offering, said *You're in Good Hands*. Directly etched above that slogan was the name *Charlie* spray-painted in bold, blue letters.

Graham placed his arm around her shoulder and pulled her close. "Charlie, you're in good hands," he read out loud.

"You see! First, the bathroom, then the airplane banner, and now this! The signs are everywhere, Graham. I can feel it. My dad is telling me I'll be okay."

"God, now I'm embarrassed. He saw what my hands were doing with you," Graham joked.

Charlie swatted his arm. "Stop!"

He swept her in his arms and kissed her. She melted in his embrace, holding his face in her hands and allowing their lips to linger together.

"Go ahead," she muttered into his lips. "I'll catch up after I call Rena."

Charlie quickly dialed Rena's number as Graham walked away. She found a spot on the sidewalk right outside the bookstore. She could see Graham walking around, pulling books off a shelf. She sat on the curb, folding her knees in and hugging them close to her chest. The sun was out in full force, and the air was warming. That was another thought that randomly hit her. From Brooklyn to Nevada, it had never rained.

"Charlie, I'm in a meeting. I need to call you back," Rena

whispered into the phone. Charlie could hear the rhythmic clicking of her footsteps against the floor and then a slow fading of mumbling voices, an indication that she was moving to another location.

"How many times have you interrupted my meetings in the past?" Charlie badgered.

"Good point," Rena said, still whispering. "Okay, hold."

In two seconds, Rena was back on the line. "What's up, love? The last time I checked, you were at some ski resort."

Charlie looked around before hushing into the phone, self-consciously cupping one hand over the speaker. "I love him. I think."

"What? I can't hear you!"

"Shhh. He's at a bookstore while I'm sitting here talking to you." She stooped her head down so it was low between her knees. "I love him."

"I heard you, and I was just kidding," Rena said, laughing.

"After ten days. Isn't that crazy?"

"No, not really."

"Seriously, Rena?"

"Charlie, listen to me. You're locked up in a car all day, driving across the United States. You talk, you get to know each other, and you're both on your best behavior. Besides, if you think about it, your time together is the equivalent of . . ." Rena paused briefly. "Hmm, let's see. Twenty-five dates. How can you not fall in love?"

"I want to extend the trip, but I know I have to figure out the next steps with my mom and all."

"How much sex have you been having?" Rena said this so loudly that it made Charlie cringe, not for her but for the people within earshot of Rena. Then she laughed. That girl was truly psychic, given what had just happened at the rest stop.

"Oh my god, Carlotta!"

"So, you don't think I'm crazy? I want him to stay longer. I want to get to know him more, but . . ."

"You don't have a job. You sold your dad's home. If anyone's got time on your hands, it's you. It's not like your mom is waiting. You don't even know where she is."

"Yeah, but it's just prolonging the inevitable," Charlie argued.

"You've always been so pragmatic."

"Speaking of," Charlie glanced over to see Graham speaking to the lady at the register. "How is Auntie Elma?"

"Dunno. Tried calling her a couple of times to check in, but Justin said she's avoiding calls. Depressed, I would say."

"Oh no! I'll FaceTime her after this. She misses my dad. She was supposed to let me know if she found my mom. And I'd been so caught up in . . ." Charlie turned toward the glass window. "Okay, I can see him wrapping up at the store. I'm gonna go, but I'll call you soon."

"Okay," Rena said.

"Oh, wait. Two more things I have been wanting to tell you."

"You and your itemized thoughts. Okay, what's the first one?" Rena said, chuckling.

"He loves *Charlotte's Web* as much as me."

"Oh god. That's impossible. No one can."

"Stop it," Charlie snapped jokingly, grunting as she unfolded her knees and leaned one hand on the sidewalk to stand. "Okay, more importantly. I'm seeing signs, Rena. Like, messages from my dad that everything will be okay."

"Oh my gosh! Me too! I dreamed of him the other day. Charlie, he was smiling at me, looking all handsome and young and well. I honestly felt so relieved after that dream. I'm glad you're watching for that, my friend. Keep looking."

"Ooh, he's coming. Gotta go. Love you!"

"Love you, Carnutta."

He appeared beside her, carrying a package wrapped in brown paper.

"For you," he said, proudly presenting it with both hands.

"What? Why? You didn't have to." Charlie went for the kill, eagerly tearing off the paper. She gasped when she saw what she was holding in her hands. "Oh no. No. Graham, you can't. I can't. I shouldn't."

"Do you like it?"

Tears filled her eyes, the corners of her mouth crumpling in an effort to stop her from crying. "This was my father's dream. That one day, he could afford to get this for me. I can't, Graham. I just can't accept this." Because, in fact, she had planned to get him the first publication of their favorite story once he got sick. They were at least twenty thousand dollars each and exceedingly difficult to find.

Papa, when was the first book published?

In 1952, Carlotta. There are still some first editions out there. One day, when I can afford it, I will get it for you. You'll be able to hold in your hands the original book published by E.B. White.

Don't worry, Papa. One day I'll be rich enough, I'll buy ten of those books for you!

"No baby, don't cry," Graham said, opening his arms to her.

She slipped right in, burying her face in his shirt, embarrassed to be causing a scene in the middle of the street. "I'm sorry, I can't take this."

"This is the least I can do to show you how grateful I am that you agreed to take me along on this journey," he muttered in her hair. "You placed this blind faith in a stranger, which is a testament to how you view the world. Hopeful."

She looked up at him. "How? How did you even pay for this?"

"I memorized the one credit card I have. That's how I've been settling my share of the hotel bills," he said, smiling.

"But," she countered, pulling away from him, "if you had that all along, you could have found your way home without me."

"No, no," he said, shaking his head. "Finding my way home means more than just buying a bus ticket. I needed you to lead the way. I wasn't ready to face the music then. Now, thanks to you, I am."

"I don't know," she said, gently placing the book back in his hands. "This is a very expensive gift."

"Charlie, the lessons you've taught me are priceless. It seems like your best memories always involve this book. Now I can be one of them."

"Even without this gift, you already are," she said, standing on her toes and wrapping her arms around his neck. She wanted to insist, but she knew he had a point. She would treasure this book and remember the lessons of love, loss, and the cycle of life that she learned with him on this journey. And so, filled with gratitude, her heart soaring and falling apart at the same time, she kissed him.

CHAPTER 23

RENO

They arrived in Reno by nightfall, greeted by the city's skyline and the Reno Arch, welcoming visitors with flashing silver and blue lights.

"Why is it called the Biggest Little City in the World?" Charlie asked, genuinely curious.

"It supposedly has all the amenities of a big city because of its status as the prime gaming and gambling center."

"Well," Charlie teased, swiping her phone as she always did when finding a place to stay. It looks like they have room . . ." she raised her phone in his direction and flashed it in front of him. "Here."

"And charging stations?" Graham asked, looking pleased.

"Yasss."

They chose to stay at the biggest casino. Charlie had forgotten what it was like to walk into a place so full of energy. For many, this was a place that alleviated the doldrums of everyday life. Slot machines filled every open space, card tables, craps tables, flanked on every side by restaurants, bars, and a huge theater off in the corner, cordoned off by red velvet ropes. The neon lights on every machine flashed and clashed with the blood-red carpet on the floor. There were people from all walks of life, all ages, all demographics. Men and women in walkers and wheelchairs, young people, middle-aged people, laying down chips, dropping in tokens to the sounds of clinking and clanging, cha-chinging and yelling and whooping.

At some point, she had let go of Graham's hand to stake out the slot machines. She chose one called Dancing Drums, dropped in a token, and clapped with glee when ten tokens came spitting out of the machine. She dropped another one in, then another, and another. The fourth token caused an alarm, a shrill, piercing sound that cut her eardrums like a blade. And then, fifty more tokens fell on the floor.

"There you are," Graham greeted. "I turned to order a drink, and you were gone."

"Look! I won!" Charlie yelled above the noise, shoving the tokens into her pockets. "I've never won anything before."

"Lucky girl!" he remarked before wrapping his arms around her.

"Let's play something else," she said. "I'm feeling lucky."

"How about blackjack? Do you know how to play?"

"No, do you?" Cards were just not a thing in her life. Board games and backgammon maybe, but never a game of cards. Within their Sunset Park community, they'd heard stories of families torn apart by a gambling addiction. Edgar always instilled in her the ethics of working hard and deserving every penny you earned.

Gambling is an industry that feasts on the poor and vulnerable. Poor men should not be risking what is well and hard-earned.

"Okay, why don't you wait for me over there?" Graham pointed to the nearest card table. "I'll go buy more chips and exchange your tokens for you. There's a line, so it will take me a few minutes."

Charlie kissed him on the cheek. "I'll wait right there."

When she sat at the table, it was just her, a female dealer, and a man at the end of the table. She watched the man play his hand, but the dealer's hand was always better. Minutes later, she was joined by two other men around her age, who sat on either side of her.

"Hi," said the man to her right.

"Hey."

"I saw you win some at the slots a few minutes ago," he said. "I'm Jake."

"Beginner's luck, I guess," Charlie answered. She was so used to small talk that she excelled at it for her job. You can't be in charge of generating revenue and bringing in millions in sales if you don't master the Art of Small Talk.

"Well, look what I'm up against," the man said, leaning close enough so she could feel his lips on her ear.

Charlie moved slightly, intent on moving to the other side of the table, except it was now filled with players.

"Oh, I'm not playing. I'm just observing, waiting for—"

"Ah, then you will be my lucky charm," the man said. "The prettiest girl in this joint."

Just then, she saw Graham's eyes on her as he squeezed between two players directly opposite her. Charlie thought she should move to his side, but everyone sat shoulder to shoulder, some standing without seats.

Graham placed a few chips on the table. The dealer shuffled the cards and gave them out. He tapped the back of the first card, which Charlie surmised meant he wanted another card. Once the dealer gave Graham two more cards, they all turned their cards up. Graham nodded, his gaze fixed on Charlie. The dealer slid a few chips over in his direction.

"I feel like a winner tonight, just sitting next to someone as beautiful as you," the man leaned over to Charlie. "Are you here alone?"

"She's not." Graham's voice boomed over their heads.

Charlie smiled before jumping off her seat. "Hi, baby."

"Hi," he said, planting a kiss right smack on her lips. "I'm ready for my real win of the night."

The man stared at Graham and eyed him up and down. And then out of the blue, "Dude, are you—"

"No, I'm not!" Graham growled, pulling Charlie away from the table.

Charlie couldn't keep a straight face. She burst out laughing as soon as they walked away.

She hooked her arm in his as they made their way toward the elevator.

"I've had it with these crowds," Graham said. "Let's go back to the room."

"Just so you know," Charlie teased once they were alone on the way to the twenty-third floor. "I don't do the damsel in distress thing. I can save myself."

"It wasn't you who couldn't save yourself," he muttered into her neck. "You looked so sexy just sitting in front of me like that, I couldn't even focus."

They couldn't reach the room fast enough, shutting the door behind them so Graham could take her against the wall. After that, they decided to stay in and order room service. They lay in bed, holding hands, aware they only had a few days left together.

"I guess it's going to be a new thing for us. Navigating the outside world around us. The world didn't stop revolving while we were driving in my car."

"I know." Graham turned to her, propping his head up on his elbows. "I guess I didn't want to think about it."

"We'll have to, eventually."

"We were meant to meet. That's all I know. It won't be the end for us, Charlie. I won't let it be."

It was a sleepless night. Charlie could sense him shifting endlessly through the night while she lay awake, trying to calm her thoughts. She didn't know how to hold on to him, but she also didn't know how to let him go. They decided to leave early, although Graham had requested enough time to go for a run. Charlie understood his need for some space. Both of them were feeling displaced. In two days, they would be in Malibu, which meant that in two days, there would be a goodbye of some sort. She couldn't bear to think of it.

When he went for a run, she cuddled up on the couch with a blanket while sipping a cup of coffee. She needed the time alone to catch up on her letters. There were two more, and the time-line suggested that Edgar was already sick by then. Sure enough, Celia sensed that something was wrong with him. In the latest one, she mentioned her concern, but it didn't look like Edgar had told her anything.

Letter #14 2018

It all started when you entered our room. The way you looked so joyful, so at peace with what we had and who we were to each other. You held a subdued smile, but your eyes told me everything. When you walked toward me and took my face in your hands, you told me that that moment was essential and gave you the strength to take on whatever life would give you next. I asked you what you thought it would be, and you said, well, it doesn't matter because I've had eight years to tell you how much I love you. And then you said, I want you to save your heart for Charlie.

I tried to decipher what your eyes were saying to me, but you hid them in the depths of the blue ocean and its dark caverns. All I could see was the beauty of your presence. Nothing alarmed me or called my attention. All I saw was love.

It was really only when you turned your back to me, and those eyes could no longer enchant me or convince me of your love that I saw it. Your body was yelling it to me, the blades of your shoulders cutting through your shirt and the waist of your jeans falling down your hips. And yet I cast my thoughts away because you were here now, and because time was all I had to hold on to, I did not waste it in worry. You stayed longer and held me for three more days.

You left me on a rainy day this time, the clouds dark and ominous, the horizon suddenly out of sight. I watched you fade into the distance until the rain obscured my vision of you. I don't know if you heard me call out, but I wanted to ask you to prolong your stay to delay your departure. I know you have something more to say.

I'm writing because there is something your heart wants to tell me. I asked you many times while we were together, and when I saw the look in your eyes—they were sad. I asked you again when your touch burned like fire on my skin, the intensity of your need scorching both ecstasy and pain inside me. Still, you said nothing. I asked you again when I caught you looking at me this morning as I slept. You had so much love and tenderness, and I saw tears fill your eyes when your fingers traced a line down the bridge of my nose.

"Do you know how much I love you?" you asked me.

"Tell me," I said.

"So much that if you were the last thing I saw before I died, I would be at peace."

I can't help but think that's a premonition, E. Why would you say that? No matter how much it filled me, how much laughter filled the room during this time together, our record-breaking sex—ten times! For forty-eight and fifty-three, wow!

I sense a foreboding. A great revelation of some sort. Something you are keeping from me until the time is right. You've lost weight, your clothes are hanging off you, your ribs are visible, and your face looks hollow and drawn. But you told me it's because you'd been working out. I believe you because you are my truth. If not you, then what good is a world full of lies?

But I won't let that spiral me back into my old self. Because what you have given me today is hope. Hope that our love is just the beginning. That finding me twenty years later is actually a gift that not many people will ever get to experience.

God, I love you, Eddie. You are the love of my life. My brain and mind may be messed up pools of crap, but my heart. It beats only for you.

I'm sorry I didn't show you the painting of Charlotta I've been working on. I wanted it to be a surprise, so the next time you come, I'll unveil it for you. We'll have an official unveiling and unwrapping event—you, me, and the painting!

Charlie was distraught, and in her despair, she remembered calling Auntie Elma. She pulled her phone out of her purse and dialed. Auntie Elma answered on the third ring, holding the phone in her hand as she padded her way out of the bedroom. Charlie was surprised to see Auntie Elma still in pajamas, given Brooklyn was three hours ahead.

"Carlotta, is everything all right?" Auntie Elma looked lopsided, the camera placed sideways on her office desk. She smoothed her hair down with her hands and then tied it in a ponytail.

"Yes, I thought I'd check to see how you're doing, Auntie Elma. Rena said she'd been trying to call you."

"Sorry, sorry. I haven't been feeling well. Are you okay? Where are you calling from?"

"Reno."

"How is your drive?"

Charlie realized Rena never told her aunt that she wasn't driving alone. "It's okay," she lied. "Were we able to get an address for my mother? I know you were looking into it."

"Getting close, hija. I was able to contact her sister, who was in Europe last week. She should be calling me back. I'll call you as soon as I have the location."

"Okay, thank you."

Auntie Elma was silent.

"Auntie Elma?"

"Yes, hija. Sorry, I am not myself." Her head hung low like a lifeless rag doll.

"I'm learning so much about my mother. Thank you for those letters. I know why she left now. I don't know why Papa didn't tell me the truth."

"He was trying to protect you, Charlie. Your mom comes from a very wealthy and powerful family. He was afraid that if you maintained contact with them, one day, they would take you away from him. You were all he had."

"Is that how you're feeling now, Auntie Elma? Are you sad because you think you've lost me?"

"A little," she sniffed. "A lot, actually." She let out an embarrassed cackle, shrill and broken, in true Auntie Elma style.

"You were like a mother to me. That is never going to change. You brought me up all those years, and I am so grateful to have you in my life. My dad would never have survived having a daughter like me if you weren't there, always guiding him and me. I love you."

"Oh, Carlotta, I needed to hear that. I've been feeling so alone. Funny, I know, because Uncle Joe and Justin are here with me. But you are my life, too. And your dad was my best friend."

"You knew, didn't you?" Charlie knew the answer but wanted to hear it from her aunt. "You knew he was traveling there to see her."

"Yes."

"And that's why you didn't—"

"Yes. I loved him. But you have to understand. He loved only her. And your uncle Joe . . ." Auntie Elma held nothing back now, her face crumpling with pain. "As an immigrant to this country, I wasn't rich. Your mother came from a well-established family. And Uncle Joe showed me a life I never knew. I couldn't do that to him or betray the man who gave me a good life."

Charlie stayed silent, giving Auntie Elma a moment to live in her tears. She thought allowing her to speak the words she hadn't uttered to anyone was important. Saying those words could cleanse them both of their secrets.

"He loved you, too," Charlie assured her. "Thank you for loving me, Auntie Elma. I love you very much. I am okay, don't worry about me. I'll call you as soon as I see my mother and as soon as I know what I'm going to do."

Auntie Elma was smiling now, using her hankie to wipe her eyes. "Maybe I can come and visit you and your mom. It's been thirty years since I last saw her."

"Of course. I'm sure she would love that."

Charlie was pleased to see the change in Auntie Elma's demeanor. She heard the swipe of the card on the door and knew she had to go. "I have to head out now, Auntie. I love you. Text me when you get my mom's location."

Charlie pressed END on her phone and lovingly offered her hand to the man watching her from the door.

CHAPTER 24

SAN JOSE

"Okay. So, I don't want to tell you this, but I know I have to."

Charlie turned to him before buckling her seatbelt. "What's wrong?"

"No, nothing. We have a choice, and I'm going to ask you to make it. It's an eight-hour drive to Malibu. We can make it by this evening."

"No," she said. "I don't want to get there yet. Where can we stop for one more night?"

"Come here," he said, leaning over to kiss her. "I like that answer. We can stop in San Jose. Thank you."

The four-hour drive to San Jose was more subdued than the others. There was little conversation, more music, more silence. Graham focused on the road, reaching over occasionally to touch her. Charlie sat in silence, clutching the E.B. White book he had bought for her. Occasionally, she would leaf through it, trying to find signs or words to comfort her and tell her what she needed to do. What she got from those pages was the message of sacrifice—for friendship, for family, for love. She had to find her mother—that she knew more than anything else.

They settled in a luxury hotel on Santana Row. This time, Graham checked them in while she waited in the lobby. The mood between them was somber. Their laughter was controlled, their conversations halted, their touches urgent. She had so much to say to him and felt like he had so much to say to her, too. Every so often, she would catch him looking at her, his eyes telling of yearning or sadness. Other times, he would look at her and just nod.

How can you love someone after twelve days? She wasn't in some rom-com where meet-cutes and marriage could take place in two hours. But what she felt for this man, she was sure she would never find it again.

"It's only five. We still have some time to hang out before dinner. Did you want to check out San Jose and walk around a little bit?" Graham asked as he handed her one of the key cards.

"Not really, do you?"

"Not really." Graham shrugged, offering her his hand. "There's a rooftop restaurant. Wanna go there and order appetizers and just sit and talk?"

"That sounds perfect," Charlie answered.

They found a secluded corner to sit in. The Spanish-style colonial structure was enclosed by a solid stone balustrade, which spanned the building and presented a clear view of the Santa Cruz mountains. They faced each other on the loveseat in front of a massive fireplace. Graham reached out to tuck a strand of hair behind her ear.

A female server set appetizer plates in front of them. A sommelier spoke briefly about the California wine they had ordered and poured a small portion for Graham, who swished his glass around, took a sip, and gave him a thumbs up.

When they left, Graham laid his hand on her thigh. "So, tomorrow, we get to where we're going."

"I know," Charlie responded. "I have so much to say and nothing to say at the same time."

"Me too."

"Before I forget," she began, trying to change the subject once again, "number fourteen was so sad. I didn't have a chance to tell you last night." She stopped short and smiled at him. "But Celia definitely knew something was wrong with Edgar. She wrote to him about how he looked sad, like he had something to say."

"Kinda like how I feel right now."

Charlie leaned in for a kiss. "She noticed he had lost some weight and looked tired. She knew something was up, but he didn't tell her."

"When was that?"

"Four years ago," Charlie said sadly.

He took a sip of his wine. "Oh no. Did you read the last letter?"

"Not yet. I have to finish it tonight, of course. I wonder if he came back?" She leaned her head on his shoulder as he wrapped one arm around her. "One thing I know is that I'm no longer angry. He tried to protect me by giving me an uncomplicated life. I'd seen so many broken homes caused by unstable parents." She paused to look at Graham. "I mean, obviously, they probably weren't diagnosed. But these kids were shifting homes all the time, and they witnessed loud fights that left them cowering in fear. Impulsive spending was another thing. There was a girl in my class who had such money problems that tuition was always late, and she was disallowed from taking our quarterly exams without a promissory note. I remember the pain on her face as she walked down the aisle, hiding the crumpled-up note in her hand. So, in a way, I had none of that. I had my father who gave me stability despite everything he was going through."

"He did give you that," Graham concurred.

She caught her own words, a lump forming in her chest and smothering her. "We all know how it ends."

"You know what I've learned from all this, Charlie? It's all about the here and now that matters. So let's pretend there is no end," he said, reaching out with the tip of his fingers to brush her lips. "Let's finish our dinner and go read that letter. I think it may help us have some closure to this journey." Graham poured her some wine and raised his glass. "And it's only fitting that we toast to the two people who brought us together. To Celia and Edgar. True love that shines forever." He paused for a bit and raised his glass a second time. "True love that shines through you, Charlie. You and the generation after you. There is no end for Celia or Edgar or Maddy. They will always live through us. And that is why I know there is no end for us."

"Oh, Graham," she said, speechless.

Just then, her phone dinged with a message.

AUNTIE ELMA: Lifesong Malibu 42 San Lorenzo Drive, Malibu

———

Letter #15 2020

You haven't come. I'm sure it's because your business has reached a frenetic pace. You told me you didn't have enough drivers and that you were taking on the influx of overnight trips yourself. I'm so happy for your success, and I know you're doing this all for us. But I miss you. It's been almost six months since I've seen, felt, touched, and loved you. Dr. Luna does not want me to call and tells me you'll be back at the right time.

When will that be? Everything revolves around time, the right time, the wrong time. I am but a slave to it, entrapped by it, always waiting, wondering. When will I be better? Will I ever be better? When will you call? When? When, E? When will all this be?

I've placed all my energy into my art. Although I don't think it's saving me. I'm on a suicide watch. Feelings of hopelessness and despair overcame the optimism I'd held for all these months. What does that mean anyway? Just an open door, a nurse assigned to me, and a million more pills to alleviate my mood swings. Dr. Luna tells me I've been acting out in sequence—first, depression and withdrawal (I did not leave my room for two weeks), followed by impulsiveness and recklessness (I've trashed a few things in my apartment and relapsed a few times. With the right amount of money, these staffers can get you the finest goodies money can buy). All textbook crazy people stuff. She said it's hard enough to experience heartache. It is doubly difficult when a manic person gets her heart broken.

One thing that will never change is that I love you, Eddie. I loved you from the day I met you and fell in love with you all over again on the day we were married. I loved you when I lost myself and loved you despite never finding myself. I will always love you. You are the only thing that makes sense in my life.

Enough of that. I am not writing to blame you or remand you for your absence. I am writing to tell you that today, in one of my lucid moments, all I have in my heart for you is peace. I am at peace with what we had, what you were to me, and the brief years we spent together. But most importantly, I am writing to let you know that I finished the painting! It is here for you, for her. Will you promise to give it to her at the right time? When you feel it is, you don't have to see me if you don't want to. You can have it picked up, and I will know that it will be on its way to her. Like Wilbur, my fate has been sealed. She prolongs that fate and defies that inevitable end for me. My Charlotte. The only good thing I can offer the world.

Charlie had made her decision. "I have to go to her. Tell her that Edgar is gone. She's been waiting for him all this time."

Graham held her tightly, allowing her tears to strengthen her resolve. She would leave him tomorrow. That had been decided.

She saw resignation in his eyes. She knew he wasn't going to talk her out of it.

This night was going to be their last. In the quiet embrace of their farewell, they kept their faces close together, their eyes conveying such conflicting emotions, the weight of their impending separation lingering heavily in the air. They clung to each other, their bodies pressed together, expressing their unspoken words through how their mouths danced together, never separating despite pulling off their clothes in a frenzy. Gently, he lifted her and carried her to the bed, laying her tenderly on the sheets, her chest rising and falling as she watched him shed his clothing. She tried to memorize everything about him—the way he looked, the way he smiled, his shoulders, his arms, every mark on his face, and his chest. And when he placed his body on hers, she arched her back to meet him, wrapped her legs around him so there was no doubt in his mind that she was his.

"Remember me always, Charlie," he gasped right before they lost themselves in each other.

CHAPTER 25

MALIBU

They left San Jose feeling at peace with their plans. During the four-hour drive to Malibu, the mood was light. They both reminisced about the people they lost—Edgar and Madison—and their impact on those around them. Charlie asked Graham to tell her all about Madison. He talked for hours about her love of music, her favorite movie (*August Rush*), and the concerts she played at the symphony. She loved how he was so proud of her. It strengthened her resolve to avoid saying anything that would hold him back. He needed to go home and get his life back on track.

Driving along the Pacific Coast Highway was an experience on its own. Charlie was enamored by the stunning vista that transitioned from mountain ranges, farmlands, vineyards, rugged coastlines, and pounding surf. Malibu was beautiful, a far cry from Brooklyn's frost and cloudy, gray skies.

As they approached the facility, Charlie was surprised at how different it looked. It was like a country club, with sprawling greenery and manicured lawns. The property sat on a cliff overlooking golden sand and turquoise blue waters. Several little bungalows, within walking distance of each other, surrounded the main building.

She could see how restorative a place like that could be—the beauty of nature providing the backdrop and the inspiration to stay alive, get well, and keep living. Her practical side couldn't help but think about how costly it must be to live there. She had never met her grandparents on her mother's side, but she loved them for taking this much care of their daughter. She held no resentment toward her father for keeping her away from them. He was protecting her from the pain of losing her mother. He was protecting her from his pain.

Graham exhaled loudly when he pulled into the massive parking lot.

Charlie grabbed his hand and squeezed it tight.

"Can we just sit here for a bit?" he asked.

Charlie nodded. "What time is your bus?"

"I need to Uber there in thirty minutes."

"That's cutting it close. Are you sure you don't just want to take my car? I can rent a car while I'm here. Gives me an excuse to hunt you down!" She laughed.

"Oh, by the way, I will send you a check as soon as I get to Portland."

"Okay," she agreed. "Just send it to Rena in Brooklyn since I don't know where I'll be."

Graham turned his attention to the back seat. "I should get my things together," he said, unlocking the door and handing her the keys to the car.

Charlie remained inside until she could no longer deny that he was leaving. She ran out of the car and into his arms, burrowing her head onto his chest to hide the fact that she was crying.

"Can we run?" he muttered into her hair, kissing the top of her head and folding his arms around her neck. "We can run. Should we run?"

"Let's run." They both knew that was impossible. She stepped back and looked into his eyes. "I'm so afraid, G. This has been my world. It has closed us up, kept us protected from everything else."

"And now?" he asked.

Charlie thought she saw a glint of hope in his eyes. "Now we have to go out into the big bad world," she said sadly.

"Without each other?" he asked.

"For now, yes." Even if she was decided, she worried about him, too. "What are you going to do?" For days, she'd been too afraid to ask. She didn't know enough about the mess he'd left behind. How long would it take to fix? How much time would he need? What would life without his sister be like?

"Head home, figure things out," he answered. "And you?"

"Meet my mom, figure things out."

They laughed quietly and acknowledged silently that this time apart was needed.

Charlie lifted herself to sit on the car's hood. Graham stood between her legs, facing her, leaning his forehead on hers.

"You lifted me when I was at my lowest. You are my saving grace."

"And you are mine," Charlie said. "I'm so lucky you trespassed in my car."

"By trusting me and taking me along on this journey, you have made me believe in people again. I know," he said before taking a beat. "I know we have things to do. I left my mom to grieve on her own. I have to go to her now so we can heal together. The trust I lost in people because of what happened to Madison, I have regained because of you."

"And I have a mom I've never met," she added. "I need to get to know her. Tell her all about my dad."

He moved away and went to grab his things from the back seat. Once again, Charlie felt the physical pain of loss: sharp pangs inside her chest, a boulder stuck in her throat. Her heart was breaking, and she knew it. She tried her best to steel herself against the car. As he slipped his arms into his backpack, she embraced him for one last time.

"You have been the best of friends to me. How will I ever give that up? Promise me we will find a way back to each other."

"Do you really want to do that?" Graham asked. "Leave things to destiny? Can't we agree on a time and place, something to look forward to, keep us going?"

"That's how we met, wasn't it? Fate brought us together. Fate will also keep us apart until the time is right. And I'm watching the signs now, Graham. I know when we are both ready, you will find me, and I will find you."

"Yes, after we figure ourselves out," Graham repeated after her. They had been stalling for some time, trying to assure themselves that this was not the end.

He cupped her face and kissed her for the last time.

"Goodbye, Graham," she whispered.

"Goodbye, Charlie. I love you."

And as he walked away, she thought of her father, the years she had taken for granted, of Celia and Edgar and their undying love, Auntie Elma's unrequited love, Lorenzo and his new chance. Of the love she had for the man who was leaving.

"Graham, wait!" she yelled at the top of her lungs.

He turned and looked over his shoulder.

She saw that he, too, was crying. "I love you! I love you, Graham. There is no end. There is no end, Graham. Come and find me. I will wait for you."

And as if to match the flow of her tears, the rain began to fall.

* * *

Charlie remained in the car for a while after Graham left, waiting for the rain to subside. She looked over at the driver's seat, longing for him to come back. She imagined him sliding in next to her and taking her away. She wished they could start all over again.

She held the E.B. White book he had given her and leafed through the pages, feeling his touch, hearing his words. She hoped to gain some insight into why this had to happen. More than ever, she believed in the power of words. Charlotte, the spider, saved Wilbur by weaving praises that showed how special he was. In a way, that's what her mother's words did for her. They changed her and gave her the impetus to live her life.

Even as the rain calmed, Charlie lingered. She wanted to remember the moment, knowing that the next time she would enter this car, her life would be different. Graham would be in the past, and she would be moving toward her future.

When the sun re-emerged, she decided it was time to go in.

She grabbed her purse and entered through the main entrance, not really knowing where to start. The reception area was as beautiful inside as it looked from the outside. A giant koi pond greeted the guests, who had to walk through an indoor garden filled with lily trees and giant terracotta planters. The reception area was hidden behind a marble wall, littered with white wicker chairs and colorful throw pillows. When Charlie approached the desk, no one was there. She noticed a few binders, one of them labeled *Sign-in Sheet*. She opened the book and filled it out with her name, whom she was visiting, the time, and her signature. After leaving the book splayed open, she went ahead and sat down on one of the chairs facing the desk. Above her, the light from the glass dome was dimming, reminding her that evening was coming soon.

Charlie observed the activity around her. The lunchroom must have been somewhere close, the sound of silverware and dishes and light, airy music wafting in the air. There were nurses in white uniforms, doctors in scrubs, stethoscopes hanging around their necks. There were two women in wheelchairs and a young couple with a child whose father was trying to convince her to say goodbye.

Lanie, say goodbye to Mom.

But I don't want to go yet.

That's okay, honey. I'll see you next weekend.

With a mother living in this facility, that could have been her life. Living for the weekend and experiencing countless goodbyes.

And then a realization . . .

Oh gosh. Charlie had been so focused on this day that she'd never thought to plan beyond it. She didn't even have a hotel. She pulled out her phone and searched for nearby places to spend the night. There wasn't an overwhelming choice of hotels in the area, but she was determined to find one. She was so absorbed in this task that she didn't hear anyone calling out her name.

A pair of white crocs filled with Disney character pins suddenly appeared in front of her. Charlie lifted her head to find a nurse trying to get her attention.

"Miss Ruiz?"

"Hastings," Charlie corrected.

"I see that you signed in to see Celia Ruiz."

"Yes, that's right." Charlie threw the phone in her bag and jumped to her feet. "When can I see my mother?"

"Your mother?"

"Yes. She lives here."

The nurse shook her head. "I'm sorry, Miss Hastings, your mother—" She paused to look at Charlie, her eyes softening as if she could now see the resemblance. "She's no longer here."

Charlie felt the wind get knocked out of her. Her mouth hung open, and her knees weakened. She blinked once, twice before hugging herself with her arms to keep from shaking. Her vision blurred, and her heart raced. "What do you mean? That's impossible."

"She checked out three months ago. She still comes to attend weekly therapy sessions, but now she lives somewhere else."

Charlie could hardly keep focus. She fought hard to keep the tears from coming, pushed her shoulders back, and tried to appear calm. They were tears of relief. Her mother was still in this world. Albeit somewhere else. "Do you know where?"

"I'm sorry. I'm not at liberty to divulge such information."

"But . . . but . . ." Charlie's voice trembled. "I'm her daughter. I came all the way from Brooklyn to see her. To see my mother." She grabbed the top of the chair for balance, besieged by dizziness and nauseated by the fact that she would never have a mother after all.

The nurse reached out to touch her arm. "I'm sorry, honey. You can stay here to collect yourself for as long as you want. I'd be happy to get you a coffee or something. Have you had dinner? We serve early here, and I can get you a pass to the dining room."

"No, thank you."

Charlie ran out of the lobby and into the parking lot. She ran from one end of the lot to the other, not knowing where to go or what to do. A beeping sound on her phone startled her. An old voicemail, dated seven months ago, lit up the icon on her screen. Charlie placed her finger on the message and listened.

Hey Carlotta. It's Papa. You're probably already delivering that grueling presentation you've been working night and day on. I want to let you know how proud I am of you. You will ace this, I know you will. You will do so because no hard work goes unnoticed. Nothing is too difficult if you set your mind to it. Everything always works out for the best. See you this weekend.

Charlie felt the world spin around her, the ground at her feet rising and falling like waves in the ocean. Her stomach churned, and her insides rose to her throat. She dashed into a row of bushes on the curb and vomited. And then she sat on the sidewalk, buried her face in her hands, and sobbed. Despondent and defeated, she cried out to her father and asked him why she had to go through this journey that made her more alone than ever. In the end, at the end of all this, she had no one.

Graham was gone, her father was gone, and now her mother was, too.

She kept her head down, hunched between her knees, oblivious of the cars that slid in and out of the parking lot. The sound of shoes pounding on the pavement caught her attention. It made her look up. A woman dressed in a suit was running back and forth, whipping her head from side to side as if trying to find someone. Charlie watched her weave in and out of the cars, shining the light of her phone as she made her way through the narrow spaces. She stopped when she looked across the way and caught Charlie's eye.

"Miss Hastings?" she asked as she approached.

"Yes," Charlie answered, swiping her hands over her face and taking a deep breath.

"I'm Gigi Lacroix. I know your mother," she said, lowering herself down on the sidewalk next to Charlie. She wrapped her arms around her skirt and tucked them under her long, slim legs. "She's my patient."

Charlie was at a loss for words. The two women sat silently side by side while the sun set and the moon came out of hiding.

"I recognized you in the lobby from her pictures of you. She has so many of them, and it always felt like she has you right there with her."

Still no words, but a slight nod and a forced smile.

"Is Ed . . ." Gigi cleared her throat. "Your father. Is he here?"

"Gone." Charlie looked away, her tone flat. "Gone."

"Oh," Gigi gasped, visibly taken aback. "I am so sorry."

A silent breeze passed through them. Charlie wrapped her arms across her chest and stared out in front of her. "Thank you."

When Gigi turned to her, Charlie could see the heartfelt despair in her eyes. It was as if she knew the impact it would have on Celia. "Your mother is the most resilient woman I know. But it was your father who gave her that perseverance. She blossomed when he came back into her life. And she wanted to get better so that she could meet you someday."

"Is she better? Did she get cured?"

"There is no cure for what she has. It's a lifelong illness, but it can be managed. She still has episodes, but she's no longer a danger to herself, which is why she was able to move out. With medications, her moods are controlled. They ensure that the highs and lows are tempered."

Charlie looked directly at Gigi and nodded.

"If I may ask . . . your dad. How did he pass?"

"Prostate cancer, which kept him in and out of hospitals. He was in remission shortly before he died. They say the chemo weakened his immune system, which led him to succumb to a virus last January." Charlie still felt the pang in her heart whenever she spoke about him. It dawned on her that the pain wasn't as bad when Graham was around. And now it was back in full force.

"He just stopped coming. To this day, she's been waiting."

"He shared her letters with me," Charlie said. "Her parents, her family . . . how are they?"

"Your grandparents love her very much. They have been with her all these years. They have spared no expense to get her the best care. But, most importantly, her mother has been around for everything. You have an aunt, Ruby, who has three beautiful children. All girls. She visits at least once a month and brings your mom her art supplies."

For the first time that evening, Charlie smiled. She felt comforted knowing that her mother was loved.

"Listen," Gigi said, looking around as if afraid someone was listening to them. "I could be fired for doing this, but I can take you to her."

This time, Charlie grabbed her hands, brought them to her face, and kissed them. "I would be so grateful if you could please take me to her. I would give anything to see her." *Even if it meant giving up the only chance I had for love.*

Gigi sighed loudly, puckering her lips as she exhaled. "We can use my car. Follow me."

Charlie marveled at the beauty of the Santa Monica mountains, dark and shadowy against the purple-lit sky. They drove through the winding roads, past cliffs and windward dunes, only a few miles from the facility.

"Your mother is so proud of you, Charlotte. She relayed every single thing your father would tell her. Everything seemed to come together for them in these past few years."

"If she will never be cured, why was she discharged and allowed to live on her own, especially after my father never returned?"

"That was precisely why she was released," Gigi answered, a veil of sadness crossing her face. The corners of her mouth stooped as she lowered her head. "Your mother's family has the means to care for her independently with the support of the facility. She has a nurse that watches her full-time, a cook, and a chauffeur. The fact that Celia has learned to live within her constraints helped with the decision to give her some space and allow her to live her life in the environment in which she thrived. That place she shared with your father."

"Where's her new place?"

"Oh, you didn't know?" Gigi turned into a side road that opened up into an apartment complex. She circled around a white stone building and found a parking spot right in front of the main door. "This was your father's place. He stayed here whenever he came to visit. Your mother was so happy when he bought it for them. She moved in as soon as she was discharged. He saved her, Charlotte. Your mother's love for him gave her the strength to fight those demons."

"Just like Charlotte and Wilbur."

"Yes," Gigi said, reaching for her hand. "Just like that."

Charlie took a deep breath and squeezed Gigi's hand. "This is it, I guess. This is the place?"

"I'm Celia's emergency contact," she said. "So I have the keys. I don't think we should ring the doorbell and surprise her that way. I'll let you in, and then I'll leave you with her. Would you be able to Uber back to your car?"

"Yes, of course. And thank you."

Gigi fished a pen out of her handbag and scribbled on a card. "Here's the emergency number for the facility in case she reacts unexpectedly and you need someone to come and help. I want you to know I'm struggling with this decision—with taking you here without a warning call to Celia. But I also know that Celia's reactions can be unpredictable. She is your mother, and you've come a long way. She needs that, too. She needs her peace. On the back is my number in case you need me tonight."

Music wafted through the hallway as Charlie stepped out of the elevator. From afar, Charlie saw that the door to her mother's apartment door was slightly ajar. She stopped in her tracks when she heard the song. It was her father's favorite one, a Frank Sinatra classic. The one they danced to when she was a little girl, stepping on his feet as he whisked her around on the kitchen floor.

He did do things his way. Loved two women all his life and lived it to protect them. Her grief was intolerable, and she yearned for his presence, his guidance, his comfort. She missed him so much that she didn't think she had the strength to keep going, to enter her mother's life and rip it apart.

She stood in the hall for a few minutes, losing herself willingly in the words of his song and in the happy memories he gave her. Her thoughts reverted to all the signs she'd encountered on her way to find her mother. And she decided that this was another one. He was there with her. He was there to help her break the news to her mother. She wiped the tears on her sleeve and kept walking.

Nothing is too difficult if you set your mind to it.

Charlie nudged the door open quietly, careful not to scare or surprise her mother. What she saw in front of her moved her to tears. Her mother's back was to the door, wisps of thick dark hair tumbling down her shoulders, while she sat in front of an easel with a paintbrush in her hand. On the wall above the fireplace was the portrait her mother had painted of her. And all over the apartment were pictures of Celia, Edgar, and Charlie, too. The missing pictures were sprinkled in every corner and illuminated by the full moon gazing from outside the window. It was a life she had missed, a family she could have had but had always been a part of.

She noticed that the ones of Celia and Edgar were in an enclosed space, one with four walls and two large windows. She realized that this place, the confines of this apartment, was the only world they knew. They were happy here. All they needed was each other.

"Lilia, is that you? I left the door open, knowing you'd have a lot of bags to take in. My mom shouldn't have sent you here tonight. It could have waited till—"

Celia turned around, her eyes widening in surprise, her jaw open, and her head tilted back in shock. The only sound between them was the crashing of paintbrushes on the floor.

Charlie took one step forward, unsure of what to do.

"M—" she stopped cold, as if she swallowed a rock, and her throat closed up because of it. She was about to utter a word so foreign to her, something she had never spoken. "Ma," she began again, forming her lips like a baby learning desperately to speak.

Mama. Mama.

But then the word forced itself out, her voice loud and clear, and her heart burst wide open.

"Mama."

"Charlotte?" she whispered, her expression changing from astonishment to joy. She opened her arms and raised them in the air.

Charlie ran right into them and buried herself in her mother's arms. Like a fever leaving her body, her sadness began to fade away. She didn't feel alone anymore. Everything had changed for her in that instant. The broken heart left by a motherless past began to slowly retrieve its pieces.

"Oh, Charlotte. You're here. Oh, my beautiful, darling daughter. You came," she cried. "You came."

"I'm here, Mama."

Celia stepped back while gently caressing Charlie's face. She scanned the room before turning her head toward the door. "Your papa?" she asked.

Charlie didn't have to say anything.

She knew, crumbling, shaking, slowly falling to the floor.

Charlie immediately enveloped her like a shield, wrapped her body around her mother just like she was the child, and Charlie was her protector. The two women remained on the floor, rocking back and forth, Charlie absorbing her mother's wracked sobs, holding her body down to control the shaking.

They mourned this loss.

Yes, they mourned. But that night, and every night thereafter, they would mourn him together.

PART 2

GRAHAM

CHAPTER 26

There he was, standing in the middle of this crowd. This maddening bunch of fakers. They didn't even know her. Most of them were his parents' friends from a long time ago. Colleagues, workmates, business associates. They had no clue about her and were there only because they wanted to see and be seen. They must have had over one hundred people at their home, at this— what do you call it? The reception for the dead? The get-together after the funeral? Even if their 19,000 square-foot home in Lake Oswego could have fit three times, no one could have that many friends. At least not his parents.

Already, he was anxious to get back to Brooklyn. The only thing that had kept him coming back was his younger sister, Madison. Born seven years behind him but wiser than the years ahead of him, she was his beacon, his light. And now she was gone. The one true thing in his life made a mistake and left him.

From the corner of his eye, he could see his mother trudging along with imaginary weights on her ankles and a huge boulder on her shoulders. She was normally the belle of every ball—tall, confident, and beautiful. That day, she looked like an elderly witch, dressed in black, stooped and hunched, her facial features exacerbated by an inordinate amount of weight loss. His father was nowhere. He was known to retreat into his den, happiest among his collection of world-class bourbon and leather-bound books. Their family had fallen apart in the one week without her. What else was there to hold them together?

"Alex," his mother called, waving her hand to attract his attention. Alex rushed to his mother's side and gently hooked his arms under her shoulders to hold her up.

"Mom, you need to sit down," he said, guiding her to the closest seat he could find. "Let me get you a glass of water."

"Oh, Alex!" she sobbed. "What are we going to do without her?"

He had no answer for that. For his heart, his torment, and his pain were all screaming the exact same question.

"Here we are, whew!" Maddy exclaimed before taking an exaggeratedly deep breath and exhaling loudly. "God, I love New York! The sights, the people. Even the smell. The buzz is overwhelming, making you feel like you're right in the middle of all the happenings!" She hurriedly peeled off her coat and followed the hostess.

"Interesting place," Alex said under his breath as they were seated at what Maddy called one of the hottest underground music bars in West Village. A male server approached and handed them a menu and a music list. When he stepped away, Alex laid the card on the table. "What are we supposed to do with this?"

The place was packed—not by the people Alex was used to seeing around Manhattan, but by a younger generation, a mix of millennials in designer clothes and Gen Zers with hoodies and trademark leisurewear. A large bar stood in front of them, flanked by wooden stools that matched the unfinished look of the walls. Above them hung a few disco balls, ensconced in foliage that covered the ceilings, branches drooping down toward the floor like willow trees. "Are those real cherry blossoms?"

Madison rolled her eyes. "Yes."

"Aren't they seasonal?" he asked, genuinely curious.

Madison held her palms up and shrugged. He knew he was starting to annoy her.

"And those walls. Grunge?" Alex pointed to the cracked, bare walls sprinkled with graffiti.

"Oh my god. What generation are you from?"

"The old one, apparently." He laughed. "Do you come here a lot?"

"Almost every night during my two-week audition. They have awesome music here. And the food is amazing. You'll see." Madison took the small pencil and scooted closer to him. "Okay, let's choose our music first, then our food." Maddy handed him a pencil before scooting over closer to her brother. Together, they pored over the list, taking turns placing checkmarks beside their choices.

"What?" Alex teased her with an elbow nudge. "That's their entire soundtrack."

"I know," Maddy said, smiling. "I love that movie."

"Yeah, but it's not as good as the way you've put a spin on it," Alex said, getting to his feet to Maddy's surprise and announcing in a booming voice. "Especially now that you've gotten accepted as part of the New York Philharmonic Orchestraaaaaaa." A round of applause ensued, everyone at the restaurant cheering and clapping in excitement. Maddy waved with a smile and pulled her brother back down on the seat.

"Stop it!" Madison squealed. "You're embarrassing me."

"Why?" Alex taunted. "Because I'm letting everyone in this place know that my sister now plays for the top orchestra in the country?"

She shook her head before taking a sip of her green tea. She was beautiful in a subtle sort of way, with light hazel eyes and honey-brown hair. Fresh-faced, young, and full of life, her eyes with hues of copper and amber, constantly changing with the light. "It's not a big deal."

"Yes, it is," he countered. "You worked so hard to get here. So proud of you, baby sis."

She sat closer to him, took his hand, and squeezed it with all her might.

"Ouch!"

"Stop calling me baby."

"Okay," he relented. "But you are."

"I'm not. But people treat me like I am. You, Mom, Dad. Mom especially keeps thinking I need to be protected. One month ago, she sent Nimfa to the dorm to bring me homecooked food straight from the casserole."

"Ha! Did she really?" Alex laughed.

"She figured I was sick of dorm food," Maddy explained. "I guess I should be thankful."

"We just love you, that's all. But yes, I agree that we have a tendency to go overboard. I'll talk to Mom, too. It was just because you were so close to her in Portland. Now you're moving away, getting out of that cocoon." Alex tried to defend their stance, knowing full well that one day, he would have to let her go, which was why he offered her a room at his Park Avenue penthouse. He traveled around quite a bit for work, giving her some independence while keeping her safe.

"Cocoon, all right. Everyone over in the dorm has a boyfriend. And I don't. I mean, who has time? I'm either practicing, auditioning, or studying the whole time."

"You're only saving yourself for the best, Moonie. It's not a rush to the finish line. You have so much time. I'm in the same boat, and I'm thirty-four."

"Shut up. You're dating a New York model and just got engaged."

Alex lowered his head and began to play with his chopsticks. "Yeah. That."

"What does that mean? You sound like you're going to the dentist. Is everything okay?"

"Yeah, of course, everything is fine. I think I'm just expecting too much from this relationship. We've just been so busy with taking the business public and all. I haven't had much time to digest what we mean to each other."

"Is she pressuring you?"

The truthful answer was yes. The diplomatic answer was, "Everyone says I'm so lucky with Libby. I know I am. I think everything is just moving a little too quickly."

"Mmm. Yeah. You know what I think. You could do better. She's just not . . . natural. Everything about her comes from a needle or a bottle. You need someone real. Someone who will be there for you without all the trappings of your success. Years from now, you won't have anything to talk about. I think she's kind of empty up here," she said, tapping a finger on her temple. "So, you'd better be having great sex till you're eighty."

"Madison Mead!" Alex exclaimed, placing one hand over his mouth, mocking her with a look of shock.

"Anyway," she said thoughtfully, pushing her teacup toward the black kettle in the middle of the table. Alex poured the tea for her. "Back to me. All my college friends are getting married. I've been a bridesmaid seven times."

"You're only twenty-five."

"And super nerdy. Look at me. I'm drinking green tea. I had nothing in common with anybody at the conservatory." She forced a laugh. "Their methods of letting loose are a little too out there for me."

"Green tea is good for you!" he countered. "And you are yourself, dear sis. Which you will learn is the bravest thing you can ever be. The world isn't that accepting, but if you stick to being who you are, you'll live a life with no regrets. Don't give in to the pressure of being who you're not."

"Says the guy who's met every expectation ever imposed on him," Maddy teased.

"Yeah, no. Don't be like me," Alex mumbled into his drink.

Their server came to take their order, choosing to stand too close to Maddy. Alex didn't think his sister had any clue about how attractive she was. He noticed the server looking at her occasionally, trying to get her attention. She was so genuine, so innocent. She had no airs, no qualms about who she was and what she wanted to be. She played the violin, spent her days writing music, doing her part to bring harmony into the world by creating beautiful sounds that brought people together.

They ordered their eight-course izakaya, a mix of classic Asian fare and some fusion dishes.

"Something's up, isn't it? You're being so profound all of a sudden." She chuckled.

"No, not really. I am just so proud of you. And," he said while fishing into a bowl of bean sprouts with his chopsticks, "I can't wait for you to move in this month. I've got everything set up for you, and I redid one of the rooms for your music."

She clapped her hands in glee, her eyes glowing with child-like wonder. In many ways, she was still so young after being educated in a private school with only sixty girls in her graduating class and spending her post-teenage years in a conservatory of music to train for her auditions. "I can't wait! I'll miss Mom and Dad, but I'm so excited to start a new life. In New York City! Thank you, G Cracker. I love you."

"I love you too, Moonie."

* * *

When Alex received the call that night, his father had already chartered a plane to take him back from New York to Portland. "She's asking for you," said his mother. He didn't know what to expect when he reached the hospital. Police cars and flashing lights blocked the entrance as his father's security guards whisked him to a private wing on the east side. Lined up along its walls were framed pictures of his grandfather, father, and whole family in the massive wing they had donated.

The first person he saw was his father, who was deep in conversation with two policemen and the ambulance tech. Words were being yelled out like "criminal" and "investigation." Right around the corner were three of Maddy's close friends from school—they looked so grown up he hardly recognized them. Machines were being wheeled back and forth, and nurses were running the phones.

"Alex!" His mother's shrill, sharp voice rang through the corridor, causing pinpricks on his skin.

"Mom!" He ran into her arms like a little lost child who'd just been found. "What happened? Where is she?"

His mother shook her head violently, thrashing it from side to side. "Oh, Alex," she bawled. "She's slipping. They're trying to get her back. Go see her. See her while you can."

Alex released his mother and dashed toward an open door. Maddy's friend, Tish, stopped him before he could make his way to her. "Alex, we don't know what happened. She was ecstatic, and we were celebrating her trip to New York. A few kids we didn't know crashed the party. The next thing I knew, I saw her taking a puff of something, and then, she just . . ." Tish's words strung together. "She just—"

Alex pushed her out of the way and ran to his sister. He broke down at the sight of her, so small and frail in the middle of this huge bed, hooked up to so many contraptions that he could hardly see her head. He couldn't control the sounds coming out of his lips. His howls silenced the bedlam caused by the machines, beeping, ticking, blowing, sucking. Everything was happening all at once. And then he saw her trying to raise her hand to call his attention.

Alex bolted to her side and grabbed both her hands. "Moonie. I'm here. I'm so sorry I wasn't with you tonight. This is my fault. This is all my fault!" Alex kissed her hands, placing them against his face and covering them with his tears.

She motioned for him to lift her oxygen mask. "Hi, Cracker," she whispered. "I'm sorry. I guess I wasn't so brave." She wheezed each word, her chest rising and falling with difficulty.

"No, no," he whimpered. "You are still the bravest person I know." He sank his head next to hers, caressing her cheeks before placing his lips on her forehead. "Now you have to be braver, okay? Use your superhero powers to fight because . . ." he cried, breathless and sinking, unable to get enough air. He saw it in her face, the paleness of her lips, the hollow of her eyes. She was slipping from his life. Slipping, sliding, floating away. "I . . . I-I c-can't be here without you!"

"I'm so sleepy, I can hardly stay awake. Can I take a short nap? Just a short one, I promise. I'll see you in New York. I love you," she said, taking one short breath and then taking in the deepest one she would ever take, opening her eyes wide to look directly at him for one last time.

And when she smiled and closed her eyes forever, he was dead, too.

CHAPTER 27

Of all the events that had been carved into his memory, the one he couldn't erase was the immediate aftermath of Maddy's death. He could still remember watching his mother slap his father on the face, a slap so forceful that the sound reverberated across the halls and walls of the hospital floor. She yelled and screamed and pounded on his chest. "See, now? What use is all this money? We couldn't keep her safe. And now, this hospital. No amount of money you've given has helped them keep our daughter alive. Your money couldn't save her. What's the point? What's the point, William?"

When Alex left the day after the funeral, Catherine did nothing to stop him. It was as if she knew he had to escape Portland if he wanted to keep living. In many ways, that was how she felt, too. Catherine was always selfless and always devoted herself to her husband and children. She left her career as a successful corporate lawyer once she was pregnant with him. Alex felt horrible about leaving her alone in Portland, but with every minute he was there, he felt himself cracking. He refused to do that, to add to her pain. He was now her only living child.

There was a sense of unfamiliarity when he walked into his home. For a moment, he didn't even recognize Zeny, his live-in maid. He had to look twice, first thinking that a stranger had broken in. Zeny approached him and tried to help him with his suitcase. He waved his hand and looked at her kindly.

"Did you want me to unpack it for you, Mr. Mead?"

"No, Zeny, thank you. It's okay. I can do it later."

"I can make you some dinner. I know it's late. You must be hungry."

"That would be good, thank you."

When she left for the kitchen, Alex became disoriented. He wandered aimlessly down the hallway, not knowing where to settle in first. He decided to sift through the pile of papers on the kitchen counter, setting aside junk mail and collating the ones he had to bring to the office the next day. He noticed a picture of Libby from one of the events he had missed. She was smiling into the camera, holding a cigarette. He tossed that copy aside and continued his task. After that, he decided to bite the bullet and walk into the room that was to be Maddy's. The place she would never see again.

He'd had the biggest corner in the penthouse renovated for her. Broken down the walls to give her a large sitting room where she could practice her music. He'd called in acoustic experts to ensure the sound carried through correctly and that the walls would be soundproofed from the rest of the home. He'd had the room painted in pink and green, her favorite colors, imported a solid marble headboard from Thailand, and displayed all three of her valuable violins—two Stradivari, one Del Gesu—and the rest of the Yamahas and Cremonas on a shelf next to her keyboard. To top it off, he'd intended to surprise her with built-in recording equipment so she could start bringing the songs she wrote to life. He'd thought he'd been fulfilling her lifelong dream—one that would never see the light of day now.

Bereft with grief and wracked with sobs, Alex sought comfort by lying down on the floor next to her bed. Never in his life had he ever felt so hopeless, such a finality he didn't think he could face. He stared up at the ceiling, praying to whoever would listen, cursing whoever it was who planned the loss of her, to the one who set the universe on fire and sentenced him to a life without his sister.

Alex was roused from his sleep by a sharp pain on his side. He opened his eyes to find a pair of pointy-toed stilettos poking at his rib cage.

"Alex, wake up!" He looked up to find Libby hovering over him, nudging him with her shoe.

"Ouch! Libby! Stop it." He still felt woozy, choosing to sit on the bed instead of following Libby out of Maddy's room.

When she saw that he wasn't behind her, she stopped and stood by the door. "What were you doing in here?"

Alex said nothing. The fact that she would even ask that question and that he didn't know how to respond set off a series of red flags in his head.

"I'm going to the living room so Zeny can get me some coffee," she said before turning on her heel and leaving. "Why don't you go take a shower, and we can have breakfast? I can't believe you're still in your airport clothes."

By the time Alex showered and dressed, he found Libby in the dining room bossing Zeny around. On the table was a spread of Iberico ham, little pastry puffs, caviar, and fresh fruit. Zeny ran back into the kitchen when she saw Alex—seconds later presenting him with his favorite, an acai bowl.

"Oh, I forgot to tell you," Libby began while pulling off a slice of ham with her fingers. "I used the card yesterday for a sale at Bergdorf's. I just had to have this divine diamond bracelet."

"How much." It sounded more like a statement than a question. Alex's tone was low and serious. He was mentally spent, distraught, and . . . who was this woman sitting in front of him right now?

"Baby," she drawled. "You've never cared about price before."

"How much?"

"Just thirty," she retorted, sticking a fork into a piece of melon so dramatically that Zeny rushed to see if something had fallen on the floor. "I'll pay it back as soon as I get my next gig."

"When?"

"Seriously? What the hell is wrong with you today? You go home to Portland and come back all cranky and mean."

"Libby, I was just at my sister's funeral," he said, filling with rage. Rage and realization. Why were her eyelashes so big? How had he never noticed how they covered her whole eye? How could she even see? And there was bronzer on her nose to make it look sharper. What was her real nose like? "You weren't even there."

"Okay, right," she said, raising her hand to appease him. "My bad. I'm just not good at sad stuff like that. But we need to keep moving forward, you know? So today, I thought maybe—"

"I have to go into the office today," he snapped. "Let's go back to what you were just saying. When have you ever kept your word with me, Libby? All those times you said you'd pay me back, or you had a gig coming up, or that you quit smoking two years ago."

"Smoking?"

Libby twitched backward when he slid the newspaper across the glass table.

"It was a social thing." She approached him and tried to place her hands on his shoulders.

He raised his palms to stop her from coming close. "Right."

"Baby, I promise I won't do it again. Not even socially," she muttered.

Alex shook his head, awash in regret and the bitterness of wasted time. "Libby. I don't care if you kill yourself sneaking cigarettes behind my back. It doesn't seem like you get the point of all this. The money doesn't even matter. But words? They define the character of a person. They give hope, and they heal wounds. And if I can't count on your words and promises, what we have is meaningless."

"But . . ." Libby was visibly shocked, her mouth agape, hands fidgeting with her hair.

"I'd like you to leave, please. Now."

"You mean . . . leave today, and I'll come back tomorrow?"

"No," he said, enunciating the word so she could hear him clearly. Cold, steely eyes met her gaze as she cowered down and stared at her shoes. "I mean, leave now and don't come back. It's over. I'll take all the money you spent and promised to pay back as a loss. And don't worry about the press. I'll have my office handle the blowback."

"But Alex . . . I love you," she pleaded, reaching for him once again.

He ignored her attempt to touch him. Instead, he focused on noticing that her palm was ten shades lighter than the back of her hand. *Moonie, stop proving your point.* "No, Libby. You love this," he said, his arms making a sweeping motion across the room. "And the thing is, what means everything to you no longer means anything to me."

CHAPTER 28

In the blur that followed, Alex was sure only of one thing: he did not spend a single second thinking of Libby after their breakup. Zeny, on the other hand, was not shy about showing her alignment with his decision. He entered his dressing room to find her neatly packing all of Libby's belongings, wiping them off, washing off, and removing every trace of her. He spent a few more days in the comfort of his solitude, most days in the dark and every day in Maddy's shadow.

The moment Alex stepped off the elevator, his point of view shifted drastically. The adrenaline rush that used to besiege him whenever he walked through the lobby painted in red, blue, and green colors was gone. The giant slide that reached four floors and the foosball and ping pong tables surrounded by five different types of coffee dispensers, vending machines with free salads and energy bars, the beanbags, the couches, the movie projectors, and television screens suddenly irritated him. The background noise, the laughter of employees scattered around to play and never to work, gave rise to just one thought—*My god, I didn't build a business. I built an amusement park.*

"Alex, so sorry for your loss," was the statement of the day as he wove through the crowd of twenty-somethings.

We loved Maddy. She was always so fun when she visited you in the office.

I remember shooting Nerf guns with her when she was here last year.

She whipped our asses in foosball. Every single time.

She loved you and told us how proud she was of her brother.

She was beautiful.

Such a loss. We are so sorry.

When he finally reached his office, he shut the door and felt relieved. He stood at the floor-to-ceiling windows over-looking Fifth Avenue, wondering how on earth he would make it through the day. Snow flurries floated slowly in the air, vanishing with the wind before they reached the ground. He'd built this company three years ago, this boy wonder who'd found a way to harness data by first developing a search engine and later integrating robotics into several software applications.

His father wasn't self-made—he was the son of Garret Mead of the Mead Tobacco family. The difference between father and son was stark. While William came from generations of family business, Alex was an entrepreneur from the day he was born. Everything he undertook seemed to turn into gold. At twenty-seven, he was a millionaire; at thirty, a multi-millionaire. And life at the top became very lonely. His professionalism separated him from men his age. He was isolated and focused on building and maintaining a business. His only friend was Jerry, his room-mate at Stanford. Well, and then there was Maddy. She was the only one he trusted with his life. He was a little disappointed when she decided to pursue music, but his chagrin quickly dissipated when he saw how talented she was.

"Mr. Mead," Tina, his assistant, interrupted his thoughts. She was the only one in the entire company who didn't call him by his first name. She was also the only one who didn't come to work looking like she was going to the beach. Tina was Zeny's niece, and he had long since learned that their culture thrived on respect. "Mr. Newby is here to see you."

"Send him in, please."

Before leaving, she asked, "Sir, would you like me to get you a cup of coffee?"

"Green tea would be great, Tina. Thank you so much."

The two men hugged as soon as Jerry walked in. "I'm so sorry, man. We will miss her so much."

Alex nodded before taking his place at his desk, looking around like it was his first time there. He couldn't explain it, this feeling of detachment. Everything around him, the things he surrounded himself with, the things he built, were foreign to him. Where did this ungodly furniture even come from? Milan, if he could remember. And why were they so uncomfortable? *Don't they make cushions anymore? Why are these modern, egg-shaped chairs so ugly? And those colored blotches on my wall—do they really call them art?*

"Alex," Jerry called out to him. "Alex?"

"I'm sorry."

"I heard what happened, man. Libby's been calling me, trying to get through to you. She says she loves you, and she's been crying to anyone who would listen."

Alex leaned back on his chair and scoffed. "Screw that. It's over."

Jerry raised his eyebrows. "Just like that?"

"It's been a long time coming. Can we talk about something else? I'm considering accepting Amtech's offer and beginning the due diligence process. We are so buttoned up that I have no doubt we will pass with flying colors. As my CFO, I'd like you to work on the multiple. I'm thinking at least five times."

"Wait." Jerry twisted in his seat. His knee bounced up and down. "You're selling?"

"Yes. And right away."

"No!" Jerry blurted before visibly composing himself. He leaned back and ironed his pants with his hands. "I mean, we should think about it more. We're just getting started. Our company is new."

"Which is why we should take the opportunity while we are at the top of our game," Alex explained. "Don't worry, you have stock options. So do all of our executives. No one will leave empty-handed. It's a win-win all around." Alex thought it strange that Jerry would not look at him.

"We can't sell, Alex." Beads of sweat appeared on Jerry's forehead. Alex watched one little drop travel down to his ear.

"Of course we can," Alex said. "It's my company. I can do what I want."

"No, you can't. At least, not right now."

Alex's grin transformed into a scowl. His jaw grew tight, and his brows turned downward. "I was supposed to be with my sister that night," he said, gritting his teeth and enunciating every word. "This deal cost me her life. I was here negotiating this deal while she lay dying. So we are selling this company, Jerry."

"We *can't*."

A cold wave of air passed through his body. Suddenly, he was no longer sure. "And why not?"

"I . . . I borrowed some money," Jerry stuttered. "From the company. I'm going to pay it back. I just need some time."

Alex brought his hands to his face. All of a sudden, his ears were ringing, and his head was about to explode. He didn't understand why money was such a problem for him. Why, once again, someone had betrayed him because of what he had. He thought of Maddy and how he would give everything up just to have her back. "I don't understand, Jerry. Help me to understand. We've been friends since Stanford. I gave you this job. I trusted you."

"I know," Jerry said, leaning forward, sweat running down his forehead, hands rolled into a ball. "And I am so sorry. I got carried away with the spending, the house, the traveling . . ."

Then, the all-too-familiar question. "How much?"

"Five million. I needed it to pay some bills, the pool, the—"

"You gave up our friendship to pay for your pool?" Alex said, shaking his head in disbelief. He was breaking. There was no one else left in his life. He couldn't trust anyone.

"No, that's not true. I thought I had time. Give me a few months. I'll pay it back."

Alex banged his fists on the table. "Words! Empty words! Do you know how long it will take to earn that money? Why promise me something you can't possibly keep? Doesn't keeping your word mean anything to anyone anymore?" He stood and leaned over, his face almost touching Jerry's. "What's your plan?"

What about a loan? Asking your father? Borrowing it from somewhere else so we can retain what we had?

Not you, too. I don't want to lose you.

Jerry buried his face in his hands and wept.

"I will cover that loan so the books will be kept clean. Consider your stock options payment. I'm selling this company, and I don't ever want to see you again."

CHAPTER 29

He was running frantically through an endless maze made out of gold. No matter where he turned, regardless of the twists and turns he followed, he always seemed to end up in the same place.

Exhausted and out of breath, he stopped abruptly and looked up at the abyss above him. "What do you want from me?" he cried. "Where do you want me to go?"

He watched as the clouds flitted by, and a big bright moon lit up the sky, illuminating the path before him. And then he heard the voice he'd been missing for weeks. The voice of the angel who was taken away from him too soon.

"Let fate lead the way. Nothing about this was your fault, Cracker. It was meant to happen. You are where you're supposed to be."

When Alex woke up, his mind was crystal clear. He knew what he wanted to do but not necessarily how he would do it. It would seem quite extreme to some, but not to him. After all, he was a risk-taker. Moving elsewhere with the same trappings of fame and fortune would be like relocating the same pain to another place. He needed radical change. He needed to walk away from everything that had disappointed him.

All this money had done nothing to save Maddy. So what was the point of it?

When his mother called on FaceTime, he told her as much as he knew.

"Alex," she said, her voice still meek, wounded. Alex wondered if she would ever revert back to the strong, opinionated woman he knew and loved. Her cheekbones were pronounced, her eyes deep and sunken. Her bleached-blonde hair had turned gray. She wore it openly—the physical toll of loss. "We received the boxes you shipped out to us. I know they're—" She paused. "Madison's things. I can't . . . I can't go through them. Not yet."

"You don't need to. I had them packed very well. They're her antique violins and some of the things I bought for her room. We can deal with that later. I just thought I'd send them before my place goes on the market." He also saw himself on camera. His hair had grown past his ears and right above his shoulders, and a thick, heavy beard covered most of his face.

"On the market? What's going on, honey? I know you sold the business, but . . ." His mother's watery eyes were not lost on him. He didn't want her to shed tears for him, and she had shed enough. But he also wanted to be honest with her. It was a chapter he needed to close, a challenge he needed to take up on his own.

"Mom, I need your help with this, okay? I need some time to leave all this behind. I'm going off the grid for a while. Nothing to worry about." He tried to lighten his tone but knew there was no sugarcoating what he was about to do.

"Where are you going? Where are you staying?"

"I don't know."

"What do you mean, you don't know?" she asked.

Alex noticed his father walking back and forth on his cell phone. He heard his father's booming voice saying something about the future of e-cigarettes and strong tobacco sales in Europe.

"I don't know yet, but even if I did, I wouldn't be telling you. I need this time, Mom. I just need this time by myself. Please try to understand. I'm floating and finding ways to survive my days without her. I was supposed to take care of her, and I . . . I can't get over this guilt. I never will, and I'm struggling to find a way to live with it."

"It wasn't your fault. How would you have known? It wasn't your fault. Do you hear me?"

"She was going to start a life in New York."

"Please, Alex. It's just us now. You're all we have. I don't want to lose you too!" Her eyes welled with tears, and her mouth started to quiver. Soon, her shoulders began to shudder, one trembling hand trying to hold the camera steady and the other covering her face.

"Mom, please, no." He wished he could run home to her and comfort her. It just wasn't that simple. Nothing in life ever was. "Listen, Mom," he said, keeping his tone gentle and reassuring. "I'll call every Sunday. Let you know that I'm okay. But you have to give me this time and space, okay? Promise me, Mom. You won't look for me or make any attempts to find me. I will be fine."

She blew her nose into a Kleenex and bobbed her head up and down. He knew she wasn't going to stop him. Just like the day he left their home after the funeral.

"Do you remember Gary, my finance guy? He's going to take care of transferring the proceeds of the sale to my accounts. They'll just remain there for now and earn some interest until I figure myself out. This isn't a permanent thing, Mom. Don't worry. I'll be home someday soon. I love you and Dad very much. We all need to heal from this, and we all need to find our own ways to do it. Do you understand?"

"I do. I do," she agreed.

He saw her smile sadly, but it was a smile, nonetheless.

In the next two weeks, he expedited the sale of the company, spending late hours in the office while the winter winds blew all over town. And when the deal was done, he walked around the office for one last time, grateful for all that had happened but devoid of any attachment to the life he once led. He thought about how everything had snowballed so fast, how he had lost control of who he was and what he really wanted to do out of life. He was a twenty-four-year-old who developed an app in the comfort of his parents' home. Something he presented one day to a group of executives who had come over for dinner. And before he knew it, his father's connections had obtained a patent for him. It inspired him to do more, modify, tweak, and perfect that little app he had made. However, the app gave rise to innovation, which led to the creation of a software company. With little or no guidance, he made decisions on his own. He had two hundred employees and $100 million in sales in one year. He chose to run things conservatively, hiring only to open contracts. It yielded him a twenty percent margin, most of which he invested back into his people. Alex became the boy wonder. And boy wonders pay a steep price to stay that way.

On the day he left, he called Zeny into the dining room.

"Is that all you're taking, Mr. Mead?" she asked, pointing to his blue backpack and rolled-up sleeping bag. "It's cold outside."

She made him chuckle. She'd been his nanny since he was six years old. When he moved to New York, he took her with him because she wouldn't have it any other way. In over thirty years, she'd never called him Alex. "Zeny, you've always been in my corner, and I am so grateful to you for that. You're the only one I trust," he said, looking directly at her. She smiled. He continued.

"I'm going to be gone for a while. I'd like to ask you to live here and manage this house until it is sold. It will go on the market on Monday, and given how well you've taken care of me and this home, I'm sure it will sell rather quickly. Take whatever furniture you'd like, and the buyer will purchase the rest as-is." He handed her an envelope, which she refused to accept. She shook her head until he gave up and laid it on the table.

"Please take it, Zeny. You deserve much more than that. It's a year's pay, your life insurance policy, and a check for Tina's tuition for her accounting degree."

"Where are you going, Mr. Mead?"

"I don't know yet. I'll be around for a bit, and then maybe I'll go home."

"Mr. Mead, I know you think that you're all alone in this. But you're not. You have people, your family, who love you. I've seen how you work and know how distant you can be. You have to be Mr. Mead. I know it's not your fault. People take advantage of you when you let your guard down. But sometimes, it's okay not to know, Mr. Mead. Sometimes, it's okay to—" She scratched her head. "I don't know how to say in English . . . *masugatan.*" She thought for a second. "Oh, I know. Vulnerable? Get hurt?" She smiled sadly. "Sometimes, it's okay not to know. To be vulnerable. Wounded. Sometimes, it's okay to let fate lead you."

Alex did a double-take, turning his head in her direction. "What did you say?"

"There is a plan, a reason for everything, Mr. Mead. You have to trust in that. Trust in fate. That is the only way we will survive this loss."

Alex stepped forward and stooped down to wrap her in an embrace. She disappeared in his arms, all four feet eleven inches of her. "I love you, Zeny. I'll see you again."

"I love you too, Mr. Mead. And thank you."

CHAPTER 30

During the day, he walked for miles, sometimes crossing the bridge from Manhattan into Queens or from Manhattan into Brooklyn. For the first time in his life, he wasn't meeting any deadlines and had no plan or agenda for the day. It was both terrifying and exhilarating. His fears had rapidly changed from delivering on expectations and keeping up appearances to simply keeping safe at night. Two very opposite sources of anxiety, but also very real.

Alex kept no cash on himself, knowing that life on the streets had no value. He filled his days by visiting libraries in every part of the city, returning to a novel from day to day until he finished it. The winter had been mild, so he slept under bridges, in train stations, and inside a church, staying no longer than he had to. Alex wasn't naïve about what could have happened to him during his time on the streets, and he also recognized that he wasn't really "homeless." How many of the others in line for a shower at the mission house had memorized the number of their American Express black card for emergency purposes? Alex had grown up in a sheltered home in one of Portland's richest areas. How much did he really know about the humanity that existed in the outside world?

There were nights when the stench of the streets made him sick. There were nights when he couldn't settle down, and his heart popped out of his chest when drunks and addicts approached him with taunts and threats. They called him pretty boy, pressed themselves against him, ganged up on him, and stole his things. But there were just as many nights when he was enveloped in a blanket of kindness, camaraderie, the generosity of strangers, shared food, and stories and experiences. Through all that, he learned that the pain he felt was nothing compared to the screams and cries of wretchedness in the streets at night and that the magnitude of his devastation was just as deep and traumatic as those who surrounded him.

During week two, he lined up at a food pantry at the Catholic Church in Sunset Park. He was familiar with this one, being the biggest anonymous donor of this mission. The irony of his current situation wasn't lost on him. He was sure no one would recognize him then. The priests and volunteers saw a different side of him—clothed in expensive suits, a beautiful woman on his arm—during charity events.

That day, he was just one of the lost ones.

By the time he made it there, the line was a block long. This wasn't his first time at a food pantry, so he was aware that the selection would be scarce by the time he got inside. Nevertheless, he appreciated having a hot meal and a decent place to sit and eat. He made it inside after thirty minutes, walking down a flight of stairs to the grade school basement. On the way down, pictures and murals of angels and saints were plastered against the walls.

He was hardly inside the room, waiting for the line to move as he stood by the doorway when he saw her. She wore her hair in a ponytail, thick and dark, swept back in a cap. He tried hard to remember what they were called. He watched as people from the church greeted her with sad faces, whispering in her ear and patting her softly on the shoulder as if offering her some comfort. She was stunning, her face in perfect symmetry, her lips the most noticeable part of her face. She smiled at him when she saw him looking at her, her eyes soft and tempered by an ethnicity he couldn't determine. They were sad, too.

Alex was a bit rattled when he stood in front of her. He slid the tray on the rails and watched as she began to scoop up some food.

"I think you forgot to get your silverware," she said, pointing at the bucket of spoons and forks.

"Yeah, sorry about that." He reached across three other bodies to grab a knife and fork.

"Would you like two scoops of mashed potatoes?"

"That would be great, thank you," he answered, staring at the tray of food as he pushed it along.

"Sister Mathilda just made these freshly baked muffins." She pulled out a big pair of tongs and placed two muffins on the side of his plate with a smile. "Guess it's your lucky day."

The winter air had thawed, turning the clouds heavy and gray. Alex was awestruck when he walked into the brand-new Brooklyn Heights Public Library. Located on the first three levels of a new condominium development, it had bright white finishings, modern exposed concrete, and interchangeable workspaces. The vast windows and high ceilings immersed the space with so much light. There was a floor dedicated to teens, equipped with a game room and furnished with bright red beanbags. Installed in the conference rooms were bas-relief artworks—lightly carved designs on a solid surface, this time on stone. Alex had commissioned this type of artwork in his former office.

He found the book in the children's section. Vivid memories

of Maddy flashed through his mind, but this time, they were good ones.

How can a cow jump over the moon, Cracker? Tell me how.

That's the beauty of fairy tales, Maddy. You suspend all doubt and allow yourself to be transported for a little while.

Kinda like when I'm lost in my music.

Yeah, kinda like that.

He read Tolstoy that day, choosing *Anna Karenina* over *War and Peace*. He chose the bright red beanbag and settled in for the day, falling asleep around ten chapters in. Alex awoke hours later, startled by the clanging and banging of doors. He saw the librarians preparing to lock up for the day and the security guards making their final rounds.

A mother and her daughter were being asked to check their books out. He jumped to his feet and ran out the door. Unfamiliar with Brooklyn Heights, he had no idea where he was going. And as he passed a street lined with condominiums, the clouds began to roar. Seconds later, he was caught in a downpour. Torrents of rain came down, blinding his vantage point, the wind pushing him back as he tried to move forward. Right in front of him sat a row of parked cars, vibrating from the force of the rain. He ran to the cars and pulled on their door handles, trying the first and then the second, with no luck. The third one, a red Tesla, automatically opened with the mere touch of his palm on the door. He crawled in, intent on leaving once the rain had passed.

He'd only been on the streets for three weeks. He had planned to be alone longer, but once he saw her, everything changed.

CHAPTER 31

Alex was awakened by the slamming of a car door, then completely rattled by the banging on the window and muffled shrieks from a woman outside. Stunned and disoriented, it took him a moment to remember where he was. He clung to the edge of his sleeping bag as the car rocked, agitated by the woman who waved her phone at him, her hands animatedly flying all over the place. He tried the car handle but was locked inside. He thought for sure she would call the police, but she didn't. Once the woman calmed down, she opened the door and released him. And then something unexpected happened. He couldn't believe his eyes. When the sun broke from the clouds and shone as bright as a summer day, he saw her face.

It was her. The woman from the food pantry. Gone were the apron and hair pulled back in a cap. It now cascaded over her shoulders, thick and dark and lustrous. Even when she was upset, she was perfect. How the hell did he end up sleeping in her car? It was ridiculous to the point of being funny. A comedy where he pisses off the most beautiful girl he's ever seen because he trespasses in her car.

Alex didn't want to scare her, so he left as soon as he was told to do so. But once he was out of her sight, he paused momentarily to collect himself. He didn't know what to think or why he needed to see her again. He felt a stirring in his heart, an attraction so strong he didn't know what to do about it. He turned back to find her pacing outside her car, appearing to call someone who didn't answer.

Slowly, he made his way back to her with the perfect excuse to see if she needed his help. And it turned out she did. For almost three hours, he sat with her, thanking his lucky stars for the opportunity to interact with such an incredible human being, and as a bonus, he met someone whose sadness mirrored his.

He wanted to ask her name but didn't want her to feel he was trying to pick her up. So, he focused on getting her car to start. In the meantime, she shared tidbits about herself, the loss of her father, and how she was just coming back into the light. She also mentioned planning a road trip to California. In her presence, he felt peace, and he didn't want his time with her to end. He had grown tired of roaming and wanted to ground himself in her orbit.

That night, to remain nearby, he slept in an indoor parking garage, leaning against a concrete pole behind the wheels of a giant SUV. It was risky, but he had nothing more to lose at that point. Not wanting to venture too far off, he filled his cup with water from an outdoor fountain and did his best to clean himself up.

Alex didn't approach her the next day, or the next, or even the next. His world felt less despondent just being close to her. He was content with spending his days at the public library, reading *Anna Karenina* and figuring out a plan to speak to her again.

Five days had passed since she had found him in her car. On the way back to the library, he spotted her leaving her apartment, dressed casually in jeans and a leather bomber jacket. He stood at the intersection and watched her cross the street to the little convenience store. It took a lot not to follow her in. But he waited. He wasn't one to act casually. No "fancy meeting you here" kind of thing, but more of an "I'm here to speak to you" kind of deal. So he waited in front of her apartment. He had a proposal, a very important one. For some inexplicable reason, he felt ready to go home.

Upon seeing her leave the store, he straightened his posture and leaned casually on the brick wall next to the entrance. A man sitting on a hardwood dolly rolled up and parked himself on the ground right by his feet. The woman quickened her pace when she saw the man waving to him as she reached her doorstep. She didn't notice Alex.

"Hey, Simon. Nice to see you."

"Well, Miss Charlie. I saw you go into the little store." He chuckled.

Charlie. Her name was Charlie. In the German language, it meant "free man," connotating strength. A warrior.

"And good thing you did." She smiled back. "Here." She fished into the brown paper bag she held on one arm. "I got these just for you." She handed Simon a submarine sandwich and a can of ginger ale. "Don't give those away now, okay? You need to eat."

"See you at the mission?" he asked, placing the food on his lap and sliding away on his wheels.

"In a few weeks, yes," she said, waving back.

When Alex saw her head toward her car, he ran across the street and waited for her.

"You?"

"Hi," he said, leaping right into his spiel. He asked her where she was going. Offered to do the drive with her.

She declined. The look she gave him was one of bewilderment that he would think she was dumb enough to consider driving cross-country with a complete stranger. But then, in a sudden plot twist, she changed her mind. Out of pity, most probably. And under the condition that her friend check him out. That was good enough for him, even though he wished he'd had more time to fix his appearance.

That was the day he knew fate was working its way into his life.

That was the day he became Graham.

"Here's the thing. Your name's not Graham," her friend, Rena, cut to the chase as soon as Charlie walked away. She wanted to have her friend sniff him out before agreeing to give him a ride to Portland. Rena stuck her palm upward so he could drop his ID in her hand. Once he did that, she brought it close to her face. "Hmmm."

"You'll see that my full name is there. Alexander Graham Mead."

She gave him a stop-bullshitting-me look. Eyes crossed and mouth slanted. "You're lucky my friend isn't into social media. She's been so focused on her work and her dad. Are you going to tell her who you are?"

"Graham *is* my name," he defended.

"You're also one of the biggest tech CEOs in the country. How will you explain that little piece of info?" she asked. "Alex Mead, sleeping in people's cars."

"I sold the company. I'm no longer that person. And if you ask me who I am, I will tell you I've left that life."

"How?" she asked, handing his ID back to him. "And why?"

"By letting go of the life that didn't serve me. And why? Because it turns out, the people I trusted had turned against me."

"Eventually, she's going to find out, you know. It's not like you're not all over the papers." Her eyes softened. "Condolences on your recent loss. I understand you were very close."

"She was my world." Alex looked away, his attention fixed on a bright yellow butterfly perched next to him on the bench. A light breeze passed between them right before the butterfly flew away.

Rena nodded, the harshness in her voice fading away. "Why, of all people, would you want to take this trip with my friend?"

"Because I need a ride home," he said, pausing to rephrase. "And also because someone taught me never to believe in coincidence."

"Well." Rena laughed. "I agree with the coincidence thing. Any other reason?"

"Nothing else, I guess."

"Really." Rena smacked her lips. "So, you're not attracted to her? Because there's such a thing as a bus. And yet here you are, offering to take a stranger on a trip across the country."

Her candor surprised him and endeared her to him at the same time. He had to think about his answer for a few seconds. He didn't want to get it wrong with this woman. It was worse than any client pitch he'd ever had to make. "I've seen her before, you know. She served me Sister Mathilda's muffins at the Catholic mission pantry. And I will admit, her beauty is exquisite. But there's more to it than that. She looked . . . broken. I am broken. And just being around her gives me hope."

Rena exhaled loudly. "Fine. I think you're legit, Alex. Graham. Whatever your name is. But just remember this." She poked a finger on his forehead. He tried to keep a straight face. "I will have my eyes on you. Tracking every single place you drive to. You may come from one of the wealthiest families in the country, but Charlie and I have connections. Mafia-type ones. One foot wrong, and I will hunt you down, cut your balls off, hang you upside down, and leave you to the ants."

CHAPTER 32

Alex hiked for miles around the ski lodge, along a winding path that meandered through plush meadows and dense woodlands. The crisp mountain air that carried the smell of pine helped to expel the amount of alcohol in his body and clear his head. He felt like an idiot for guzzling those drinks down, but then again, all he wanted to do was to disengage himself from what was currently happening. The pain of remembrance was so intense he didn't know how to carry it. It was obvious why he hadn't told Charlie about Maddy. He just didn't have the heart to do it, to add to her grief with stories about another death. After all, the trip was in honor of her father's wishes, not of his sister. But that didn't mean he hadn't been thinking about her every single day.

The morning of the one-year mark, Alex was awakened by an email from the mission, a reminder about a mass he had requested in honor of Maddy. He turned to Charlie and held on to her for dear life, reminding himself that his heart had not been lost. He decided to tell her that day. He was in love with this woman and intended to be honest with her. What he didn't expect was the subtle coincidences that occurred as time went on—the way Charlie constantly brought her name up, the songs he heard on the tram to the mountain, the boy named

Alex goofing around on the floor. All those signs led back to Maddy, his anguish, and his torment. He'd forgotten about all that for almost ten days, lived in the newness of love and lust for this woman, and he hated himself for it. Most of all, he felt so selfish for leaving his home, his mother, and the people he loved. They were hurting, too. The story of Maddy wasn't just about him. It was about a fractured family that needed to be put back together.

He walked, trudged, and ran up the mountain, encountering deer and squirrels while ascending slowly until he could go no farther on the trail. When he arrived at the top, he sat under towering evergreens, blending into the shadows that they cast on the forest floor. He lived in Maddy's memories, his childhood, their friendship, and their bond. And from where he sat, he had a glimpse of the ski lodge below, its rustic structure a beacon of hope and warmth but also of love. She was there waiting for him, the woman of his dreams.

Three hours later, and with renewed hope, he felt like a new man. He was eager to get back to her. But first, he needed to do one more thing.

His mother answered on the first ring and appeared on camera a second later. She wore black, her hair neatly rolled up in a bun, her eyes still solemn and hazy, but her smile full and unencumbered.

"Alex!"

"Hi, Mom. Did you just go to mass?"

"Yes, it was a lovely service for Madison. All her old friends were there, and we're on the way to the house for a little reception."

Alex forced a smile. He didn't know what to think about his mother's disposition. She looked too accepting, too amenable to what the universe had thrown at them. He could feel her vibes through the phone, radiating peace.

"Is everything okay, honey? Are you all right? I'm so glad you called."

Alex began to shiver uncontrollably, his cries echoing among the trees. "Mom, I am so sorry!" he wept. "I am so sorry I'm not there with you and Dad. I shouldn't have left you all alone to deal with this. I was so selfish, thinking of how the loss of her affected me and ignoring your pain. You were her mother, and your loss was even worse—"

"No, no, my sweet boy. We all needed to deal with it in our own way. Grief has no measure, no limit, no timeline. I had to let you go so you could find your own way back. And if I learned anything today," she said. "It is that she is remembered well, Alex. Your sister was loved by many. And that gives me comfort. I have to live again. I have you and your father to take care of. She left us here for a reason—maybe some unfinished business she knew we had to tackle. But whatever the reason was, I had to go on. You do, too."

"I spent the last few hours remembering her. Those mornings, she would play in the garage with her dolls and serve tea all day long. She wouldn't let me enter the house before sitting with her and having tea. And god, she was so nurturing. At one point, we had two ducks, one pig, six dogs, and three cats."

"And don't forget the goat!" his mother blurted with a giggle.

"Oh yeah, whatever happened to the goat?"

"He pooped one too many times on my rose garden, so we asked Albert to take him to his farm."

Mother and son laughed, their tears drying in the sun, their sadness erased by good memories.

"I'm on my way home, Mom."

"Oh, Alex! I am so happy to hear that. Where are you?"

"In Salt Lake City at a ski lodge. Look, do you see that deer?" Alex rotated his phone. The deer lifted its head from the patch of grass and stared back at him.

"Salt Lake City! Why? What on earth?"

"I hitched a ride with a woman I met weeks ago. She's driving to California. Long story, but you'll hear about it when I get home. She's going to be in my life for a long time."

His mother gleamed widely, her affliction dissipating as she reached out to touch his face on the screen. "I love you, Alexander. You are my light. Come home soon."

"I'll be there in a few days, Mom. And I promise. I won't leave ever again."

CHAPTER 33

If someone were to ask him when he realized he loved her, he would say that it happened early in the trip. Maybe it was the first time he touched her hand when she held it while watching the kayakers paddle down the Scioto River. Or the first time he heard her laugh at their dinner on The Hill. Or the night he watched her sleeping in the bed across from him, both hands tucked neatly beneath her cheek. By the time he held her in his arms during the slow dance at the dive bar, he knew that the twelve-day journey wouldn't be just that.

He held mixed feelings every time they pulled into a hotel. For one, it meant that they were getting closer to their destination, but it also gave him a few hours of pleasure, lying next to her, holding her, touching her, discovering who he was inside her heart and her body. He was careful not to push his agenda. Not to lose sight of the purpose of their journey. For Charlie, her mother's letters had affected her so much that she was anxious to reach her, meet her, and share a life with her. For Alex, it was to find his place in the world without his sister. And to devote his time to helping his family recover from their loss.

They arrived in California on the first day of May and said goodbye in the parking lot of a mental health facility. He didn't—no, he couldn't—make any promises. However, he saw in her eyes that she was searching for one. Whatever he found when he was with her had to stand the test of time. She needed to be with her mother. And he needed to find a way to stay alive.

Ten months had passed since Graham last saw her. He still thought about her every single day.

He'd worked hard to pick up the pieces with his family, moved in with them for three months, and focused on showing his mother that he was healing and that she needn't worry about him anymore. He'd also repaired the bonds of his family by moving to his own house a few miles away, having dinner with them on the weekends, and taking his mother to visit Maddy's grave whenever she wanted.

A foundation was set up in Maddy's name, a scholarship for underrepresented young musicians. Graham took some of his earnings from the sale of Power One and invested in a video game company, this time as a silent partner. One step at a time. He'd taken all the steps he could without her.

Now, he'd never felt more ready in his life. It was time to find Charlie.

The thing was, he didn't want to upset her progress if, indeed, she had moved on or if she had found someone else. They'd both had issues to work through, and they'd given each other the space to do that. Better to ease in than to charge into her life and destroy all that progress.

In mid-March, he contacted Rena and asked if he could fly to Brooklyn to see her. There was no need.

If you can wait until the end of the month, I have a CPA conference in Seattle. Could we meet there?

He spotted her from afar, her tiny frame standing out among a crowd of men and women in business suits and dresses. She was the only one in jeans and a leather jacket, clearly debunking the stereotypical notion of someone in her profession. Something about her looked different. Granted, the last time he saw her was almost a year ago, but she looked lighter and smilier.

"Alex!" She waved at him and pointed to a row of bright blue chairs in front of him. He waited for her to come closer, kissed her on both cheeks, and sat beside her. "I just finished a keynote," she said, waving to a server and asking for a glass of water. "A little parched, I guess."

"Not a bad location for an accounting conference." He glanced around at the stone tiles and monochrome abstract paintings. "The Four Seasons, no less."

"Yeah, well, it's all the fees we have to pay to be a part of this event," she said, laughing. "How are you, Alex?"

"Graham," he corrected.

"Graham," she affirmed. "Thanks for sending the reimbursement for the hotels and food, by the way. I was surprised you sent it so quickly. And so organized, too. Three thousand seven hundred nineteen dollars and twenty-one cents. It is so exact and supported by all the receipts. You're an auditor's dream."

"Well, I didn't want to insult her by paying more than the actual amount."

"You spent twelve days with her, and you know her that well?"

He said nothing.

"Seriously, though. How are you, Graham?"

"I'm well, Rena. Took a few months to get back on track, but here I am."

"It's only been ten months. I would have expected you to take more time. Both of you."

"The thing is . . . I can't take more time. I know what I want, and I know what I need. I need Charlie, Rena. I need to have her in my life. None of the progress I've made means anything without her."

Rena planted her heels firmly on the bland, gray carpet and leaned forward. "Tell me about your progress. How have things changed for you?"

"Well," he said, smiling. "I moved in with my parents for a few months but have since bought my own place. I live on Lake Oswego as well, so I am making sure I stay close. My mom has good and bad days, but I'm always there for her now. We take comfort in knowing how much we loved Maddy and how her passing has changed our perspective. My dad actually retired! He built a greenhouse by the pool, and he and my mom are flying to Hawaii to fill it with orchids. Maddy has a foundation for underprivileged musicians, and I am an investor in a start-up tech for video games, so I'm not building anything. It's funny, but it was a connection I made with her at the gaming convention," he said. "And the most fulfilling part of these past few months? My nanny, Zeny, is back at my house, taking care of me. And I've forgiven my best friend, Jerry, for what he did."

"Jerry, the guy who—"

"Ha. I forgot. That was the only story about my personal life that I couldn't quell with the papers. But, yeah. I was also so uninvolved in his life that I didn't see how much he was struggling. If I listened more, I would have been able to help him before he had to resort to desperate measures. He got caught up in the shiny objects," he said, shaking his head. "We didn't know how to handle the trappings that come with success. We lost our way and grew blind to what really mattered. In different ways, I suppose. But lost all the same." He paused to look at her. "Enough about me. How is she? How is Charlie?"

Rena exhaled loudly before answering. Her tone turned low and soft. "She cried a lot of tears for you, Graham. It wasn't easy for her, trying to cope with her grief, saying goodbye to you while having to manage through Celia's grief, too. I flew there a couple of times to help out. Celia suffered a relapse shortly after getting the news about Edgar. They had to re-admit her for two months. They're doing fine now, living in Edgar's apartment. Her Auntie Elma also visits once in a while."

"I want to see her, Rena. I *need* to see her, please," Graham begged.

"Can I ask, why didn't you tell her your real name?"

"Oh, but this is my real name. The old one is dead and gone forever. She gave new life to the man she knows. She knows me more than anyone else."

"By the way, I saved the newspaper article—the one with your picture at that diner. I sent it to her months ago. She totally understood why you didn't tell her. She wanted to give you more time. Which is why I never connected with you."

"What about her? Does she need more time?"

"It wasn't her who gave up everything she stood for, Graham. Hers was a simpler kind of pain. She may have forgotten it, but she still had us."

What he learned these past few months was that pain was subjective and that various degrees of healing made it personal, too. "May I see her, please, Rena?"

Rena's attention was no longer on him. Instead, it was a tall, handsome man with wide-rimmed glasses walking in their direction. "Hi!" The man leaned down to kiss her on the lips. "Graham Mead, this is Brian Lopez, my fiancé. He's an accountant, too."

"Oh, wow! Nice to meet you. And congratulations!" Graham shook his hand while Rena whispered something that made him wave and walk away.

"Were you engaged when I met you last year?" he asked.

"Nope," she said, beaming. "It's pretty new. I owe it all to Charlie, actually. She came back a changed woman, and she convinced me to take the leap. And then when you know, you know," she laughed. "Charlie believes that no matter what happens in the future, you were exactly at the right place . . ." She rolled her eyes. ". . . even if it was in her car, at the right time."

Rena stood and took Graham's hands in hers. "Listen, you must think about this clearly before seeing her. You've both gone through such trauma in the past few months. It hasn't even been a year yet! I know you've both worked hard to give each other the time and space you both needed. She hasn't contacted you, and to my knowledge . . ." Rena paused and scowled at him. "You haven't tried to contact her."

"I have not."

"Okay, so now you feel you're ready to do so. And only you can know that. But if and when you decide to see her, you have to promise this will not be a stop-gap-finding-yourself type of thing. You have to be found, Graham. Promise me that by the time you go and see her, you will be found. Get your shit together, okay?"

"I promise."

"Okay, I have to go. Give me your phone," she ordered, holding her palm up so he could drop it in her hand. There it was, the kickass girl he'd met last April—pushy and direct. He was relieved to know that she was still the same. "And you know that mafia speech I gave you last April? That still stands. Snip, snip." She laughed, making a cutting motion with her fingers before walking away.

CHAPTER 34

He cherished the tranquility in the garden, his retreat. Surrounded by nature and comforted by an atmosphere of serenity and solace. Tall, stately trees gifted him with a canopy of shade as he walked a stone pathway leading him to where she was. Gentle blooms dotted the landscape, a sign of the birth of spring. Roses, lilies, and other blossoms added vibrant splashes of color—celebrating her life, beauty, and memory. A simple headstone adorned her resting place, a violin carved on the surface. Inscribed on the stone were the words Graham had chosen:

The sunsets,
The moon sets,
But they are not gone.

Graham knelt to place a bouquet of flowers on the ground, allowing himself to be soothed by the sounds of a babbling brook. The sounds of life whispered back to him, reminding him in subtle ways that there was so much more life to be lived. He said nothing for a few minutes, closed his eyes, and tried with all his might to recall everything about her. There were times when he couldn't even remember her voice, and he would cry and hate himself for it. But that day, he knew more than anything else that she was right there with him.

"Guess what?" he asked, beaming. "I specifically didn't bring Mom with me today. Because you and I—we need to talk. What I'm going to be telling you isn't something you don't already know, though. I saw the signs, Moonie. I know you know. I may not have known that this was part of the plan when I met her at the food pantry, but did you have to make me end up in her car?" He laughed. "You see, it wasn't just serendipity. She came at the exact moment that I decided to find myself. And then, who would have thought I would be sharing twelve days with her, and her mom and dad, for that matter? And what a love story they had! Whoo. That was another sign, Moonie. I wanted that so much for myself."

A yellow butterfly settled on the headstone, flapping its wings but going nowhere.

"The loss of Charlie's dad mirrored the loss that I felt when you left. We may have handled it differently, but I learned that this emptiness, this hole in my heart . . . although it will never go away, can be filled with something greater than me. It can be filled with love and purpose and channeled into making the most out of life. You have inspired me to make sure of that. So that when we see each other again, Moonie, you will be so proud of me like I have always been of you."

Gently, he touched the headstone, prodding the butterfly to sit on his hand. It did.

"So, anyway. The reason I'm here is because I want you to be the first to know. I'm ready. I'm ready to go and see Charlie, tell her I have always loved her, and ask her to be in my life forever. Wish me luck, Moonie. And if possible, can you please throw in more signs that you will always be here? I love you so much."

And with that, he lifted his hand in the air. "Go now, Moonie. Kiss the sky for me."

Exactly one year to the day after she found him, Graham arrived in Malibu. Unlike their last meeting, the sun was out in full force, the smell of the ocean hung in the air, and the palm trees swayed in the gentle wind. He looked at his phone and smiled. Rena was never going to make it easy for him.

3712 Pacific Coast Highway
You'll know when you see it.

She was right.

Nestled among a string of stores in a high-end mall was a lone brownstone in the corner, its sandstone façade standing tall. His heart leaped out of his chest, and he laughed out loud.
Brooklyn Books.

He stared for a few minutes, shaking his head, giddy with excitement. *She did it—she really did it! She brought her father along for the ride and reunited him with her mother.* People were coming in and out. He wanted to surprise her and didn't want to be noticed, so he followed a couple inside, slipping between them right before they walked through the door. Proceeding directly to a shelf opposite the front desk, he began to wander around.

"I will be with you shortly," the woman at the cash register said. He recognized her accent, thick and heavy with a rolling of the r's and an emphasis on the consonants. Her wide-rimmed glasses slipped off her nose, and her orange floral dress matched the ribbons in her hair. He was sure it was Auntie Elma. Quietly, he moved around the store, smiling to himself when he saw the mural on the walls. Every chapter of *Charlotte's Web* was painted against a white, whimsical background—there was Wilbur, Charlotte, Mr. Zuckerman, and Fern, as well as pictures of the farm and all the animals.

Salutations are greetings. It's my fancy way of saying hello.

Everything in that store represented a piece of her heart. He was overwhelmed to see the book he gifted her in a collector's section, locked in a glass case and surrounded by pictures of her mother and father. He was overcome with joy to think that he was a part of that, too. His heart leaped in his chest when he saw the *Not for Sale* sign right next to her treasures. Just around the corner was the children's section. Storybooks and picture books filled the bright-colored shelves while little desks with matching chairs were scattered in the middle. The next thing he saw stopped him in his tracks: painted against a backdrop of midnight blue and bright yellow stars was a cow with his legs splayed out, floating directly above a giant yellow moon. He took a few steps back, unable to contain his astonishment, unaware that there was someone right behind him.

"I'm so sorry," he said, turning around as soon as he stepped on some toes. "I didn't mean to—"

"Can I help you?" a woman with long black hair asked as they faced each other.

It was Celia. He recognized her from her pictures. She had hardly changed.

"I'm—" he began.

"You're . . ." she interrupted and swallowed loudly. "I know you," she said, opening her arms to him. "You're Graham." She hugged him quickly, then stepped back to look at him. "You're more handsome in person. Come," she instructed, leading him by the elbow up to the front of the store. "Elma, look who's here."

Elma looked up from the register and shuffled her way past the line of customers. "Oh, my goodness! You are here!" And then, in a sudden turnaround, she frowned at him. "You took quite long, huh? And what is your real name anyway?" she asked, whipping her head from side to side. "Charlotte? Where is Charlotte?"

"She's managing the deliveries right now, but she'll be back," Celia said calmly before waving toward the counter. "In the meantime, Elma, will you ring the customers up and come join us afterward?" And then she turned to him. "Come, Graham, have a seat." She pointed to a leather couch right behind the non-fiction section. "What luck for you to come while Elma is here visiting. She comes every few months to check on us. We've become her mini-vacation spot."

"I'm too nervous to sit," he said. "I'll just stand, thank you."

"You've made quite an impact on my daughter," Celia said, smiling. "I wanted to thank you for bringing her to me."

"It was Charlie who wanted to go to you," Graham said. "I was just along for the ride."

"I want to tell you what has happened in the past ten months," she said, warming his heart with how she beamed and glowed. He saw the goodness of Charlie in her, remembered the effervescence of her laughter, her tears, her passion. It hurt his heart to think he'd been away from that light for so long. Celia reached for his hand and clasped it tightly. "I was a mess for a while, you know, when I found out Edgar was gone. I knew he was sick because Elma ended up letting me know."

Graham furrowed his brow in confusion. He looked up at Celia with a quizzical expression. "Elma knew where you were?"

"Edgar told her quite a while after we had gotten back together. You have to understand something. Everyone was trying to protect Charlotte from me. She would have had a messed-up life if I was in it. Elma tried to prolong giving her my location until Charlotte had a chance to read all the letters. And she understood those reasons. She holds no ill will toward Elma. Or me."

Graham stayed silent.

Celia continued. "Anyway, I also knew that after the chemo, Edgar had gotten better. There was a time I expected him to walk in the door like no time had passed. I waited for two years. My main focus was on Charlotte. I didn't want to ruin her life by contacting her. So, I waited. In many ways, I still am. I am waiting for the time we can be together again. But in the meantime, I have a lovely life with a daughter who loves me. We spend time together when we're sad, but even that grief has slowly eased. Charlotte brings vibrancy to my life, which Edgar once showed me. There is so much of him in her."

Graham smiled at her and squeezed her hand. "I can't live without her."

"You and me both," Celia said. "Don't get me wrong. I have my bad days, and I have my medication. I have mood swings and outbursts, and I have regrets. But love. Edgar and Charlotte—their love has healed me. Anyway, my parents set up a trust fund for her many years ago. Even without that, as you know, Charlie had been very successful. She paid for this bookstore with the proceeds from the sale of Edgar's home and lives off her investments. The reason I'm telling you this is because you are here now, and there's so much to get to know about each other. But the fact that you're here reminds me of the time Edgar came back to me. He fought for me. And if you fight for her, you will make it just like we did. Because love is unconditional, it transcends torment and suffering and grief."

"Thank you" was all he could say. For the first time in his life, he was hopeful.

"How do you like the store?" she asked. "I'm amazed at how much work she put into this in such a short time. That girl. So much like her father."

"When she puts her mind to it, she gets it done," Graham

completed her thought. "This place. It has everything she's ever loved."

Graham heard the wind chimes by the door, signaling a new customer. He looked up to see Auntie Elma whispering in a woman's ear. When the woman turned around, his heart stopped. *Charlie.*

His pulse raced at the sight of her, and his heart banged like a drum against his chest. It drowned out every noise and sound around him. His knees weakened. He wanted to fly, float in the air, toward her. Graham pushed his way through the line of customers. He couldn't wait to get close to her, see her face, and touch her. He knew that the feel of her skin against his was all he needed to be saved, to feel brand new. Soon enough, they stood facing each other. He'd waited so long for this day.

"Hi," he said, lost for words. Everything around him turned bright and effervescent. It was like he had never known darkness.

"You found me," she whispered, tilting her head and blinking her eyes, now hazy with tears.

He stepped forward and gently cradled her face in his hands, his thumbs caressing her cheeks. Her skin was the sun, the source of endless light, reviving his heart and soul and breathing life into his weary spirit. Her eyes laughed and sang of this moment's joy as if the hours, minutes, and seconds of anguish had never existed. He had no doubt she was the home he'd been searching for all his life.

"I keep asking myself," he began, "how could I have ever let you go? Walking away from you that night last year was the hardest thing I'd ever had to do in my life. And for you to even doubt that what we had was real. I had to fix myself and rebuild what I had lost, but on my own terms this time. And through all the days I'd been away from you, I realized that no matter what I did, whoever I was, none of that mattered if I didn't have you."

"Graham," she said.

"No, wait. Let me finish," he insisted. "I want a lifetime with you, Charlotte Hastings. And a lifetime after that. I want to sit in the car with you for hours, go to dive bars, and carve our names on bathroom doors. I want to listen to your voice reading *Charlotte's Web* over and over again. Most importantly, I want to see and share all the signs with you, Charlie. There will be many more, and for the rest of my life, I want to see them all with you. I love you. I always have. From the first day I met you, when you gave me Sister Mathilda's muffins. It doesn't matter where we are or what we do. Every road will always lead me to you."

Charlie smiled before she wrapped her arms around his neck and pulled his head down for a kiss. In the background, he heard Auntie Elma shushing the customers away, leading them out the door and locking it behind her.

They both turned around and laughed.

Aunt Elma shrugged.

"You cut your hair," he said, admiring how it showed off her delicate ears and smooth, long neck. Lovingly, he traced his finger down the bridge of her nose. "It suits you so well, shows off your true beauty."

She self-consciously ran her fingers through it. "I needed a change."

"I love it," he declared again, kissing the top of her head while pulling her close to his chest. "We did need a change, didn't we?"

"We did."

"And all that time?" he asked, waiting to hear the words she spoke ten months ago when he left her in the middle of a parking lot, full of hope but with no promises.

"All that time, I've been waiting for you," she whispered.

"We all have!" echoed Celia and Auntie Elma.

And as they burst out in laughter, Graham heard a familiar

tune. He took her in his arms and twirled her around while Auntie Elma and Celia joined in, laughing, clapping, and swaying. They danced to the melody in their hearts: Graham, to the sweet sound of violins, and Charlie, he was certain, to her father's favorite song.

"There is no end, Charlie."

And when he kissed her, he kissed their pasts away, absolving it from all its suffering and offering up a lifetime of dreams and ambitions, both unfulfilled and complete. Like the pieces of a puzzle coming together and the final notes in an unfinished song, Graham would trust that fate would always lead the way.

PART 3

EDGAR

TO BE OPENED ONE YEAR
AFTER MY DEATH

To: Mrs. Celia Ruiz–Hastings
From: Ed Hastings

29 January 2022

This is getting ridiculously routine. Ending up in the emergency room
for the past year and staying longer than I ever want to. They keep
sending me up to the oncology floor, even if all I have is a horrible
cold! And what's worse? I've become a mainstay on the ninth floor,
and a nurse named Gabby Santos has taken care of me during every
single visit. This nurse is the smartest, well, second smartest (your
daughter still takes the cake) person I have ever met. She's only in her
twenties, quite serious, and extremely diligent. She knows every vein
and artery in my body. She inserts that IV into my arm so painlessly
I fall asleep while watching her do it. She's pretty, too, this nurse. Her
boyfriend is named Ivan. He brings her Kung Pao chicken for lunch
and picks her up after every shift. Young love gets me all the time.

Charlie is on a business trip but will return in a few days.

Today, I am in room 906. It doesn't feel like a good day. My fever
has been oscillating between extremes, and my body temperature

can't be regulated. I am wistful and philosophical. I want to tie up the loose ends of my life, just in case.

And so, I pull on the cord hanging on the edge of my pillow and accidentally knock myself on the head with the giant white, clunky remote. "Son of a gun," I mutter before pressing the red button on the keypad. Why is everything in a hospital so big and old and outdated? I make a mental note to ask Gabby about that.

I hear her shuffling about before her white shoes appear at my door. Today, the nurses are wearing pink scrubs, and I think about you and how you love this color. I smile at Gabby, and she smiles back. I'm never treated like a burden in her care. Sometimes, she sits by my side, and we have actual conversations. She sneaks in my favorite food. I feel safe with her. I feel at home. I know Charlie has a lot going on at work, so I try not to bother her by checking myself in whenever I feel bad. And Elma. Don't get me started. That woman would be here in a flash if I called her. But she has a life with Joe and Justin, and I also want to respect that. She's done so much for Charlie and me already.

"What's up, Mr. H?" Gabby circles around my bed, checking the IV tube on my arm and then looking up to watch the speed of the drip. "Are you in pain? Is it time for your Tramadol?"

"Not yet," I answer.

"What can I do for you, then? Bathroom? Need to go?"

"I've just been thinking a lot," I start. I don't want to be dramatic, so I'm trying to make conversation first.

"Oh, about Charlie? She called to say she's flying home first thing tomorrow." Gabby knew Charlie well from the days of the treatment and the inpatient chemo sessions.

"No, no," I say. "I don't want to scare you, but I don't think I'm going home anymore."

"What?" she asks, tapping me on the shoulder. "Stop that, Mr. H."

"My fever is back."

"And it will subside again," she said, her eyes growing tender. I can see her face grow slack while she nods. "We're managing it, and Dr. Torres is monitoring."

"Okay," I say, just to appease her.

"I'll tell you what. My shift ends in an hour. I'll stop back for another chess game. You keep beating my ass, and I want you to make me win this time, okay, Mr. H?"

I laugh. I should let this kid win tonight. For a minute, my tears begin to form. I reminisce about those days in Sunset Park when Lito, Boy, and Noel would challenge me endlessly to chess games under the white mulberry tree. But first, I need a favor. "Could you grab me a pen and pad? I'd like to write some notes for the home repair I'm doing."

Didn't I tell you how smart she was? She knew where this was going. "Okay, but no last wills or testaments on my watch. You are going to live to see your grandchildren."

"Ha, can you please tell Charlie that?"

We both laugh.

When I get my pad and paper, I will write this for you.

My love, I am sorry for being so selfish. For disappearing from your life once I knew I would be leaving. I didn't want to do it. Didn't want you to see me this way, didn't want to curtail your progress. You were loving life, getting better. We planned a future together. Dreamed of having grandchildren, of finally being a family. I thought I had more time. I really did. Maybe I do. Have more time, that is. Maybe I am wrong.

But I'm sad to say I don't think I am. I can feel it, Cel. I can feel my life slipping away each time this fever burns through my skin. It eats away at my insides. I feel weaker.

So please, indulge me for a moment while I write these words down for you. I loved you from the first time I saw you, even when I didn't understand why you were sad, angry, or just plain unhappy all the time. Even when you thought the world was out to get you. Yes, you may scream and kick and throw things (plates, mostly) in your fits of rage or laugh so hard until the tears run down your elegant face. But that only affirms one thing to me. It tells me that you're alive. And life, Celia, is precious, and sane and divine.

You are life. And you are mine. And that's all that matters.

I didn't want to leave, you know. But I had to protect our daughter. If I stayed, she would have been taken away from us. And I just couldn't let that happen. She was the product of our love and proof that it will exist long after we are gone.

I hope you know it was a privilege to be loved by you. While it pained me to separate my life the way I have, I always knew that one day, we would bring the two halves of my heart together. I planned to tell her about you and take her to see you. But when I got sicker, and my health began to deteriorate, I was confined to our home and only allowed out for hospital visits.

Today, I was thinking about how Charlie didn't pursue finding you when she turned eighteen, even when I gave her the choice to do so. I'm afraid she won't follow through once I am gone. Although our daughter is resilient and determined, she harbors a broken heart that only motherless daughters can understand. Because of this, she's guarded and shielded. I know I must find another way to slip you into her heart.

I have to keep her curious. And what better way to do that than to introduce her to your letters? I know she will fall in love with you once she gets to know you. Your letters have kept me afloat. They enabled me to grasp and accept our situation without any resentment toward you.

I will give her your letters. When she hears your words, she will search for you. And find you.

In the meantime, I will ask Gabby to hold onto this letter until you and your daughter are reunited.

I love you, Celia. You and Charlie have been the joys of my life. I am a very lucky man to be living this life with someone as special as you. I am sorry for the pain my silence has caused you. But in time, you will see how this was all for the best. You can imagine how a child feels as she watches her father's eventual departure. I am the only parent she knows. I want to show her every day how much I love her and how her efforts to prioritize me are so much appreciated.

You always tell me how I rescued you, how your life would have taken a worse turn if not for me. In reality, it was you who saved me. Without you, I would not have known what real love truly means and how it heals the heart and becomes a refuge from life's daily battles. Without you, I would not have had the honor of raising our Charlotte. You have given my life meaning. I am alive because of you.

All you've ever wanted in your life was to be loved. And you were. You are. And you will always be. That love will now multiply in the years to come because you have a daughter, and she will bring you many days of joy and laughter.

We've said goodbye too many times over the years, and I never want to do it again. I am never going to leave you. I am never going to say goodbye.

I'm still here. I haven't left. And I will always be with you.

I am with you every day. Look for me in the stars at night or in the vibrant colors of the sunrise.

Until we see each other again.

I love you, my Celia.

Your Eddie

EPILOGUE

TODAY

Charlie digs her heels in, burying her feet in the powdery sand while losing herself in the rhythmic sound of the waves caressing the shore and the cry of the seagulls above. To her left is a woman in a black swimsuit, her dark hair held up inside a big, white bucket hat. To her right is a woman in a red swimsuit, the frills of her long blonde hair peeping out of a black straw hat. Charlie holds their hands as they sit on beach chairs, each of the women relaying a story, giving an opinion, giggling at a joke or an anecdote or two. There are many words between them now. Nothing is left without saying. Maybe it's because their stories started with so many things unsaid.

This is life. This is her life. The bookstore, her mother, grandparents, aunts, uncles, three sassy little cousins, and her husband's mother.

And yes, her husband.

Charlie shields her eyes from the sun as she watches him rise out of the water with the dark brown hair and the sparkle of emeralds in his eyes. When people call him a business mogul, he tells them he's just a normal person, a man filled with faults and fears like everyone else. He knows that the value of life is not in what he owns but in what he carries in his heart.

He's holding a small boy's hand, a boy with sun-kissed golden hair and a little button nose. Celia thinks it will grow in time, but Charlie hopes it stays that way forever. Together, father and son walk against the tide, the boy squealing as the foam crashes between his legs, holding on to the shovel and pail in his hands while his father lifts him over the rushing sea.

For the past four years, he's been her home, her respite. His arms have given her solace, peace, and a sense of belonging she had never felt before.

You found me.

"Wook!" the boy exclaims, placing the pail in front of the women. "Wowa and Cat, I got a tiny cwab."

"You did!" both grandmas said. Each one takes a turn, pulling him in and squeezing the life out of him.

As the day wears on, Graham takes his mother back to the hotel. Celia, Charlie, and the little boy have returned from their nap. They are glued to the same place, watching him make snow angels in the sand, sorting seashells, and running back and forth with the rise and fall of the tide.

"I see so much of your father in him," Celia says, turning to face Charlie.

Charlie nods with a smile, takes her mother's hand, and kisses it. The women remain silent for a while, watching the sky change colors as the sunset begins.

"Charlie, am I easy to love?"

"Yes, Mom. So easy," she responds. And then, she leans forward on the chair and calls out to her son.

"Will! Come here, baby. What did you want to tell Lola last night?"

Will puts the last shell in the bucket and jumps to his feet, wrapping his arms around Celia while rubbing sand on her skin and sprinkling it in her hair. "I wuv you, pweetty Wowa," he says before planting a big, wet, salty kiss on her lips. "I wuv you."

ACKNOWLEDGMENTS

In my previous book, I mentioned that I live a "never say never" kind of life. This has been proven once again as I write these words of gratitude. I really thought it was time to move on to other ventures, heed the call of other opportunities brought about by my career. And yet, here I am, grateful for the chance to share another story that is so personal to me. With this book, I honor my parents, whose real names have been used.

I am indebted to **Christine Gillespie** and the Open Road Integrated Media Team, including Emma Chapnick and Sara Kapheim, for taking a chance on this journey with me. Libby Turner and Jonas Saul are my outstanding editors, and **Camila Grey** has created the most beautiful cover I have ever seen. It truly depicts the story of Charlie and Graham, and I hold it close to my heart.

Many thanks to my agent**, Italia Gandolfo, LK Griffie** at Vesuvian Media, and the ladies of our **Braes Butterflies** group for sticking it out with me through life's many changes. My friends, Gayle Meyer, Rachel Schneider, Missy Geneken, Suzy Stork, Suzanne Wendolski, Karolyn Davityan, Amanda Jones, Pepsy Bolton, Ashley Good and all of you! It's been a privilege to have you in my life. Thank you for your love. To **Joyce Lamb** for your invaluable input in every story I write. To **Meryl Moss**, as well as all the bloggers who graciously promote my books, and **Kiki** with The Next Step PR.

I've been so lucky to have the guidance and support of two authors. Everyone knows that true friends in this industry are few and far between. Thank you, Mary Ting and Leylah Attar.

And to my family, my daily blessings—Bill, Tim, Katie, Gigi, Marco and Izzy. Thank you for lighting up my life with your love.

And last but certainly not least, THANK YOU, dear Readers. You have inspired me to write these words over and over again, with the hope that they will touch your heart.

xo

ABOUT THE AUTHOR

Anna Gomez was born in Makati, Philippines, and relocated to Chicago after an education abroad. Sometimes writing under the pen name Christine Brae, Gomez's titles include *My Goodbye Girl*, *In This Life*, and the From Kona with Love series, cowritten with Kristoffer Polaha, which has been optioned for film and television. Her works have been covered in *People*, the *Hollywood Reporter*, *Variety*, and *Publishers Weekly*. Gomez has also been featured on CNN Philippines and Ad Age. In addition to her creative works, Gomez is the CFO of Mischief at No Fixed Address. You can find her at annagomezbooks.com.

INTEGRATED MEDIA

Find a full list of our authors and
titles at www.openroadmedia.com

FOLLOW US
@OpenRoadMedia